TUNNEL OF DEATH

Stryker felt the shades of darkness inside the tunnel slowly lighten, but he didn't move. He knew one or more Viet Cong guerrillas were in front of him — he could feel it, and he would let them make the first move.

Even if it took all day.

He was prepared to wait them out all day and into the night. But all that changed when he heard the soft, confident voice a few feet away announce, "We outgun you."

The guerrilla's tone was confident. It told Stryker he need not even offer to surrender — he was already cold meat. . . .

THE SAIGON COMMANDOS SERIES
by Jonathan Cain

SAIGON COMMANDOS

SAC MAU, VICTOR CHARLIE

#7

JONATHAN CAIN

ZEBRA BOOKS
KENSINGTON PUBLISHING CORP.

ZEBRA BOOKS

are published by

Kensington Publishing Corp.
475 Park Avenue South
New York, NY 10016

Grateful acknowledgement is made to Paramount Pictures
Corp., the owner of Star Trek ® Properties, for permission
to use the passage on p. 194, and especially Sandra Delaney,
for her assistance in this matter.

"The Leroy Eltinge" by Mike Clodfelter, and "Open Season"
by John P. McAfee were reprinted with permission of American Poetry and Literature Press of Upper Darby, Pennsyl-
vania. Special thanks to Jocelyn Topham for bringing this
and other Vietnam veteran literature to the public's attention.

First printing: April 1985

Printed in the United States of America

For Elaan of Troyius, whose loyal fans — the true trekkies — know her better as France Nuyen. And for my star cousin, Tom DeCesaro, who showed me how to turn a model rocket into a S.A.M. You would have loved the intense swirl of excitement and emotion when the .122s fell across the streets of Saigon and the air raid sirens cried. Suddenly reaching Corapouri no longer seems so important.

Sac Mau, Victor Charlie is a novel. But it is based on several true stories the author swapped with other MPs at Mimi's Bar in Saigon, where he was assigned to the 716th Military Police Battalion.

The phrase "Saigon Commandos" was a derogatory term invented by infantrymen in the field to refer to almost any soldier stationed in the "rear." But some of the Military Policemen fighting snipers, sappers, and other hostile hooligans across the sleazy Saigon underworld affectionately adopted the title, proud to be lawmen and not jungle grunts, battling crime in the toughest beat in the world.

—*Jonathan Cain*
August 1984
Bangkok, Thailand

Acknowledgments

A special note of thanks to Gary Johnson, Pat Callahan, and Skip Foy, of the 281st MPs Thailand. Had they not rolled on my Ten-2 at the Ding Dong Club in Newland, this series of military police novels would not be possible.

OPEN SEASON

They say war affects a man;
Don't believe it.
If he looks at Dogwood white
Blossoming spring on mountains
And thinks of phosphorous marking
Rounds calibrating death;
If the peaceful bee sounds
Like the ricocheting bullet
Off concertina, or the bee-sought
Rose seems an open wound—
What of it?
(The night will gauze them closed
and find the bee home.)
But the man—
He sleeps fitfully,
Lost in a firefight between sun and moon,
Calling for help down petal trenches,
Trembling under the wife's helpless touch.
They say war affects a man;
Don't believe it.

—John P. McAfee
Asheville, North Carolina

from: *Vietnam Heroes: A Tribute*

THE LEROY ELTINGE

We boarded the Leroy Eltinge this "Ship of Fools"
savage in our sincerity
and hell-bent for hell;
we carried green-dyed underware
and olive-drab optimism,
and sailed toward certain glory.
A year later we flew home in the Freedom Bird — most of us —
returning in khakied contempt
and with a duffel bag stuffed with silence

—Mike Clodfelter
Lawrence, Kansas

from: *Vietnam Heroes III*

Vietnam was what we had instead of happy childhoods.
—*Michael Herr*
Dispatches

Prologue

Mytho Vietnam, 1962

His eyes still hurt from the brilliant flash of red tracer. His ears ached, too—five rifle slugs, fired in rapid succession beneath ground in a VC tunnel, will do that to you. He fought to steady his nerves, to keep the gasping breath locked in his lungs. He kept his right arm locked at the elbow, straight out, the cool steel of the .45 automatic in his fist almost soothing, comforting, but not quite. The heat in this earthen tomb was drenching him in sweat. Beads of perspiration trickled down from the edges of his close-cropped hair into his eyes. The salt burned, but the stress lines beneath the jungle green orbs—dark and tough as leather from years under the tropical sun—did not flinch. His trigger finger tensed. He could feel his prey cowering in the darkness, a few feet away.

Sgt. Mark Stryker finally blinked his eyes once, but he swallowed the urge to cough at the gunsmoke choking the air in the pitch-black tunnel. His purple vision—that term the DIs back at The School had given to man's ability to eventually see in the dark—had still not returned, but every fiber in his body was prepared, animallike, to dodge from harm's path; evade the blind tigress that was Lady Death. Stryker's mental reactions had shifted to phase red — a form of discipline he felt put him a heartbeat ahead of his opponent. The MP sergeant knew the bright flashes from the guerilla's carbine had also temporarily blinded the Vietnamese, so they were fighting on even terms for a change. Under cover of *this* darkness, the Cong had no advantage.

"You okay down there, sarge?" A distant voice invaded his suddenly silent battleground, and Stryker's lower lip moved up to tug on the tip of his mustache. This was not the place — *or the time* — to respond. Any movement would signal the man somewhere across from him his exact position, and more hot lead would fly. *This time* he might not survive. The tracer might not slice through the muggy air an inch from his ear, impacting against the dirt wall behind him in a shower of crimson sparks.

"*Sergeant Stryker!*" Another voice was calling from the tunnel entrance fifty yards back. "You Code-Four? We're gonna send a dog in, sarge!"

"And tear gas!" the first private added.

Stryker gritted his teeth. The men above ground had heard the rattle of discharges. They thought he was dead. He couldn't blame them: In the last two weeks a half dozen military policemen had been killed in the line of duty chasing the communists through their tunnels on the edge of the airport.

At least they were affording him the courtesy of a warning, in case he *had* survived hell underground. Stryker grinned: What were his men up to — a bluff? They didn't have any attack dogs in Mytho anymore.

12

Not after the kennel had been hit by sappers and most of the animals destroyed in the raging fire that followed. Sure, the PM had that old dope-sniffing mut he terrorized the Arvin potheads with on Saturday mornings, but all the real K-9s were up in Saigon with the 716th.

Overhead the ground trembled slightly as a massive vehicle of some sort rumbled past. Clods of dirt bounced off Stryker's shoulder, and a swirl of dust hit him, coating the sweat on his face and chest.

He considered firing blindly in a fanning, left-to-right motion. He had eight rounds in the pistol, including the hollow-point he always kept in the chamber — the hammer cocked back on safety. (Stryker believed an automatic with an empty chamber was a farce: By the time you drew the weapon and pulled back the slide to chamber a round, your ticket would already be cancelled.) There was no telling how many were standing, crouching, or lying prone a few yards in front of him, even now.

The first MP to radio in the foot chase — one of his best men, a double vet on his second extension — had reported a dozen guerillas fleeing the surprise sapper attack on the edge of the airfield south of the city, across the Song Cua Tieu. Stryker had been exchanging riverine sit-reps with a PBR unit at the ferry crossing, and two gun jeep patrols had been returning from Cho Gao after escorting a payroll convoy east, so several MPs had eagerly converged in on the Ten-100 Call-For-Help.

Stryker had been the first to arrive. He hardly noticed all the South Vietnamese Air Force jets smoldering beneath billowing fireballs on the steaming

13

tarmac—there'd be plenty of time to gawk at the carnage later. As a heavy pall of oily smoke rolled in across the sea of swaying elephant grass, his eyes watched the scrawny terrorists piling into the narrow hillside tunnel entrance. Stryker's own legs pumped him forward frantically as he watched the American between the tunnel and himself fire off a wild burst of rounds on rock-and-roll from the hip. The slugs threw up dirt and torn reeds but no blood or limbs, and the MP sergeant soon found himself yelling at the other American not to follow the guerillas into the tunnel.

"You'd be chasing them into *their* territory!" He pulled the corporal back up out of the huge "snake hole." As both men stood in the waist-high reeds beside the entrance, breathing hard after the thousand-yard run from the roadway, Stryker pulled the pin from a grenade and rolled it down into the tunnel.

"Fire in the hole!" he called out as the two gun jeeps, their drivers' automatically forcing the gearshift into four-wheel drive, flew across the bumpy field and roared up to the scene. They did not even duck as the blast sent a geyser of smoke and dust skyward, and before their wheels rolled to a stop, Stryker was waving them to the far side of the hill. "Spread out!" he advised. "And keep an eye open for an exit!"

"Or grenade smoke drifting up through air holes!" the corporal added as he slung his M-2 over a shoulder and unsnapped the rainflap on his holster.

Stryker smiled broadly as his eyes took in the scene —this was what he lived for! A grizzled police veteran poised for action on an Asian hillside, knees bent slightly against the eighteen-hour shifts, hair plastered to his scalp with sweat, shirtless, with an open flak

14

jacket hanging from broad shoulders.

The corporal's eyes had narrowed defensively after he was prevented from chasing the terrorists beneath the ground, but in the pit of his gut he knew — and Stryker knew he knew — his watch commander was right. Chapped lips assaulting a smoldering cigar stub, the man eyed Stryker silently, waiting for the big NCO in starched fatigues to take over.

In a flash of the moment, Stryker's eyes raced across the terrain around them. A thunderstorm was rolling in from the south. Lightning danced in the black clouds hanging ominously along the horizon. Air raid sirens up in Mytho were filling the humid air with their mournful cry, and firetrucks, loaded down with more heavily-armed SPs than firefighters, coasted up to the torn and mangled Canberra bombers and A-37 Dragonflies. In the distance, F-100 Super Sabres and F-105 Thunderchief jets rolled onto their sides as landing gear collapsed from secondary explosions. And beyond the blossoming fireballs where fuel tanks were going up, he could see fishermen floating down the wider Mytho River in their sampans, oblivious to the commotion and excitement of the attack. Where the Song Mytho forked and gave birth to the murky Cua Tieu, he watched the endless stepping-stone network of shimmering blue-green rice paddies rise up through the valley to the edge of the rain forest.

He wanted to cheer because this was what Vietnam was all about — this was where the job satisfaction was really at, but he could not cheer because death lurked beneath his feet, and you did not make fun of Lady Death because she jealously guarded a funny little secret and always had the last laugh.

15

In that split second spent sucking the sweet beauty of Vietnam in through his eyes, Stryker wondered if any jungle tigers sat on that faraway stretch of treeline, drawn from the depths of the rain forest by the sound of explosions and panic. He wondered if all the activity drove them into a frenzy, or if they just sat there patiently, slapping at the clouds of mosquitoes with their tails, unimpressed.

As more patrol units arrived on the scene, he wondered if their were any big cats in the hills north of Mytho at all, for this was the Delta, and you were more likely to run across a twenty-foot python.

"Who wants the honor?" said a short, stocky lieutenant with a waxed, handlebar mustache who sounded bored as he remained standing behind the windshield in the front seat of his jeep.

"It's Mark's turn," answered a lanky NCO who pointed at Stryker, but the corporal who had called in the chase protested.

"It's *my* crime scene." He waved his arm out to encompass the entire airfield in the background, a dense cloud of smoke now hanging over it.

"Hell of a crime scene," Stryker said with a laugh as he kept his .45 trained on the tunnel entrance. He was agreeing with the corporal, but it wouldn't do to have a crafty Cong pop up without warning to blast them in the backside as they argued.

"This ain't no fucking *crime scene*, boy!" the lieutenant yelled good-naturedly, refusing to dismount from the gun jeep. Additional explosions from a jet fuel tank rocked the airfield. "It's a goddamned battlefield!"

"Well, it's *my* call," the corporal replied, edging closer to the tunnel entrance, then hesitating. "And as first

16

man on the scene, *I'm* in charge."

"*He* makes the decisions," added a fellow enlisted man leaning against an M-60 in another unit. But he blushed as all eyes turned on him, and he looked away.

"Then have at it." Stryker's grin had grown ear to ear as he motioned toward the menacing-looking snake hole. Its camouflage cover gone, the entrance now appeared wide as a tree trunk. Spiderwebs lined its walls.

The corporal glanced up at Stryker, then back down at the hole. His feet refused to move. "I hate spiders," he muttered, and the sergeant across from him took that as an open invitation to assault the tunnel himself instead.

Stryker placed the grenade in his left hand back in the pouch on his web belt, flipped the lieutenant a thumbs-up, then locked eyes with the private in the gun jeep.

"Nobody has exited on the other side of the hill," the MP said, lowering his head closer to the radio receiver as if trying to decipher the nonstop stream of transmissions that clogged the net following the sapper attack. "No air shafts located either, sarge."

Stryker nodded then vanished down through the sharp reeds into the tunnel.

It descended at a forty-five degree angle for several feet but quickly leveled off, and he was soon faced with a bend in the narrow underground corridor. Using a log pillar for cover, he carefully moved into the larger shaft without meeting any resistance, but after crawling a few minutes through the dust, he found what he was searching for: damp sections in the floor of the tunnel. Blood. The frag had done its job. Now the guerillas were dragging home casualties. And sometimes wounded men were more trouble than body-bagged corpses.

Stryker frowned as his nostrils detected the stench of an open intestinal wound. He had never known Charlie to carry body bags in their rucks.

A moment later the rifle discharged a score of feet in front of him. The tracer zinged an inch to the side of his face, and his sight was temporarily chased away.

Not that it had been that clear before the shots rang out, but at least he had been able to perceive shifting shades of grey and black where obstacles filled the tunnel ahead. The shapes told him he was fast approaching the main storage point of the tunnel: the ammo or weapons cache. Or possibly an underground field hospital, though the NVA had long ago taught the Cong not to build medical facilities so close to an airfield.

Stryker felt the shades of darkness inside his eyes begin to lighten as his sight slowly returned, but he did not move any part of his body. He knew one or more men were directly in front of him — he could *feel* it, and he would let them make the first move.

Even if it took all day.

Even if they *did* have a police dog topside and were taking the leash off it this very moment. Again, something rumbled past overhead, and dust drifted down into his eyes. Stryker began blinking uncontrollably as the particles worked their way in under his lids.

"We out-gun you," a confident voice announced softly a few feet away.

Styker's ears perked at the sudden sound, and he immediately placed the exact location of the man. The guerilla's tone was overconfident, in fact. It told Stryker he need not even offer to surrender — the MP was already cold meat.

Using the training he had received not at The School but at the VNP combat survival camp, his gunhand moved to the right slightly as it followed his mental line of sight. Stryker pulled the trigger slowly, smoothly at first.

The flash from the kicking discharge lit up the tunnel for a brief moment, and he saw the startled Vietnamese, eyes wide and mouth open, stop the slug with his chin. The next two rounds were jerked off with as much precision but less care — the barrel flame had also revealed that a half dozen guerillas were huddled in the dark behind the now dead spokesman.

The MP sergeant listened to the hollow-points smack into shoulder flesh as two more Viet Cong were disabled, and as he fired off five more bullets in rapid succession, additional Vietnamese toppled to the cool floor of the tunnel.

Stryker rolled to the side, hitting a support log with his ribs, but the return fire he had expected failed to materialize. During the roll, he had ejected the empty pistol magazine. He now pulled a fresh clip from his ammo pouch and slapped it into the butt of the automatic. He flipped the slide forward, and after a cartridge was forced into the chamber again, he fired three rounds down the dark, narrow tunnel. Screams answered the ear-splitting reports, and the barrel flash showed one man still running away.

The air against his ears began to tingle suddenly, and the tunnel started taking on an eerie pressure. He thought of the rainstorm moving across the airfield overhead, but then he remembered the ground shaking earlier, and he stumbled over groaning bodies in his haste to catch up to the guerilla running for the exit. For some reason they had called in the heavyweights: *tanks*!

They were going to burn him out with a flame thrower!

Stryker concentrated on forcing all his strength into the sprint. Leg muscles pounded across the damp, packed earth as he ran. Even the swinging of his arms added to his momentum. He didn't waste time looking back over a shoulder. He could sense the fireball chasing down after him through the tunnel. His boots moved faster until he was almost on top of the fleeing guerilla; almost climbing over the Vietnamese's back.

The slender Cong threw his shoulder into the exit hatch as he leaped up and away from Stryker at the last moment. The MP sergeant followed the tiny man into sunlit, fresh air, and a second later, as they were tumbling down the hillside through the blades of elephant grass, the hungry ball of fire from the flame thrower exploded forth after them.

Stryker watched the smoke plumes rushing out of the earth alongside the steady stream of flame. His mind envisioned the tank on the other side of the hill, directing its long barrel down toward the tunnel entrance and suddenly belching the all-powerful wall of swirling yellow and orange: a dragon which had descended from the huge, castlelike clouds looming overhead, searching out its Heaven pearl beneath the surface of the earth.

Stryker knew the legend. If a dragon were ever lucky enough to capture the Heaven pearl — and some were — it became an emperor, and therefore, a god. But the military policeman was not thinking about man-beasts just then. His side aching because he had rolled into an old water buffalo carcass and had been jabbed by a protruding shoulder blade, Stryker's wary eyes scanned the steep hillside.

The Viet Cong was running at full tilt through an old trail in the distant treeline—straight for a small village beyond! MP gun jeeps were swooping down toward him from opposite directions, but they'd be unable to intercept him before he reached the sanctuary of the hamlet. One rook fired a short burst from his Hog-60, but the rounds strayed wide—a tracer missing the oncoming patrol by only a few feet—and the terrorist vanished behind the thick curtain of bamboo.

As Stryker sprinted down between the patrol jeeps, steadily gaining on the Vietnamese, he thought of the RVN Service Medal crazy Jake Drake, the company clerk, had presented him halfway through his Tour. Three hundred sixty-five. Below a saffron ribbon with three vertical crimson stripes, a dragon prowled a similar field of bamboo. Stryker abandoned trying to take aim while running and allowed his eyes to dart back and forth through the tall wall of flora surrounding the village, but there were no serpents lying in wait for him, not even a Cobra or twostep viper.

The guerilla bowled over an old man blocking his path—a feeble attempt at proclaiming the hamlet would not hide a communist from the authorities—and raced up the narrow planks into a bungalow on stilts.

Stryker was forty meters behind the man now and rapidly gaining. He skidded to a stop and took aim on the doorway, breathing in slowly despite his pounding heart, waiting for the Cong to top the flimsy stairwell. *Twenty-five meters is the maximum effective range of your side-arm, MP,* the sergeant-major back in Korea had proclaimed during an argument at his oral board for promotion to NCO, *and that's final!* Stryker begged to differ with the man, and the entire panel followed the two out to the range behind the Orderly Room, where, at fifty meters, Stryker calmly placed seven .45 slugs into the middle of a seven-inch-square plank of wood. An hour later he had his sergeant stripes.

He now carefully squeezed off a round so gently that it was a surprise when the trigger finally released the hammer. A pane of bamboo in the doorframe split down the middle from ceiling to floor as the bullet slammed into it.

Stryker frowned, pulling off the second round with a slight jerk this time, and the slug surprised everyone watching by punching the guerilla in the lower back. He was propelled into the dwelling with knees bent, as if some invisible force was throwing him down onto an altar to pray for his life. A woman inside the bungalow screamed.

Stryker flipped up the thumb safety and started running again, but suddenly the air erupted into a funnel of dust and twigs and torn reeds, and he had to shield his face with his forearm as he ran bent over beneath the landing helicopter's downblast.

A warrant officer from Military Intelligence jumped off a skid and bounded after him, and both Americans rushed into the bungalow, abandoning all caution, long before the gun jeeps located the access road and pulled up to the clearing.

Stryker did not immediately see the terrorist lying in

the shadows next to a sleeping mat, dead from the back wound. His eyes locked onto the wildly flapping breasts of the woman who had been nursing her child. She was now rushing out the back door, behind a man in black pajama bottoms. Two teenagers, a boy and girl, sat frozen beside a rice cooker, their fingers still clutching chop sticks that didn't move now, their chins hidden behind the small porcelain bowls, their un-blinking eyes wide in terror.

"Dung lai!" yelled the man from MI who jumped in front of Stryker and fired a burst of rounds from the submachine gun on the sling riding his hip. "Dung the fucking lai!" He repeated the order to stop after the spray of hot lead caught the male in the feet, toppling him instantly, but the woman continued to flee.

When their father somersaulted into the dust, screaming, the children in the hut dropped their meals and rushed for the doorway, but the warrant officer knocked them back with his forearm. "Sit down!" he growled, then took aim on the woman's back and fired off another burst just as Stryker knocked the weapon up.

"This is my footchase!" Stryker yelled, disregarding the man's rank and forgetting he wasn't in a Saigon back alley but a jungle hamlet deep in the Delta. "Who the fuck are you?"

One of the bullets from the MP40 caught the woman in the back of the right shoulder and spun her around. A splinter of lead passed completely through her and struck the child in her arms with such force it was thrown through the air in a shower of blood, its tiny heart no longer beating.

"We're MI!" The warrant officer waved his arm back

23

in the direction of the chopper, its rotors still beating slowly in the thick, sticky heat. His eyes reflected none of Stryker's rage. His face was a mask of shock and surprise at the rebuff.

"You suspect's right *there*!" Stryker whirled around and pointed at the body in the shadows. "You got no call gunnin' down these people, sport. You're on *my* turf, and —"

"That VC sonofabitch beat feet into *this* hut, *sergeant*!" The man from MI emphasized Stryker's lower rank, but his eyes lost none of the hurt and insult lines at their edges. "That makes this whole dump a friggin' free-fire zone, okay?"

Stryker holstered his pistol and turned away from the agent. "No, it's not okay," he muttered as the children rushed past him and flew down the steps to their parents. "This is my goddamned beat, and it's not fucking okay!" He started after the teenagers dressed in peasants' garb.

Another helicopter was landing in the narrow clearing between the hill overlooking the hamlet and the peaceful river on the other side. Stryker glanced at the man lying in the dust. His son and daughter had both run to him. His feet were mangled beyond repair—he would surely lose them. The infant was dead. The teenage girl stared at her tiny body, lying facedown in the dust, flies already swarming over it. Their mother was also facedown in the dirt. A pool of blood was slowly spreading out from her right shoulder. Her left hand reached out to her family, but the children would not run to her. She was naked except for the loose sarong wrapped around her hips. Perhaps the children sensed the soldiers were not through with her yet.

24

Stryker went down on one knee and checked the dead baby for a pulse. Finding none, he turned to face the approaching warrant officer. The man still had his finger on the trigger. Stryker could read his mind: *Never trust any of the bastards—you can't tell the good guys from the bad—not in this stinking war.*

He appeared to be in his late thirties, with a receding hairline but with a thick tuft of black hair in the middle. He was a large man with a boxer's nose and a wide chin. A facial scar looking almost filmy against his darkly tanned features, ran diagonally across his left cheek. His eyebrows grew together over his nose, and that made Stryker chew his lower lip slightly—he sensed evil in the man.

The bungalow was full of people now. A half dozen MPs were starting down the rear steps of the dwelling. Additional MI agents were scurrying to leapfrog past the soldiers from the gun jeeps.

"Cuff his ass." Stryker could hear Kip Mather directing one of the privates to handcuff the guerilla they had evidently found lying in the shadows by the doorway.

"But he's dead, sarge!" the enlisted man replied above all the commotion.

"I said cuff his ass!" Mather repeated, and then their conversation was lost in the loud stampede of boots rushing down the stairwell. Stryker grinned inwardly: It was procedure. Clamp on the metal bracelets even if the suspect was now a corpse. Especially in the jungle. The jungle was a crazy place: Charlie Congs had a bad habit of rising from the grave.

"You need any help, Hoyden?" Three agents from Military Intelligence were rapidly approaching now.

25

"Naw," said the big man with the submachine gun and he nudged the wounded woman in the side slightly with the boot of his toe. "Chased down one lousy VC and ended up with a nestfull of 'em—that's all. This bitch won't make it—got a DB back in the hooch there—and we'll transport that one there." He pointed to the father with mangled heels. "Ourselves," he added.

"Just thought you might need a hand." One of the men smiled, eyeing the teenaged girl holding her father's head up out of the dirt. She looked about twelve but already was filling out nicely. Someday she'd be a real looker, he thought, if her country didn't kill her first.

"That's a negative," Hoyden responded. "But thanks for the assist."

"We were just on our way up north," the MI agent in charge of the second chopper added. "To interrogate some sappers a squad of Saigon Commandos captured outside Tan Son Nhut—monitored the Signal-Three hundred from your MPs here and thought we'd drop in to see if we could help."

To see how much blood you could see, Stryker was thinking when he said, "The MPs belong to *me.*"

"What's that?" The senior warrant officer halted in mid-stride on his way back to the choppers. His eyes narrowed with irritation.

"This is my turf, mister. I don't even know who you guys are with! Though I've got my suspicions." Stryker matched the man's scowl.

A small black plastic identification holder was flashed in the MP's face a second later. "Show a little cooperation, my friend." The ranking MI agent displayed a sudden smile but no compassion whatsoever. "I don't know what you had going on thirty minutes ago, but now *we* got a tunnel system to check into, and this matter has become *our* matter. I'll clear it with your C.O. Show Hoyden there every manner of cooperation he requests. Or you and I will be seeing each other again," he said, focusing on the sergeant's nametag, *"Stryker."*

The big MP bit his lower lip and remained silent. Arguing with chopper jockeys was a waste of time. The MI agent turned and headed back up the steps through the bungalow, and several Vietnamese militiamen met him in the doorway.

Stryker watched him point back to Hoyden, who was still standing over the wounded woman. Then the warrant officer was looking directly down at Stryker. "These boys are Arvins detached to us!" he yelled before disappearing inside the hut. "They'll be assisting Hoyden now, so you and your men can resume doing whatever MPs in Mytho do."

Stryker's eyes took in the bristling weapons of the young Viets. He wondered how many of them actually knew how to use them. He nodded his head from side to side in resignation and turned to walk back toward the injured woman. Moments later, one of the helicopters was ascending through the trees atop a whirlwind of twigs and dust.

"I'll ask you one more time," the agent said, and nudged the toe of his boot against the woman's torn shoulder. He was speaking in pidgin Vietnamese. She grimaced in pain but did not cry out. "Who's the Cong cell leader in this hamlet?"

Stryker began to intervene, but some of the militiamen had already rushed up to Hoyden and were adding their own torrents of accusations. They included some descriptive threats, but the woman only spat out at them.

Stryker's eyes shifted to the man lying in his daughter's arms a few yards away. His features were no longer a mask of tortured agony. The eyes were fixed tightly on his wife. They told her to remain silent, not to cooperate, yet not to resist with angry actions either. To insult and intimidate their captors would only make things worse later for themselves and their children.

Hoyden glanced over at the wounded man. "Well, maybe *you'll* talk, asshole!" He grinned evilly, sliding his boot under the woman's body and starting to turn her over. This time she cried out in pain.

Her husband's features went tense, and his mouth became a narrow, horizontal line, but he said nothing. The woman, racked with sobs, stole a glance at him after Hoyden removed the boot, and the wiry Vietnamese only nodded his head solemnly. As if they had discussed the possibility of this happening before and had rehearsed how they would react.

Hoyden raised his foot above the woman's wound. "*Talk*, you commie sonofabitch!" His eyes remained on her husband. "Or I'll smash her ribs under my—"

"Back off!" Stryker moved forward, but several of the militiamen drifted between the MP and the man from MI. "You're abusing your—"

"I'm not abusing shit!" Hoyden retorted. He waved a hand out at the helicopter fading beyond the treetops. "Like *they* said, this is a matter for MI now. *You* back off."

Stryker stared down at the woman lying half on her

28

stomach now and half on her side. Her breasts still swollen with milk so soon after childbirth, they ballooned outward slightly as her chest pressed against the damp earth. Lines of blood streaked her smooth, amber skin, but her face was flawless. The anger in her eyes enhanced the beauty, Stryker thought to himself. Even with her long hair soaked with perspiration and clinging to her shoulders and back, he found himself suddenly aroused. Lusting. The form of evil desire that was never found in the bedroom of his hooch back in the city, or even the whorehouses downtown, but only on the battlefields, when soldiers fought for days, watched their buddies die, then won the skirmish only to discover the enemy had abandoned a woman or two behind during their hasty retreat.

"You beat cops." The warrant officer's words were drenched with disgust. "What do you know about the war here in Vietnam? People like this . . ." He grabbed the woman by an ankle and jerked the leg off the ground, eliciting another scream. "People like this are behind incidents like the one last week where a village bitch fragged a whole chopperful of our agents. Or the week before, where a so-called baby-san ran up—all smiles, mind you—to three field agents with a claymore taped to its back!" The woman's thighs spread apart, and her sarong fell away from her hips as Hoyden began dragging her over to a nearby hut, ignoring her wound. "All you Saigon Commandos know about are VD card checks and recovering stolen toilet paper at the static posts!"

Stryker's hand went to his holster, but two of the militiamen raised their rifles waist-high and he froze. None of the MPs back in the bungalow seemed to notice what was going on outside, and the few men behind Stryker followed his example and did not move forward to interfere. Hoyden did not call off his people but disappeared inside the deserted structure as if this village were his kingdom, and the woman merely another maiden from his harem.

Stryker swiftly counted the Vietnamese militiamen. More had arrived on a troop lorry. Nearly a dozen now mingled between himself and Hoyden and around the wounded man and his two children. The MP sergeant had to consider the boy and girl, too. He could draw, take a round or two in the flak jacket and hope for the best. Or he could wait for Mather or one of the men up in the bungalow to sense something was wrong and make their dramatic entrance atop a roaring gun jeep. He glanced up at the sun. Time was on his side. Hoyden had just crossed that invisible line, regardless of his motivations or loyalties. You could rationalize why cops sometimes enjoyed gunplay in the streets, but rape was another matter. By nightfall, Stryker would have the man's career in his backpocket.

The MI agent's eyes darted about the small interior of the single room hut before thrusting the woman across the floor. She slid against the far wall and rolled onto her back. Whimpering, she tried to raise herself up, but the pain was too much for her to overcome. Her head fell back against the floor. Her left leg was against the ground, straight out. The other was bent with knee in the air and the sole of her foot flat on the thin sleeping mat beneath her.

Hoyden slowly maneuvered around in front of her so that he was standing just at the edge of her feet. He stared down at her mangled body, and a surprised grin creased his harsh features upon realizing that, even in this condition, he found her desirable. Never mind the exit wound over her right breast. Both were still wide and full, and he had never seen nipples so large in his life. Never mind the blood caking her chest: Red was the color of passion, Hoyden thought to himself with an evil little laugh. He did not know the nipples that appeared so erect were not aroused by him or the danger of the moment. And Hoyden's ego would have been bruised if you told him they were only stretched taut from nursing a child for the last four weeks. He had no children and knew nothing about rearing them.

Instead, his eyes fell to the flat stomach, then the flaring thighs. Then they returned to the woman's defiant snarl.

Hoyden growled back. He slid his left boot between her ankles and kicked her foot out, spreading the thighs wider. "Today you find out the penalty for cooperating with the VC, mama-san." The woman was in her mid-thirties, at most. Her eyes were ageless, possessing both the culture of thousands of Vietnamese women before her and the innocence of the dead baby outside. Her fear, her terror and bewilderment were displayed in an almost childlike manner by those eyes, yet in their depths Hoyden saw the anger of a thousand years of persecution, subjugation and resistance. And the defiance came as a challenge to him.

Unbuckled now, his web belt clattered to the ground. He unzipped his trousers, let them fall to the ground, and slowly stepped forward, stopping between her knees.

He unbuttoned his shirt and threw it behind him,

then went down on one knee and ran his fingers lightly over the wound in her chest. She arced her shoulders back in pain, but Hoyden clamped his other hand over her teeth. "We both know you are going to die from this wound, my dear," he whispered into her ear then drew his face back to gauge her reaction. Her lips trembled, but her eyes remained locked on his, radiating hate.

He glanced at the blood on his fingers, then ran them through the hair on his chest. "But your life will not have been lost in vain." His smile remained intact, and he took her left hand and placed the fingers around his erection. Her eyes widened slightly at the shock of its size, and then, his fingers tightly around hers, he made her guide it in between her legs. "Your life will not have been lost in vain," he repeated, pausing as the head of the shaft touched flesh. "Because my chest will slide against yours, dear. Your blood will mingle with my sweat as I enter your body. And when you expire, because the shock of my making love to you is more than your body's defenses can handle, I will suck in the life that leaves you because my lips will be pressed against yours. My eyes will be, like now, still locked on yours."

The woman shuddered, and she turned her face away: This was no foreign intruder, invited into her homeland by only the politicians. *This man was a demon!* Surely he escaped from the dark depths of the rain forest, she thought.

When the woman felt his chest lower itself on top of hers, she screamed at the top of her lungs, with the last of her strength, and then he plunged into her. The pain in her breast seemed to flow to her entire body, and she heard the scream chasing after her long after she had blacked out.

When the children heard their mother cry out, they ran from their father's side and bolted through the soldiers' legs until they were inside the doorway of the hut. The first thing they saw were two white haunches, like crescent moons arguing as they bobbed up and down in the dark. Then the long-nosed foreigner was looking over his shoulder to face them—a demonic flash of teeth greeting them. And then they saw the small, fragile feet spread beneath the mat, unmoving, and they knew it was their mother.

The tiny daughter rushed up and began pounding at the man's back, but she did no harm. The boy's eyes darted about the room, but he saw no weapons with which to strike. He, too, attacked, but the man kicked him away.

When the foreigner was finished, he rose up off the woman and kicked both children from the hut. Then he quickly slid on his clothes, never once glancing over at the woman whose lifeless eyes stared back at him, and sauntered out into the blinding heat.

"The VC bitch is dead," he announced. His eyes met Stryker's and his smile faded. "From the stress of the interrogation," he added.

"Yah, I'll bet." The MP sergeant's words sounded noncommittal, and the MI agent cocked his head to one side, wondering perhaps if it was worth his time to try and figure Stryker out.

"Now it's time to chopper that bastard." He pointed to the wounded Vietnamese: "And his brats back to the city—for an—interview." His smile returned with the last word.

Stryker glanced back over his shoulder to the bungalow where he had last seen Mather. His fellow sergeant had sent most of the patrols back into service, and the few men left in the structure fifty yards away had still taken no interest in the scuffle escalating outside their crime scene. This was where Stryker would have to make his stand.

"Get them three commies into the chopper!" Hoyden was directing some of the militiamen standing beside the wounded father and his children. "And sergeant," he said, shifting his gaze to Stryker, "I'd like you to come with us. There's some things we have to discuss." The MI agent's mood softened and his eyes grew sad, or so it seemed. "Vietnam looks different from the sky. The situation—the whole damned quagmire takes on a different meaning at two thousand feet. I want you to come along."

Stryker's gunhand lost its tenseness. He glared at the men standing across from him, and their carbines slowly lowered from chest height. He stared at Hoyden for a few seconds, frowned, then turned and started for the helicopter. It was obvious he really had no choice in the matter.

1. Silk and Steel

Saigon, Five Years Later

He shoved his arms out in front of him, but that failed to break the fall. A vast carpet of silver clouds below was rapidly rising up to meet him. Behind and above him, the drone of powerful rotors slapping at the air as the helicopter flew into the sun. Before it disappeared, he spotted Hoyden's face again, leaning out the hatch, an ear-to-ear grin on it, as he directed one last salute down at the helpless MP sergeant. As he began passing through the wisps of cumulus, the turquoise expanse that was the South China Sea appeared several thousand feet below his tumbling, out-of-control form. And he remembered all the childhood stories he had swapped with friends about how striking water at this distance would be no different than slamming feet first into a concrete parking lot.

Mark Stryker's eyes popped open moments before his dive-without-a-parachute culminated in rough, shark-infested waters along the eastern shores of South Vietnam. Drenched in sweat, he was sitting up in his bed, alone, trembling. His hands felt about the silk sheets frantically, but he found no water. His head tilted back, and his eyes scanned the ceiling, but there was no chopper fading in the distance; no MI agent waving him bitter farewell after pushing him out the side of the Huey—only the precinct map he had tacked up above the bed.

Stryker focused on the map, scanning past the blue and red and gold stars that forever marked shooting scenes, murders, and his latest afterhours conquest. His eyes stopped at the date above the legend: 1967.

A shiver went through him, and his body tingled with relief: He was safe. Roy Hoyden was five years in his past and ten thousand miles away—in a Leavenworth stockade.

Stryker checked the bed again. More carefully this time: He was alone.

Shafts of moonlight filtered in through the bamboo drapes separating the bedroom from the balcony. The constant hum in the air—the electricity that was Saigon—had lessened somewhat, and by the crystal clarity of airport noises drifting in from Tan Son Nhut, he could tell it was about three o'clock in the morning. A warm breeze swirled in through the drapes, and he stared out at the temple across the street, rising up through the mist. And at the charred and blackened tenements rising up beyond the golden spire.

A harsh aroma in the room teased his nostrils suddenly, and he glanced at the Buddhist altar hanging on the far wall. A small, silver smoke trail still snaked out from the assortment of joss sticks in front of the jade statue, and the sight almost made him chuckle: Had he actually fired up the incense again last night? Or had some housegirl followed him home from work, walked on his back all night, sucked him silly, then said his prayers for him?

Stryker nodded his head from side to side in resignation. Trying to remember her face would only bring on another headache. Better to just forget it. And perhaps he had just lit the damn things himself anyway: Ever since Kim had left him he had taken to superstitiously lighting a candle or joss stick now and then to ward off the temple curse she claimed to have cast on him. He took in a deep breath, savoring the wet air that hung over his bed when the ceiling fan was off, then forced his legs over the edge of the bed and sighed.

He was never able to fall back asleep after the nightmares. He glanced at the clock on the wall. How long had he gazed out at the damn temple *this* night? It was nearly four o'clock now. Guardmount briefing in two hours, and he felt strong, vibrant, charged with the power of the city. If he went back to sleep, he'd just awaken more exhausted and sapped of the energy he now possessed.

Stryker pushed himself up off the bed. He wrapped a towel around his nakedness and started over toward the balcony. Ah-*hah*! he thought. Totally naked. Proof he had not been alone after all. But he still couldn't remember her face for the life of him.

It was not until his hands were resting on the balcony railing that he looked back toward the dresser bureau—her nightgown was draped across the desk chair. Crimson red.

"Well if it ain't Malarkey Mark!" A husky voice drifted up to him from the street below, and Stryker glanced down at the two MPs walking their beat.

Smitty and Murphy.

"How's tricks?" The off-duty NCO leaned hard on

the railing of the third floor hotel balcony. He had been living at the Miramar a lifetime now, and it seemed almost as much like home as Pleiku had. Before Lai had left him.

"Same old shit," the stocky, forty-year-old staff sergeant on the right responded. His grey hair cropped close to his scalp, the man had a perpetual smile — even when the chips were down — and an evil gleam in his eye.

"Got all the ladies of the evening tucked in tight." The private with the wire-rim glasses and round face sported a toothy grin that outflashed Smitty's. His broad shoulders seemed to roll from side to side as he walked. Both men were clean-shaven.

"Yep, the streets are safe in ol' Saigontown tonight." Smitty hummed the words up to Stryker as both MPs stopped and braced their hands on their hips. "The question is how many underaged cherry-girls you got stashed up their in your pad, Stryker?" Smitty's nightstick came out almost magically, and he began patting a rough hand as if he wasn't beyond breaking Mark's door down to find out.

"All by my lonesome tonight, fellas." Stryker produced his most innocent expression. His hands were held out dumbly, palms up, as if for inspection.

Murphy wondered what the gesture was really saying. "You just happened to be star gazing at this hour of the night, eh sarge?"

"That's right, Murph." Stryker folded his arms across his chest, and the towel around his waist came loose and fluttered to the floor. "Plottin' the trajectory I'm gonna boot your ass if ya don't resume pounding your beat instead of your meat."

A high-pitched wolf whistle broke the eerie silence, and all three Americans gazed up at a fifth floor balcony across the street. A Vietnamese woman was zooming in on Stryker's frame with a pair of binoculars, but the ex-Green Beret did not move. Instead, he smiled up at her and extended a casual salute with his left hand.

"Shit, Stryker," Smitty muttered under his breath. "Salute her with a hard-on!"

"Maybe she'll come down and pay you a visit, sarge." Murphy was all smiles again.

"Maybe she'll pay you a visit and *go down*!" Smitty corrected his partner, then motioned the private to resume patrol by pushing him roughly from behind.

"You gentlemen watch yourself down there," Stryker called, keeping his voice low. They already had enough problems with rooftop snipers: He didn't need irate neighbors dropping trash cans from balconies at four in the morning added to the list of potential hostiles in the City of Sorrows.

Stryker glanced back up at the woman across the street. She was wearing a filmy gold nightgown that didn't hide a thing. Her feet were braced apart as she kept the binoculars to her eyes, and, as flares ringing the neighborhood drifted slowly above the rooftop behind her, the curves of her body were silhouetted by the brief string of bright lights. As the shafts played across her, he watched her curves seem to shift about, though her feet failed to move. When the sizzling orbs of gold drifting on the breeze revealed the untamed bush between her legs, he tore his eyes away and searched the street.

They came to rest on the two black MP helmets fading from view down the block. He thought about calling a retort down to them but reconsidered at the last moment. Just the sight of the two men made him chuckle out loud softly. Smitty had recently transferred in to the 716th from some isolated outpost in the Central Highlands. His reputation had preceeded him by weeks: He was one of the meanest, bravest, craziest NCOs in the Military Police Corps. By far, the most notorious in the brigade! The VC in Pleiku Province had a million-p bounty out on his crew cut, and the NVA hierarchy were offering a battlefield commission to the first soldier who delivered his ears to Hanoi. Murphy, on the other hand, was what made the duo so comical. None of the other MPs would walk beat with him, because, just like Murphy's famous law proclaims, anything that can go wrong *will* go wrong. And that was how most Saigon Commandos felt about ol' Murph. He was a nice enough guy, and dedicated beyond reason to the battalion, but disaster seemed to follow the Pfc wherever his jungle boots took him. Stryker smiled again: Only Smitty possessed and polished the balls to challenge fate and walk beat with Private Murphy. The two cops deserved each other.

Again, the urge to call down something insulting to the MPs raced through him, but Stryker remained silent, and after their forms vanished in the mist, he glanced over once more at the temple looming up between the tenements of Tu Do Street. He wanted to direct an obscene gesture at the structure—surely it was the source of whatever power Kim still had over him—but he only gritted his teeth, wondering why he didn't just move to another hooch where palm trees or a bus stop filled the window view instead.

40

He was about to return to the bedroom when a man's voice called down to him from the fifth floor balcony across the street. "Get your ass in gear, Stryker!" He recognized Sgt. Raul Schultz's voice immediately. "You got less than two hours, chump, before dayshift guardmount." A wry laugh drifted down from above.

Stryker fought the urge to look up. He tried to act like he hadn't heard a thing. *I'll just turn and slowly walk back into the bedroom like I didn't hear a word*, he decided, but he *couldn't* resist, and his eyes shot up to where Raunchy Raul was standing behind the beauty in the see-through negligee. His hands were cupped across her wide breasts and the mandatory shit-eating grin was plastered across his face.

Stryker's first impulse was to yell, *Well if it ain't the rolly-polly policeman!* But circumstances prohibited that: Stryker was apparently alone, and Raunchy Raul had his hands full of more than he could handle. So he just stood there, returning the smile from above.

"Yep, sure feel sorry for you *working* boys!" Schultz called down loudly as he turned the woman around to face him and propped her up in his massive arms. Several lights in tenement windows all along the street were slowly flashing on. The woman, her nightgown hiked up around her hips now, rested her haunches atop Schultz's shoulders and wrapped her legs around the back of his neck. "Me?" Raunchy Raul feigned total innocence at his luck. "I got the *hole* day off, Marcus!" And he buried his face in the woman's crotch. He turned and carried her in off the balcony and back into the bedroom. "The *hole* day off!" His last four words were appropriately muffled.

Stryker frowned as their fifth floor storm shutter slid

41

shut, and he was left alone again with his thoughts.

He turned and returned to the bed, suddenly exhausted from the distant confrontation with a rival sergeant. He felt empty, unfulfilled, even trapped by where his life had taken him. He sat down on the edge of the bed and stared at the poster on the far wall. It was a blown-up black and white photograph. One a combat photographer friend of his had taken long ago. It showed a Vietnamese woman in an *ao dai* walking along down a deserted city street, the sheer gown clinging to her slender body. Her long black hair danced in the breeze as it billowed out from beneath a straw, conical hat. The book in her hands made him think of a student, or perhaps one of the Catholics that paraded down Thanh Mau Street toward the basilica with songbooks or Bibles clutched to their breasts. But the black highheels made her look so sensuous Stryker had to drop his eyes lest the poster arouse him at this late — or early hour — depending on how one looked at it. He doubted even the porter Chay, down in the cavernous lobby below, could fetch him a *xo lam* at this time of night.

But his eyes were drawn back to the poster again and again. He was in the most exciting city in the world, and the picture symbolized all Saigon was to him. So why did he feel there was something lacking in his life? Especially at this late stage in the game. He was on his upteenth extension of his original Vietnam tour and still had a minimum of eight months to go, though he knew the provost marshal would gladly nullify the paperwork if it meant getting the ex-Green Beret out of his hair. So where lied the problem? He was a line sergeant in the toughest beat in the world, with the greatest bunch of guys working for him. He was living in a city at war where the romanticism was exceeded only by the intrigue of the situation and the danger lurking close as the nearest back alley. Vietnam was all he had left. Where else was he to go?

He leaned back against the headboard and allowed his eyes to close. Immediately visions of plummeting through space filled his mind's eye again and he sat bolt upright. But even with his eyes wide now he still saw himself falling helplessly from the helicopter high above the South China Sea. The flashback seemed to project itself across the blank wall in front of him, like a home movie shown without a screen. He blinked several times in terror, and the picture of himself slamming into the shark-infested waters east of Mytho slowly faded in front of him, flickering out as if the projector's cord had been jerked from the wall by a prankster. Yet wasn't it all inevitable, especially in view of the way he had gone tripping through these last few years of his life?

Stryker couldn't purge the memory from his mind. It hadn't been *he* they had thrown from the chopper five years earlier, but in the nightmares *only* he plummeted down through the clouds without a parachute.

He slipped a cassette tape of Thai Hien into the small recorder beside the bed, fast-forwarded the music to his favorite tune, *Em ben nha*, then turned up the volume so that the slow song's mixed Vietnamese and English verses filled the room. He felt himself relax as the woman's soothing voice caressed him, and he was soon drifting back again to those events of five years ago. . . .

The agent from Military Intelligence, Hoyden, had

not only persuaded Stryker onto the chopper after raping the wounded woman in the village outside Mytho, but he brought along the two children, a teenage boy and girl. Their father, his feet mangled by bullets from Hoyden's submachine gun, was bandaged by the man from MI himself, then roughly thrown into the helicopter beside his son and daughter.

As the craft's rotors whipped up a dust storm before pulling its passengers up toward the clouds, Stryker had locked eyes with a bewildered Kip Mather down on the ground. And Mather had gotten the mental message: Something was wrong. He ran to one of the gun jeeps and began following the chopper as best he could, radioing to other units along the way to keep the craft in sight.

Of course they lost it when Hoyden directed the helicopter out over the sea.

He unleashed torrents of rapid Vietnamese at the prisoner, but the man ignored him, sitting silently beside the open hatch, staring at his children. The daughter, her blouse drenched in tears, reached out to him without touching. Her lips were drawn back in silent sobs. The boy remained quiet as the helicopter ascended, but after it leveled off, he rose to his feet and confronted Hoyden. "My father is not Viet Cong!" he yelled at the tall American. "The man who ran into our hut was a stranger!"

"You murdered our mother!" the girl cried, rising beside her brother.

"He raped her." The boy turned somberly to his sister. "He raped her first."

"And you killed my baby brother!" she screamed, hitting at his chest with tiny fists.

44

Hoyden pushed them both onto the floor of the craft, and the girl nearly tumbled out the open hatch. Stryker grabbed her at the last second and held her to him. "What do you expect to accomplish by all this?" Stryker waved out at the endless expanse of turquoise extending to the horizon. "You'll have to kill me, too, you know. Use your head, Hoyden. Take this bird down and let me handle it from there." He glanced up at the men in front of the craft. The pilot acted detached, like he was in another world entirely.

The whole event was like a living nightmare — unreal, but Stryker had pressed on. "You're going about this wrong, Hoyden. You're acting like a madman! It's not worth it. Your career is not worth torturing a few tidbits of information from a wounded villager, and I tend to believe the children, my friend. I think you got the wrong guy. I think the wrong people got hurt down there today. But I think there's still time to salvage the situation. You need a rest, brother. MI's been working you a little bit too hard."

But Hoyden had ignored Stryker. He unleased another barrage of accusations at the wounded Vietnamese, and after the man remained silent, choosing to stare out at the clouds and the sea now instead of his children, Hoyden lost total control and kicked the prisoner out the hatch.

Stryker, like a jungle cat, sprung at the interrogator. With the children screaming and scrambling beneath them, the two Americans wrestled for the submachine gun and rolled right up to the opening in the thin wall of the chopper. Hoyden's finger jerked in on the trigger, and a burst of smoking tracers tore a zipper of holes across the green metal ceiling. As Stryker pinned the man on his back and knocked him senseless with a flurry of fists, the ex-Green Beret's eyes stared past the bloodied face to the dark speck of a man plummeting down through space toward the sea. Already a thousand feet below the helicopter, his legs kicked wildly as the manacles held his arms in behind him. And then he disappeared into the haze of clouds between the ocean and the aircraft.

Mather and six gun jeeps were waiting for them when the Huey finally landed back at the airport outside Mytho. The interrogator was taken into custody, and the pilots were detained for questioning. Seven long days and nights of questioning.

Hoyden was jailed on three counts of homicide. Stryker testified at the court martial, and the former MI agent received six hundred years of hard labor at Leavenworth. Had the victims not been Vietnamese, he probably would have been executed outside the sprawling stockade at LBJ.

Stryker had personally accompanied the children to the psycho ward at Third Field Army Hospital. He brought them presents every day, hoping the stuffed elephants and plaster buffies would soothe the mental wounds of seeing their parents murdered right before their eyes. But the children had just stared straight ahead at the cinder-block walls, unblinking, ignoring him.

And Sgt. Mark Stryker had added another nightmare to his collage of after-dark memories. Many people dream of flying, of soaring up through the clouds on their own power. Stryker's nightmares were of plummeting down through those same clouds, a smiling Hoyden saluting him from the open hatch of the fading chopper—the two Vietnamese children laughing insanely in the unseen background.

Stryker's eyes dropped from the poster girl on the wall. A dim shaft of light had caught his attention: under the bathroom door. A shadow moved across it.

Someone was in there!

He felt no fear but bewilderment. Was his memory really getting that bad? Perhaps it was all the drinks from the night before. He groped in the dark for excuses. Then his eyes darted back to the chair beside the desk and the cherry-red nightgown draped across it.

Wann.

He remembered now. He saw her lying next to him, still fully clothed, earlier that night. Tears in her eyes as they talked about Johnny Powers and the hail of bullets that had torn her husband and her child from her earlier that year. Mark had visited her in the hospital every week, and after her own wounds had healed and she was allowed to leave the ward, men from her husband's shift had chipped in to rent her an apartment only a couple blocks down from the headquarters compound. And Mark had increased the visits, seeing her three or four nights on some weeks, talking with her through the lonely hours till pre-dawn, slowly gaining her confidence, her trust.

Wann had started preparing intricate meals for him only the month before, and after he took her to the cinema for the first time, they went straight back to her apartment and he said goodnight at the door. And didn't even try for that midnight kiss, let alone her pants.

He knew that this woman was special—that she had

47

gone through hell and survived it—that he was walking on thin ice when he was with her: The wrong words, the wrong sights or sounds—*anything* could cause a major setback in her recovery. So he had gone slowly with her, showing her the utmost respect, becoming a close friend more than any kind of suitor.

And last night she had visited his hotel room again and asked to stay.

She had lain in his arms for hours after the movie at the Rex, and she had cried out the memories, and after they were both emotionally drained from reliving the shooting all over again, he said it was time to take her home, and she had hugged him tightly, refusing to let him up as her tears coated his chest. "I am so lonely from playing the grieving widow," she had said, "so very very lonely. Please let me stay with you tonight."

And she had pulled the neatly folded nightgown from her purse. She had been planning this evening for a long time. How could he forget?

Stryker sighed as the memory of her against him flooded back to him. He lifted the satin pillow to his face: He could smell her perfume now. And when he propped it back against the headboard, he could still sense her fragrance, heavy on the air. *That's* why he had turned off the ceiling fan before they slept, he remembered now. He wanted her aroma to settle over him, follow him as he fell back into his dreams.

The bathroom door creaked open slightly, and the light went out, but he could clearly see her standing in the doorway, brushing her long hair. She did not smile down at him or taunt him with her nakedness, but merely stood there in the dark, staring into him, the line of her mouth expressionless as he tried to read her thoughts. And it was not difficult. He knew she was wondering if they had done the right thing. If it was too early. If she should not have waited another month — or another year.

"You are very beautiful," he whispered as she switched hands with the comb and continued brushing the silky, waist-length hair. The outline of her hips in the doorway aroused him, and he slowly pulled a sheet across his own body. "Come here." Her breasts seemed to jut out from the shadows at him, but the tips were flat. Unaroused. He could barely discern the outline of the scar running from her throat to the flat belly.

"What was all the commotion about?" she asked. He detected the irritation in her tone at their secret rendezvous having been interrupted by somebody down on the street.

"Just some of the boys walking their beat," he answered softly. "Come here." And he held a hand out to her.

"Will you speak to them about me in the morning?" she snapped, and he thought perhaps he saw a spark of anger in the cold eyes. "Will you compare me with the other women you've had?"

Stryker was taken aback. "What?"

"Will you tell them I was a good fuck or a bad fuck?" She finally began walking across the room to him.

"I will speak nothing of you to them," he said seriously.

"Then I was a bad fuck." A frown creased her features as she rested one knee on the edge of the bed. Stryker's eyes raced up the firm thigh to the dark shadow above it. He thought of the woman taunting him earlier from the fifth floor balcony, and he wanted

49

to throw Wann across the floor and leap into her, but he resisted.

"You were wonderful." He held both arms out to her, but she did not move closer. "And you are my little secret for as long as you want our relationship to remain that way. I do not talk to my men about women. It is very boring, Wann: I talk about the street, and the crime statistics, and how many of my MPs are out on sick leave, and how I've never got enough cops to cover the patrol roster—"

Wann grinned and fell forward, grabbing his crotch through the sheet. She squeezed hard, and Stryker winced but did not try to pull away. That would have just made it worse. "Johnny used to talk about your guardmount *briefings*!" She laughed aloud as she twisted playfully. "He said that's all you *ever* talked about—is pussy!" She shot her tongue out at him, snakelike, then bared her teeth as if planning to slice down into his groin. Stryker tensed involuntarily. "He said you keep a street map tacked to your ceiling, preserving forever with little red stars the sights of your conquests of hearts!" His face sunken in guilt, Stryker's eyes drifted up to the ceiling map. Wann's eyes followed his, as if she were noticing the display of precincts for the first time.

The phone on the nightstand beside the bed rang just then, startling them both.

Stryker made no move to pick it up but stared at the clock on the far wall: Who would be calling him at four-thirty in the morning? Wann grinned wickedly and reached for the phone. "Expecting a phone call at this time of night?" she asked, suddenly excited and not in the least jealous.

Mark tried to grab the receiver first, but she scurried across him, pinning him down with a knee in the shoulder. The sight above his face just then was irresistible. Ignoring the phone, he clamped his hands around her buttocks and pulled her pelvis down across his lips. She squealed in delight, and, unable to reach the phone, allowed him to pull her closer, tighter, in deeper.

The phone continued to ring undaunted as Wann pulled the sheet out from between them and slid off the hungry sergeant's face. His tongue moved along the flat stomach, up her chest over the ripples of her rib cage, and his lips engulfed half of her breast against her heart.

Wann moved her legs apart, guiding him within her with her free hand. He slowly released the taut nipple from between his teeth, and she brought her lips down across his.

Her hands locked behind him now, she rolled over onto her back, and he plunged in deeper with the thrusts, forcing her lips from his as her head drew back in the pleasure and the pain of the moment.

Something happened to Stryker just then. Something he had never experienced before while making love to a woman. The hairs along the back of his neck were rising in warning: *He was actually drifting into phase red!* And he could not remember even being in the cautionary state: yellow. Perhaps it was the phone, ringing harsh against his ears.

But no. There was a shrill sound in the night air. Outside the window. Beyond the balcony.

The piercing cry of an air-raid siren.

Stryker continued pumping into the woman beneath

51

him, her limbs spread wide for him — her body actually the victor for she was consuming *him*. They thrashed about on the slick sheets, and then she forced her legs closed within his, and he knew she was preparing to climax without him. A familiar fluttering sound filled the air.

The hairs on his neck rose again: Visions of a sea of elephant grass being whipped about by a landing chopper's rotor downblast flashed through his mind. Stryker instinctively rolled onto his back, pulling Wann back on top of him again. Her lips drawn back in wild ecstasy by the unexpected manuever, she screamed her pleasure in his ear as the building trembled and the rocket crashed down through the two floors above them.

Failing to detonate, it came to rest protruding halfway through the ceiling of Stryker's room, nose cone poised a few feet above Wann's humping haunches.

Stryker's eyes went wide with disbelief as the building shuddered again, and the rocket swayed slightly from side to side but failed to drop from the ceiling into their bed. Screams filled the air in the rooms overhead and the streets below, and slabs of plaster and other debris crashed to the floor around the princess bed Kim had left him.

Shocked into inaction by the gravity of the situation and dumbfounded — he had survived the ultimate intrusion, where the odds were stacked so highly against him — the MP sergeant did not dash from the room but merely continued working his hips against the woman's until Wann collapsed across his chest, oblivious to the attack.

And though street lights in the block had dimmed,

flickered, and finally gone out altogether, the phone continued to ring throughout the commotion.

Forty-five . . . forty-six. . . . Stryker did not even realize he was counting the rings to himself as their world crashed down around them.

Finally, Wann braced herself up off his chest, shook the dust from her hair and licked the tip of his nose. She glanced over her shoulder at the rocket hanging motionless mere inches above the crack in her buttocks, then licked his nose again.

"So we live to screw another day!" Wann raised both her hands in the air and smiled broadly down at him. Her breasts swayed back and forth in front of his face, glistening with sweat.

"We have cheated Lady Saigon," Stryker muttered, his tone irritated now: The phone was beginning to give him a headache.

"Do you realize the implications of all this?" Wann arched her shoulders back so that her breasts jutted out at him like smooth, amber ski slopes. "Can you imagine the odds against our surviving a rocket attack?" Screams filled the night outside. Flames crackled in the distance. Air-raid sirens sounded everywhere as fire trucks roared up to the scene.

Stryker thought of his old girlfriend Kim's temple curse, and how she vowed it would forever destroy his future lives, whether he stayed in the Orient or fled back to The World. He thought about all the times he had lain with his women in the middle of the night, listening to the surprise VC rocket attacks, wondering how many lovers had perished in the flames of the distant explosion; wondering how fate decided upon which random tenement the solitary rocket would fall

53

that evening. "You mean — you knew?" Stryker motioned at the dangling projectile with his chin.

"But of course, lover." She winked seductively at him as she reached for the phone. "You're good, Mark Stryker, but nobody's *that* good!"

"Then how — why?"

Wann hesitated picking up the receiver. She did not want a third party listening to what she had to say just then. And she did not want to keep the words inside her, trapped in her bosom. "Many nights I have wished the rockets would claim me," she said, growing suddenly sad. "I have prayed I would not wake from my sleep, so lonely have I been — can you understand? And tonight — well, I can think of no better way to die than in your arms, beneath the searing flash of an explosion."

"At the same time your insides are exploding," Stryker added with a wry smile.

"Yes!" Wann let out a deep sigh as her shoulders wavered, and she stared into the depths of his eyes. "*Yes!*"

"Answer the phone," Stryker muttered, breaking the spell. He cared for her, but this was no time to fall in love: A 122mm rocket was about to fall in their laps. "And tell whoever's on the other end that we could use the bomb squad up here," he added as an afterthought.

"Hello?" Wann's eyes lit up slyly as a feminine voice spoke several words to her. Without saying anything else to the caller, she directed an accusing stare at Mark and handed him the phone. "It's a woman," she hissed, leaving the smile on her lips as her eyes narrowed into sharp icicles.

He picked up the receiver and tried to shift into a

more comfortable position, but Wann tightened her thighs around him, and he winced, remaining the way he was. "Yes?" he finally said.

"Who was that bitch?" A tigress on the other end of the line screamed into his ear. "I'll kill her!"

"Who the hell is this?" Stryker's manner stiffened as he braced himself up on his elbows, but then he remembered her. The woman who had been taunting him with obscene phone calls the last several weeks.

"You know very well who this is!" She was yelling so that Wann could hear every word. "I have been trying to reach you for days!"

"Well—" Stryker hesitated as he glanced down at the woman lying across his chest, but Wann was staring across the room at the poster on the wall. The poster of the woman in the form-hugging *ao dai*. "I've been putting in a lot of overtime lately." The words stumbled forth from his mouth, fooling nobody. "I've been staying at the barracks with my men."

Wann giggled and reached down to grab his buttocks by sliding both her hands beneath him. Then she pulled up with all her strength, forcing him deeper within her. They both gasped, for they were still in the sensitive stage after lovemaking. Stryker didn't doubt their groans carried clearly across the phone line.

"Nobody stays at the barracks anymore!" The caller refused to believe him.

"*I* stayed there—" he began, but she cut him off.

"I called, Mark. A dozen times. They said you were taking a week R and R downtown, but they said they didn't know your address. Dear, dear Mark—" There came a pause on the line. Then she said, "How loyal of them to protect you from the women of Sin City.

How—*brotherly*! But they didn't know I already had your address and phone number, honey!"

Stryker gritted his teeth. Over the past several weeks, he had tried to arrange meetings with the woman, but, perhaps sensing he only wanted to trap her, she had never showed up. And once, the open-air cafe where they were supposed to meet was rocked by an explosion moments after he left without seeing her. It was, strangely enough, a bombing the VC never took credit for publicly. "What is it you want?"

"I told you before." She shifted personalities on him. "I want to unbutton your shirt and run my fingers through the hair on your chest, Mark Stryker." Her voice grew soft and seductive. "I want to suck you erect with my lips and bury my face in your crotch, draining you of all your energy, lover boy, all your juices."

Stryker's face turned red, and Wann struggled up closer to the phone, trying to overhear the other woman's words.

"I want to feel you pumping me up like a hot-air balloon, Mr. MP. I want to wrap my thighs around you while you—"

Stryker hung up the phone. He let out a strained sigh, and only then realized he had been holding his breath ever since the woman spoke her first words.

"One of your chippies?" Wann cast him a disapproving wink, but the smile remained on her lips.

The phone rang again, and Mark picked it up a couple of inches but replaced the receiver on the dialbox without saying anything.

"Hardly," he muttered, his attention returning to the rocket hanging halfway through his ceiling. "I don't know *who* the hell she is."

"On come on, *lover boy*." Wann pinched him in the side, keeping her strong, firm legs wrapped around him.

"No seriously, Wann." Stryker feigned total innocence. "The voice is vaguely familiar, but I can't place it for the life of me."

"Well, *I* recognized it with the first word out of her mouth." Wann ran her fingers through the hair on his arm.

"*No.*" Stryker was sincerely confounded. And mildly shocked at her matter-of-fact comment.

"You know who she is." The woman pressing into him like a hot earthen mold drilled a thumb into his navel. "Don't treat me like a child."

"No really, Wann—" He could not believe they were lying there arguing while fourteen and a half pounds of high explosives dangled above their tangled legs.

There came a scraping against the balcony railing, and both Stryker and the woman in his arms shifted about on the sheets to get a better look at what was transpiring outside.

A tall fire ladder was being braced against the railing from below, and soon a wiry form was racing up the rungs.

"*Stryker!* Mark Stryker—you all right in there?"

A small, wiry Vietnamese policeman appeared against the balcony railing moments later, and as he stared in on the naked couple tangled atop the plush princess bed, his narrow eyes widened, contrasting sharply with the ashen features of his soot-covered face.

"Why Jon Toi!" Stryker shouted past the unsteady nose cone separating the two men. "Welcome to the party! Glad to see you could make it. This was one choir practice that would have bombed without you!"

Stryker slapped the steel tube affectionately with an open palm, and Toi the *canh-sat* slid back down the ladder up which he had just climbed, using only his hands.

2. Splitting Headache Numba Ten

The roaring blast rolled up through the maze of back alleys and knocked MP Murphy off his feet. Chunks of smoking shrapnel arced overhead from where one of the rockets had impacted against the wall of an already leaning tenement a few blocks up from the notorious intersection of Tu Do and Le Loi. Smitty, Murphy's partner and an E6 at that, heard the three .122s fluttering overhead an instant before they detonated. Instinctively, he made himself slim beside one of the jutting concrete lamp posts that hadn't worked in years. The concussion whirled past him and shot on down the side street, knocking trash cans over and shattering windows on those few shops that still had glass panes behind the iron security grills.

"You all right, Murph?" Smitty peaked out from around the lamp post, his pistol already drawn, barrel in the hot, sticky air, ready to smoke one.

Murphy pretended he was in the mood for push-ups and lifted his aching frame off the blacktop. "Yah, I think so, sarge. Feels like I'm all broke up inside. But—"

"But you feel that way all the time anyway."

"Right."

"I think one of them rockets took out Stryker's hooch, Murph." Smitty eased out from behind cover and stared down the dark street in the direction of Tu Do. Air-raid sirens in three locations across the city were beginning to wake those who had somehow slept through the explosions. The sound both saddened and invigorated Smitty.

"Was that what it was?" Murphy shook his head back and forth and made a quick inspection of his limbs. They were still there, but his nose was bleeding. As usual.

Poor guy ends up with a bloody nose answering every call except a goddamned barfight, Smitty thought to himself as he motioned The Murph closer.

"Yah. Sounded like a one-twenty-two. I'm pretty sure one slammed into the Miramar."

"Sounded like a fucking locomotive to me." Murphy rubbed the bruise on his cheek. He checked his holster. The pistol was still there.

"They tend to come across sounding like a real bad ass." Smitty tapped his partner on the shoulder. "Come on, let's go. One of them suckers sure 'nough got the building across the street from the Miramar." Flames licked out at the darkness down the block.

"That goofy Stryker's probably down there roastin' marshmellows over the crispy critters," Murphy commented as they cautiously started toward the flames. Neither MP ran. In Saigon, you froze after an explosion. And after dark, even the police moved slowly toward all the commotion when not in a marked vehicle. Rookies tended to shoot at anything that moved and ask questions later. Sometimes even the old grizzled vets, who had worked all-night curfew checkpoints for

60

years, were unpredictable; it depended on which stage of burnout they were currently in. "I doubt his room took any rounds. With the arsenal he's got stored under the bed and in the closets, this whole precinct would be tits to the wind already."

"Yah." Smitty peered down a dark alleyway as they crossed an intersection. Now that the explosions had died down, dogs slowly emerged from their lairs and were howling at the stars with hurt ears. But Smitty was searching past the small animals. The scourge of the city, the underworld denizens tended to slither out from their holes after the rockets fell. Prowling the scenes of destruction while emergency crews were still arriving and tending the wounded, the man-animals looted wherever they could, stealing from neighbors who were now dead or buried under the rubble. Smitty had even caught a cowboy trying to rape a dead woman after one barrage of steel from the night sky.

It had happened in Cholon, the predominately Chinese district. Only the woman's lower torso protruded from the landslide of charred brick and cinder blocks. The man had hiked the bloodied nightgown up over the woman's hips and was busy pumping her—his trousers down around his ankles and his arms holding onto a splintered section of light pole—when Smitty happened down the dark side street and spotted him.

Dropkicking the cowboy all the way back to his patrol jeep, Smitty broke his nightstick over the prisoner's head when he bolted and ran. Hampered by the trousers still around his ankles, the man would have been an easy recapture, but Smitty slowly drew his .45 automatic, muttered, "*Dung lai*," under his breath, then popped off three quick rounds that tore away one ear

61

and split his back down the middle.

When the MP—a buck sergeant back then—walked up to the groaning Vietnamese, the suspect rolled painfully over onto his side, a dazed look in his eyes. In his right hand, he sluggishly brandished a stiletto.

Smitty just grinned—even after the man weakly jabbed out with the sparkling blade and the tip failed to penetrate the green canvas top of the MP's jungle boot. Smitty's smile broadened as an idea came to him. A flash of headlights down the block signaled a vehicle was approaching, but Smitty didn't seem to notice. He moved closer and stepped on the steaming coil of intestines protruding from the exit wound across the man's belly. "Bye-bye, buddy boy," he muttered as the man thrust the knife at him again. "You're just another Buddha toy."

And as the beams of red light from the MP jeep coasting up to the scene illuminated Smitty's gunhand, the sergeant sent a fourth round into the dying man's flaring nostrils. His head slammed back into the pavement with the impact, but he still refused to die. With one eye trying to focus on the glowing white letters across the black MP helmet liner, the man, his words drawn out and smothered with blood, gurgled a final insult at the American. "I—laugh—last—" And a shallow chuckle escaped through the heavy wheezing. Then he was dead, the one remaining eye still staring up at Smitty.

"Not *quite*, gutterball!" And as he holstered his weapon, the stocky military policeman bellowed out a laughing roar that echoed back off the tenement walls rising up all around him. Then he turned to face the men in the patrol jeep, a sad look in the dark eyes above the ear-to-ear grin, for Smitty knew the man *had* had the last laugh in this crazy Asian game.

"I saw it! I saw it!" the private driving the duty officer to the sector involved in the rocket attack had screamed for his favorite sergeant's benefit, trying to prevent another internal investigation by the MPI Shoot Team. "That sucker pulled a blade on Smitty, Lou! It's a justifiable homicide in my book!" The young MP was standing up behind the windshield of the jeep now. "Definitely a righteous shooting!" His words were growing defensive, on behalf of the NCO standing in the street in front of them, uncaring. "I'll testify to it, too, in any court martial — *I'll testify!*"

Lieutenant Slipka had stared across the drifting cloud of gunsmoke at Smitty for several seconds, silent as stone, then he turned to look back at the woman's body protruding from the pile of rubble. Her legs spread apart and blood smeared across the inner thighs, she had obviously been savagely violated. And all of it *after* she was crushed by the cinder blocks, the line lieutenant thought, disgust in his expression. A flare drifted slowly overhead, shedding even more light across the ghastly scene, and then an entire string of flares — a starburst — floated past on the warm Saigon breeze, and as he waved his driver back in the direction of the command post, his eyes remained locked on Smitty's.

Lt. Tony Slipka frowned as another patrol coasted up and two enlisted men hopped out and began slapping the NCO on the back. But he was not disturbed by the routine show of frontline comradery. It was the uncertainty clouding his mind that bothered him: the self-doubts over *who* had raped the woman back in the

63

shadows. A bolt of brief shame lanced down through Slipka's gut as they drove away, and in the ensuing weeks he would dismiss the whole notion. But much later, the suspicions would return to him, and that mental picture of the woman's mangled body was always in front of his mind's eye whenever he saw Smitty smiling about something, or when their eyes happened to meet. As time passed, he stopped trying to avoid the man, and at the guardmount briefings he was even able to joke with him about this or that. The usual waves were exchanged when they passed each other on street patrol, but a chill always shot down Slipka's spine, and he knew they were never smiling about the same things.

The men had made him an instant celebrity of course, after rumors of the shooting circulated through the many companies in the battalion and were slowly blown out of proportion. But fame was short-lived in Saigon, for there were always shootings, and the VC sent sappers after the MP patrols every weekend like clockwork, so there was someone different in the spotlight with each new X slashed through the short-timers' calendars.

Gunfighter.

That was the inscription in Smitty's customized belt buckle. It always brought a frown to Slipka's face during the uniform inspections. The lieutenant knew men who so revered and respected the weapons on their hips often died with them drawn. At least his buckle wasn't as brazen as that goofy Writter's: *Gimme Head Till I'm Dead*.

Murphy stopped in mid-stride as they crossed the intersection with the barking dogs. The flames down the road had engulfed a second building, and the sky was aglow like a false dawn.

"Did you see that?"

A shadow had rushed across the narrow alley: a cowboy, heading for the rooftops.

"Yah." But Smitty continued toward the crackling flames in the distance. He could bag a cat burglar anytime. They were like traffic violations on Le Loi Boulevard or uniform gigs at the MACV annex. Shards of broken glass, sparkling down at the MPs from atop high concrete fences, were quickly left behind (to be logged in buried memories of the city's scars). Then they were approaching another alley in the complicated maze running off the lively nightclub district of Tu Do Street like branches off a tree trunk.

"We're not gonna circle around and nab his ass?" Murphy was shocked, but his feet kept walking.

"Nah." The faint click of metal against metal could be heard as Smitty toyed with his pistol's slide safety, flipping it on and off with his thumb as they approached the raging fire. "First we gotta check on Stryker-san—just to make sure. I'd want him to do the same for me."

When they reached the final block before Tu Do, they routinely split up, taking opposite sides of the street and keeping to the rare shadows as the blinding inferno sent a pulsing glow through the neighborhood.

Military Police privates Derek Ramsey and Benny Harcourt had been sitting in their parked patrol jeep moments before the VC rockets descended on Saigon. They were on their short-7, or midnight chow break. And since Tan Son Nhut's USO was out of their sector, they sat at the smoky intersection of Le Van Duyet and Yen Do, munching on steaming sugarcane cubes and sipping ice coffee from plastic baggies with colorful straws protruding from them.

Harcourt enjoyed this time of the shift, an hour or two before dawn, when the city was in its most quiet mood but still humming with electricity and the potential for hidden excitement in the air—if one was only motivated enough to search for it in the dark back alleys. *Seek out And Destroy* had come to mean SAD in more ways than one.

Ramsey, on the other hand, dreaded these last few hours of the 6 P.M. to 6 A.M. night shift. He felt it was the most dangerous time for cops on the street. Derek Ramsey held as much respect for the Viet Cong and their sympathizers as he did contempt. He often spoke of their cunning and knew *they knew* when the MPs were most vulnerable: toward the end of their shift, when they were glassy-eyed and apathetic about the threats of routine patrol. Hadn't the last dozen snipings come about a half hour either side of four o'clock in the morning? And you can bet he had a map downtown in his hootch with little gold pins all over it to prove his theory. Harcourt called it his voodoo veneer.

A total of five streets came together where Le Van Duyet meets Yen Do. Some people maintain it's six, but they count the railroad tracks that cut straight through the large platform in the middle of the intersection. A fountain and numerous flower stalls once decorated the sprawling space, but one night terrorists blew up the statue next to the fountain, and the flower merchants slowly moved their stalls elsewhere. Martial law curfew roadblocks now crisscrossed the boulevard arteries, a tank and two gun jeeps were parked in the heart of all the concertina wire, and checkpoint fires burned within the rims of countless sand-filled oil drums. Ramsey and Harcourt often parked on the Yen Do side of the intersection at this time of night, gambling on how many civilian vehicles would brave the streets after curfew—Vietnamese confident they had bribed the appropriate *canh-sats*, only to find other officers working the roadblocks when they got caught. Ramsey usually won the wagers, but all they ever involved were military ration cards, and since he didn't drink or smoke, they were of little value to him. He always ended up selling them back to Harcourt for comp days or the latest Star Trek fanzine. Harcourt's sister was always sending him boxloads of the stuff, and though he wasn't the least bit interested in the exploits of Mr. Spock or Captain Kirk, Ramsey was a trekkie of the first order.

Parking on the Yen Do side had its other advantages also. Their spot was catty-corner to the Pink Pussycat nightclub, and brazen bargirls were forever venturing out into the night, attempting to run drugs back and forth for their pimps or score that last trick before the sun rose. Never mind that the only warm bodies out on the street that late were cops and militiamen—the whores never learned. Stryker maintained they were more sophisticated than most of the MPs gave them credit for. Richards often defended them, claiming the girls were really trying to bed down the nightwatch MPs. "What safer place to be after dark than in the arms of a dirty copper?" he lamented more than once.

Bryant bragged his favorite sergeant got *that* idea from the T-shirts Thomas always wore when they were working undercover: Feel Safe Tonight — Sleep With A Cop.

"Ain't that Little Oral Annie?" Harcourt's eyebrows did a thirty-mile-an-hour dip as two buxomy women sauntered out of the Pink Pussycat. Both wore tight hot pants, black silk blouses cut low, and high heels.

"Yah," muttered a disgusted Derek Ramsey after he spat a wad of juiced-out sugarcane into the gutter beside their unit. "And I'll lick their assholes if that ain't Moanin' Lisa struttin' her stuff right beside her."

The two women symbolized a segment of Vietnamese society that turned Ramsey's stomach. He didn't want to hear about how American policy in Saigon turned poor girls into prostitutes (because he'd argue nonstop with you about that) and he didn't want to hear about how war orphans often learned no other way to survive and support themselves. Maybe this was why the night shift so rattled him. On day watch he could eat lunch in Le Loi Park and watch the pretty, shy secretaries pass by without so much as sneaking a glance at him. He could admire the Catholic girls strolling down Thanh Mau on their way to the cathedral, prayer or songbooks in their arms, blue and white *ao dais* the uniform of the day. And when the sun was up, mothers who would never dream or dare to speak to hairy foreigners supervised their children in the playground or inspected goods at the open-air markets, totally ignoring him. And he admired them for that — for the strictly Vietnamese behavior in them. They were petite yet fiery women to be treated with respect. They were flowers to make the day shift pass by much swifter. They were an ocean breeze — a floral fragrance on the warm Saigon wind, elusive yet ever present.

But no — that goofy Stryker had put him back on night shift just because Slipka caught him putting Hang Traitor Jane stickers on the jeep bumpers in the brigade motorpool.

He stared at the two women across the street and frowned. They had already made contact with one of the checkpoint militiamen and were no doubt offering a vulgar proposal in return for allowing them to pass through unchallenged.

Little Oral Annie was the bigger of the two women though they were the same height. She wore her hair in a swirl style that rose up slightly off her shoulders and had on a layer of red lipstick that was so wide her lips appeared twice their normal size. She was in no way overweight, but her thighs were so muscular many men were frightened by them.

Moanin' Lisa, on the other hand, contrasted sharply with her partner. Her face was slender, with high cheek bones, and she wore no makeup whatsoever. Her hair, jet black and shiny, was worn straight and hung to her waist. Her legs were shapely but she had no hips, and Ramsey was of the opinion her bra merely propped up inward breasts which were otherwise sagging and withered. Both women chewed bubblegum like it was against the law — the MPs could hear the loud pops clear across the intersection.

"You wanna go over and card 'em?" Harcourt sounded enthusiastic, like he had just finished a double dose of coffee and was remotivated to return to the streets and chalk up some stats for Gary Richards, his squad leader.

"Naw." Ramsey tossed a cube of sugarcane in the air, and it disappeared between his lips. "Let the Viets have 'em. I don't wanna get *near* them broads, pal."

"Yah, but they're sure bouncin' their butts down that sidewalk." Harcourt felt himself growing hard. "Maybe we could score a skull job or something."

"And go home to The World with a perpetual case of the black syph?" Ramsey sat up in his seat, an incredulous look on his face.

"You can't get the clap from a lousy skull job." Harcourt's eyes grew big and sad, like an old, burnt-out hunting dog that had been kicked off the welcome mat by an ungrateful owner.

"Of course you can." Ramsey wadded up the empty plastic baggies, tossed them over his shoulder onto a pile of trash in the gutter, and folded his arms across his chest. He belched in silent protest as the two Saigon Commandos watched Moanin' Lisa rub up against a militiaman across the street. Her hand went straight for his crotch, but the embarrassed soldier brushed it away.

"I'm callin you on this one, Derek," Harcourt countered. "I'd even bet a week's pay on it: You can't get no fuckin' VD from a skull job."

Ramsey's smile returned. "A week's pay?"

"A week's pay, hot shot."

"And on whose expertise do you base such overconfidence?"

"Raunchy Raul taught me everything I know—who else?"

"A week's pay, huh?"

"A week's pay. Hell no, asshole—make it *two* weeks

70

pay!" Harcourt imitated his partner and also folded his arms across his chest. They looked like two yoga instructors preparing to lead the street life in a meditation class. "I just fucking *know* you can't catch it from a skull job."

Ramsey turned slightly in his seat to make eye-to-eye contact with the man behind the steering wheel. "You're willing to wager forty bucks on evidence provided by a man who thinks babies are the result of rear-end whiplash?"

"Do I stutter, homo-head?"

"Look, Benny." Ramsey dropped a rigid arm across Harcourt's shoulder. "You're my partner, for Christsake. I'm not in the mood tonight for tearin' anybody a new asshole—"

"*Homo-head* was no exaggeration," Harcourt cut in, feigning intense disgust.

"So I'm gonna cut you some slack. Why do you think they call that cunt Little Oral Annie?"

"Don't mean nothin'." Harcourt was adamant. "You can't catch the clap from a simple—"

"Why do you think her voice is always so hoarse?" Ramsey interrupted this time. "Why do you think she's so—*throaty*?"

Harcourt's eyebrows came together as he seemed to reconsider.

"I'm tellin' you, son." Ramsey punched the older private lightly on the arm with his free hand. "Little Oral Annie has sucked so many whangers her *tonsils* are all scabbed up and stranglin' her from inside!"

"That's dis*gusting*!" Harcourt pulled away from the man beside him. "*Ughh!* Gross-out, Derek. You've gone too far this time!"

"I shit you not, Benjamin baby."

"Some women just naturally talk—*husky* like that."

"*Some women?*" Ramsey smiled broadly, victorious in his own eyes over the other man. "You ever heard a *new* girl talking with such a deep voice?" He didn't give Harcourt time to ponder over his reference to Vietnamese virgins. "Fuck no, Joe! Only the *business* girls got a permanent case of the sore throat. And you know how they get it, Benny? You know how they get a dose no cough drops or hypo of penicillin will cure?"

Harcourt shifted about uncomfortably in his seat but didn't say anything.

"From suckin' worthless whangers like yours, boy!" Ramsey slapped his partner on the back, hard this time. "From applying a gold medal liplock on swollen rods that already been drippin' for days! For twenty-five hundred p they'll swallow you whole, brother, and won't let go till you blow up on 'em. You don't believe me? Go over and French-kiss ol' Annie then, smart ass! Go ahead! Trot on across the street and show your balls!"

"You're disgusting, Ramsey." But Harcourt was still smiling.

"Go on over there and ask Little Oral Annie why she does it, sport—she'll tell you. Go over there and ask her why she loves suckin' cock more than spreadin her legs! You know what she'll tell you? She'll confess her ulcers don't hurt no more when her stomach's coated with semen!"

"Nah." Harcourt shook his head from side to side in disbelief.

"You think I'm shittin' you, sonny-boy?" Ramsey stood up in the jeep and yelled over to the women.

72

"Hey Annie! Hey Moaner Lisa! Get yo buns over here, girls!" The women displayed startled faces at first, but when they recognized the American MP jeep and realized a couple of fat wallets awaited them across the street, they ignored the Vietnamese PFs and helped each other down through the gutter so they wouldn't trip over their high heels with eagerness.

"Oh, now you've gone and done it!" Harcourt gazed up and down the street. "What if Richards drives by — or worse: Stryker!"

"Hi boys!" The girls, still fifty yards away, were all smiles now as they waved to the patrolmen.

"I'm in such a good mood tonight, Benny, I'm even gonna amend our bet a little bit." Ramsey stepped out of the patrol unit.

"Amend our bet a little bit?" Harcourt's grin warped into a suspicious scowl as his eyes watched the restrained breasts bouncing within the women's silk blouses as they maneuvered across the scattered piles of debris in the middle of the street.

"I'm not even gonna hold you to three weeks' pay on this one like I planned on — "

"I thought you said — " Harcourt's mild protest was lost in the swirl of emotions coursing through him as he watched Little Oral Annie's thighs brushing against each other with each swaying step, and he envisioned his face between them.

"You know Phuto?"

"Phuto racetrack?" Harcourt wasn't the least bit interested in the new proposal. He could already smell the perfume preceding Moaning Lisa and Little Oral Annie. Actually, the scent was a mixture of alcohol, sweat, and stale sex, but the nostril-twitching odor excited him even more than perfume.

"Yah, where they run the horses every night: Phuto."

"What about it?"

"I'm willing to call off our bet if you'll agree to finance a week's worth of my wagers out at Phuto." Ramsey's slight hint of a smile faded as he locked eyes with Little Oral Annie. Ramsey didn't like the women of the night the way so many of his brother cops seemed to take to them. Especially Annie and her sidekick, Moanin' Lisa. He had booked both of them a dozen times in the past. Prior to, during and after the arrests, the girls were constantly giggling behind his back and making fun of the way his eyes darted to the corners of their sockets and lingered there when strangers approached or when he heard suspicious sounds off to the side.

"A week's worth of wagers?" Harcourt was asking, but Ramsey's eyes narrowed with caution when both Moanin' Lisa and Little Oral Annie's faces seemed to light up suddenly — as if dim headlights from somewhere behind the MPs had briefly played across their features then vanished. The girls skidded to a halt, their smiles abruptly disappeared, then a brighter flash illuminated the fear in their eyes and bathed the tenements behind them with a powerful orange glow. And then the sound hit them: rolling, thunderous blasts that shook the ground, made the street lights flicker, and sent the tenements all around them to trembling violently.

The twirling buzz of descending rockets reached their ears in-between the secondary explosions, and moments later the night erupted with air-raid sirens from government rooftops across the city.

"VC come!" Moanin' Lisa screamed as her hands flew up and the fingers draped the edges of her cheeks. "VC come Saigon!" Ramsey's eyes shifted to the bright red fingernail polish she wore. Cherry red.

"No, no, no, no!" Harcourt glanced over his shoulder at the ascending fireballs a few miles away and the pall of inky smoke creeping across the city's edge. "Come here, honey, come here! MP protect you from the bad, bad Cong. VC no come Saigon tonight!" His hands reached out to them. "Come to papa."

Little Oral Annie was already running back across the street from the direction she had just come. "VC come Saigon!" She agreed with Moanin' Lisa, who was still standing in the middle of the street, mouth open as the distant flames danced in her eyes. "VC find all whore girls boom boom GI! VC march them naked through streets—lop off head in Le Loi Park—you bic, MP? Time to *di di mau* or die!"

Moanin' Lisa whirled to follow her girlfriend, broke a high heel and twisted her ankle, stumbling to one knee. Harcourt made to rush up and assist, but the woman rebounded like a ostrich trying to fly and zigzagged through the sand-filled oil drums and was gone.

Ramsey was already back in the jeep. "We better beat feet down there to see if they need any help," he muttered, trying to sound unemotional as he reached in the back seat and turned the radio volume up full. With his other hand he twisted the starter button on the dashboard, and the powerful engine under the hood rumbled to life. The dual red beacons on the front fenders began twirling lazily against the midnight mist creeping up out of the back alleys.

"It looks outside our sector," Harcourt argued, wondering if he was displaying cowardice toward combat or fear of the supervisors. They had all been on the rag the last few weeks, ever since all the commotion in Bien Hoa where a payroll convoy had been ambushed. Thirty-five MPs had died. Nine KIAs were lost trying to round up the bandits responsible. "We better hang tight till we hear from WACO."

The radio net was nonstop chatter interspersed with bursts of static, the wail of sirens, and straining jeep motors as units raced about the city. The criminals in Saigon did not call a cease-fire merely because the communists had mounted a surprise rocket attack. The hoodlums took full advantage of all the confusion and excitement. A multi-pitched electronic yelp scrambled the dual WACO channels, silencing most of the transmissions from the street, and Horatio Schell, notorious NCOIC, legendary desk sergeant, and much-loved all-around good guy, broke squelch as he simulcast across all channels in a deep, confident voice:

"Attention all units. Sectors two, four, six and nine—this is Waco—switch to Channel Two—Code-One Channel One at this time—Signal-Three hundred coming in from one, two, and three hundred blocks of Tu Do and Nguyen Hue—also Newport Bridge and Checkpoint Six-Alpha—Cars Twenty-two-Echo, Niner-Alpha, Thirty-five and Thirty-six-Delta disregard the barfight on Le Van Duyet, over. . . ."

"Tu Do Street!" Harcourt sighed, a pained expression in his eyes as he watched the flames on the building skyline grow. A trio of Vietnamese firetrucks

rushed past, their engines roaring and roof lights revolving but sirens strangely silent, as if they were
merely the ghosts of firefighters killed years ago in a
long-forgotten inferno.

Ramsey switched the radio to Channel Two. He was
biting his lower lip so hard blood began trickling from
the chapped cracks.

"All other units responding to non-priority calls Ten-
Twenty-two at this time," Sergeant Schell continued.
As he keyed the mike, enlisted men could be heard in
the background at headquarters, rushing about. Pa-
pers shuffled loudly, banana magazines were slammed
into their M-16 receivers. Harcourt thought he heard
the provost marshal's voice telling Sergeant Farthing to
fire up the Assault Tanks.

"Alert Teams report to your V-One hundreds,"
WACO droned on, and Ramsey commenced tapping
his fingertips against the eager barrel of the Hog-60
mounted in the back of the military police jeep. "First
shift Mike Papas remain in your assigned precincts.
Third shift will respond to the Signal-Three hundreds
from the International and Capitol compounds."

Ramsey jumped in the back of the gun jeep and
grabbed hold of the big machine gun's handles. He
whirled the weapon around so that the barrel faced the
fifty-foot flames off in the distance, and he sighted in
on the dark stretch of jungle beyond the snaking river.
He wanted to send a sustained burst of tracers out at
the terrorists hiding in the trees. (For how could you
call scum who'd launch exploding metal into civilian
housing projects guerilla fighters?) But he knew they
were long gone now. He beat his fist on the top of the
bulky radio clamped to the side of the jeep.

And Waco droned on, unaffected by the assault. "Car Twenty-two-Echo—respond to the Embassy Hotel—number thirty-five Nguyen Trung Truc—see the woman, a Victor November Foxtrot—report of a stabbing victim that one-four, over. . . ."

Ramsey listened to The Uke acknowledge the call, then he beat the radio again. "Christ!" he muttered. "Saigon's burning to the ground, and they still got the gall to air assault victim calls!"

"Maybe The Uke can save the guy." Harcourt's tone sounded bored, though his fingers were nervously wrestling with each other. He knew their number would come over the air anytime now. He dreaded the waiting game the most.

Ramsey could see the young MP they called The Uke beating his jeep, too, as WACO forced him to miss out on the action downtown and respond to the CAP call instead.

"Car Eleven." The desk sergeant at Dispatch went on with his list of little goodies. "At the Pan Am office—number twelve Nguyen Hue—report a heat-seeking missile was launched through the plate glass windows at the model Boeing hanging from the ceiling—perpetrators missed—took out the whole back wall instead . . . V.F.D. Ten-Seventy-six to assist—secure the scene for the *canh-sats*—MPI sending a squad in to cover from MACV annex. . . ."

A garbled acknowledgement broke through the intense static on the radio set.

"Car Thirty-five-Alpha—"

Ramsey's frown deepened. He hated the term car used as a call sign. He had long ago submitted a memo suggesting Dispatch call the street patrols gun jeep this and gun jeep that, but the duty officers only laughed out loud after reading then circulating it among themselves. It never reached the C.O.'s desk — of that he was sure — and the lieutenants on duty at the time had probably shit-canned the lengthy report.

"Car-Thirty-five-Alpha — report of a Ten-Thirty-two — at number niner two-uh niner Nguyen Van Thoai — possible murder-suicide involving a Uniformed Sierra — Code-Zero that fourteen, Greenlee — several reports flooding in of shots fired. . . ."

"Car to cover?" A tired voice immediately followed the dispatcher's transmission. Both Ramsey and Harcourt instantly recognized Lieutenant Slipka's unemotional drawl.

"Car Twenty-two-Echo's Ten-Twenty-three the Embassy Hotel," a different voice cut in. A dying siren could be heard in the background, then the transmission broke off.

"Roger, Twenty-two-Echo." The dispatcher acknowledged the unit skidding up to the stabbing incident. "On scene zero four forty hours. WACO to Lima Three: negative on your last, lieutenant. I've no cover cars available at this time and five more ASAP calls to air — over. . . ."

"WACO — This is Lima Three — roger. Covering from the Calypso on Pasteur street — Ten-Thirty-nine."

Ramsey felt the tic in his eye going to work. Harcourt swallowed hard. The desk sergeant had said there were no backup units available and that five calls were pending. That meant their number was rapidly coming up without doubt now. Their instincts told them to race across town to assist 35-Alpha. But their training demanded they stand by for an assignment.

"WACO, this is Twenty-two-Echo." The Uke's voice betrayed the slightest hint of excitement for a change as his transmission cut through the surges of intense static. The energy in his voice merged with the power flooding the net, and every MP near his radio cocked an ear closer, anticipating what was to come. "Requesting a Ten-Seventy-nine this one-four—victim is Delta Oscar Alpha—suspects GOA—no witnesses, no descriptions, no nothing, over. . . ."

Harcourt quickly translated all the MP codes in his mind. The Uke was requesting a coroner. The stabbing victim was Dead On Arrival, which was a peculiar police play on words for the dead man had been at the scene the entire time in the first place. GOA meant Gone On Arrival and was a civilian law enforcement term Schultz had brought over with him from working the streets of Fort Carson. The PM had been unsuccessfully trying to discourage its use for months—it just was not GI!

"WACO, this is Car Eleven!" a high-pitched voice screamed across the net. "Been hit by an RPG at—" Static drowned out the transmission.

A second cut through the interference on top of it. "WACO, WACO—this is Caaaar Toowelve-Bravooo." An oldtimer with nineteen years on the street stretched out his call sign out of habit. "Can we get some flare ships out over the Saigon docks? Gots lotsa acccction down on wharf Charlie-niner. Unable to tell if they're friend or foe, over. . . ."

"Send a blooper round down at 'em!" An anonymous voice came across the net, fading just as quickly. It was obvious the MP to blame never heard Car Eleven calling for help.

The desk sergeant sent the tonal scrambler screaming again. "*Code-One* on Channel Two!" he demanded. Then, for the record: "Units responding from headquarters to assist Car Eleven. WACO to Car Thirty-six-Charlie. . . ."

Harcourt brushed his knuckles against his brow, wiping the sweat and grime away. Then he reached for the telephone lying on the seat. "WACO," he said softly, almost in resignation, "this is Thirty-six-Charlie—send it."

"At the warehouse—number one one six Nguyen Dinh Chieu—respond to report of suspicious activity in the area. Your call is Ten-forty." No siren.

Ramsey shot a questioning look at his partner as Harcourt slid in behind the steering wheel. *Why were they airing a lousy Ten-37 in warehouse row when so much flak was falling on Tu Do?*

"Roger," Harcourt said simply, almost in a whisper.

"Your location?"

Ramsey reached forward and grabbed the mike as Harcourt was about to hang it back on the dashboard: He wanted his partner's hands free as they started down Yen Do hill.

"Le Van Duyet and Yen Do!" he almost yelled.

"Roger—responding from Le Van Duyet and Yen Do at four forty-one hours."

Then both MPs in unit 36-Charlie remembered what was at 116 Nguyen Dinh Chieu: a huge stockpile of S.A.M. missiles!

Visions of sappers in black pajamas flashed through their minds as the two privates cut corners on two wheels. Harcourt doused the headlights three blocks before they reached the scene, and they coasted up to the fence line, silent and swift as panthers.

But the American military warehouse was intact. Security had not been breached. There were no signs of forcible entry anywhere. An infantry unit security guard was found sleeping on duty. *How could he snooze through the rocket barrage?* Ramsey wondered in amazement. *If you snooze, you lose.* But he bore no injuries and still had his carbine cradled in his arms like a teddy bear.

Ramsey and Harcourt walked around the warehouse with the guard three times, but they were unable to find anything out of the ordinary. In the distance, explosions lit up the southern horizon.

Ramsey was still biting his lower lip: He wanted to be in the middle of the rocket attack. He wanted to feel the heat of the rolling blasts. He wanted to feel the intensity of emotions that always swirled about when the air-raid sirens screamed against the oppressive night. *Derek Ramsey loved the stench of cordite on the pre-dawn breeze!*

"You didn't hear *anything* earlier in the evening?" he asked the guard for the fifth time.

"You didn't *see* anything?" Harcourt added, though he didn't really care one way or the other.

"Well, there *was* this strange buzzing noise about an hour or two ago," the infantryman finally admitted.

"A buzzing sound?"

"Yah—you know, like a buzz saw at a wood mill."

"Never been to a wood mill," Harcourt revealed.

"A buzz saw?" Ramsey stopped walking back toward the MP jeep, and the others halted beside him. "Where?"

The security guard glanced up at the stars as if trying to get his bearings, then down at the fireworks show over Tu Do.

"Well?" Ramsey grabbed the soldier's arm, growing rapidly impatient.

"I think it was coming from *that* warehouse," he decided, stammering as he pointed to a building in the middle of the vast compound. "But the whole string of structures are supposed to be empty. Maybe there was a small light on inside, too, come to think of it. But at the time, I thought it was just street lights in the background, shining through the holes."

"Could anybody be working a late shift in there?" Harcourt asked. "Technicians or somebody on a government project? Maybe a—"

"Fuck it," Ramsey interrupted, guiding his partner away from the infantryman as he started down toward the warehouse. "Let's check it out, then get back to the jeep so we can code in-service!"

They found a side door to the building ajar. A lantern in a far corner of the long structure sent a dull yellow glow up against the ceiling but left the doorway dark.

Both men routinely drew their automatics.

Without speaking, Ramsey—the senior MP as far as rank went—motioned toward the left side of the entry corridor with his fingers, and Harcourt moved off as directed.

Harcourt was miffed. He was certain they'd find nobody inside the warehouse: The door was open but showed no signs of having been forced. But he proceeded up ahead of Ramsey like the two military policemen always cleared dark buildings. And after he got as far as he could see safely, he paused and waved

Ramsey up to his position. Then they switched off, and the senior MP took the lead up to the next corner or wall divider.

Harcourt could smell wood shavings in the structure. Minute particles floated about in the air, settling on his lips. Your typical carpenter's workshop.

The heavy odor of spilled blood reached him an instant after he rounded the last corner of the interior maze of panels and came upon the grizzliest sight of his brief law enforcement career: A woman's body lay on a high metal table on her back, her limbs strapped to hooks on the edges. She wore nothing beneath a thin flowered skirt that was hiked up around her hips. A buzz saw had split her head down the middle and was imbedded against the column of thick bones inside her neck.

"My God—" Harcourt muttered under his breath as he slowly walked closer to the blood-soaked body, his eyes glued to the grotesque expression on half of the victim's face.

Ramsey was not so careless. He allowed himself a brief glance at the corpse then immediately commenced clearing the rest of the building.

He was back beside Harcourt thirty seconds later. Benny was staring down at the red film smeared across the woman's exposed vagina. He jumped when Ramsey put a hand on his shoulder.

"Bitchin' sight, ain't it, Benny?" Ramsey asked matter-of-factly.

"She's been raped." Harcourt pointed to all the blood drying between the woman's legs.

Ramsey peered closer, careful to keep his hands behind his back. "I don't think so, brother." He glanced

84

around again, just to make sure they were still alone. It wouldn't do to have the murderer sneak up behind them when they were so engrossed with the mutilated slab of meat lying before them. "I'd say she was on her period."

"That didn't stop some lowlives we've arrested before."

Harcourt stopped breathing and began to turn slightly red.

Ramsey moved to the side a couple of feet and lowered his face an inch above the woman's chest. Then he slowly scanned left to right, from her navel to her throat, like a human x-ray machine.

"What the hell you doing?" Harcourt finally asked after he resumed breathing and succeeded in keeping the sugarcane cubes down in his stomach.

"Her breasts—" Ramsey said softly, as if he was mesmerized by the sight of them. Once full and youthful, they were now settling flat across her rib cage, cold and lifeless.

"What?"

"See how the nipples are all swollen? They've got some awful bite marks in them."

Harcourt moved closer beside his partner, then jumped at the sound of water trickling from the edge of the table down onto the floor.

Ramsey was not so unnerved by the noise. "Urine," he said simply. Harcourt relaxed somewhat, but he directed a questioning gaze at his partner. "From between her legs. The muscles inside her are loosening. There's no automatic control regulating her bodily functions anymore, Benny."

"Oh—"

85

Private Harcourt was beginning to feel like a botanical garden inside. His stomach was filling with butterflies that *wanted out*! The hairs along the back of his neck were starting to rise. He feared the dead woman might rise from her icy table at any moment and charge them. And that old childhood fear of monsters lurking out in the dark, beyond the dim circle of light, was returning to haunt him. And we all know a .45 caliber automatic is useless against such creatures.

"Let's get the fuck outta here, Derek." Harcourt rested his fingers on Ramsey's wrist. "This — *crime scene* gives me the creeps — "

"Gotta hang around for CID. You know that." Ramsey reprimanded him lightly.

"They're all out chasing down the rocket-launchin' Cong, for Christsake. They won't make it down here till high noon, at the earliest."

"Then she's gonna be awful ripe by the time we turn the scene over to Investigators." Ramsey smiled almost demonically. The corners of his eyes arced up and were accented by the yellow glow from the lantern on the floor behind them. "Bring your nose plugs, *Jacques*?"

"This is a Vietnamese affair," Harcourt countered, irritated the woman's skin was so light. She just might be Caucasian. "All we have to do is turn it over to the *canh-sats*."

"Not when it occurred on a U.S. military compound." Ramsey nodded his chin up and down, then started upon seeing something he had missed earlier: a necklace hidden in the thick layer of blood congealing along the throat wound.

Harcourt swallowed hard as his partner slipped his fingers into the clotting gore. He turned away as Ramsey dug out the ring attached to the stained gold necklace.

"I think I know this bitch from somewheres," he said after a thoughtful moment scanning his memory banks.

"How the hell can you tell?" Harcourt glanced back at the split skull and swallowed again, once more fighting to keep his stomach down.

"Well whatta you know—" A broad smile creased Ramsey's normally grim features as he polished the bloodied ring with an olive-drab handkerchief.

"I don't think you should be touchin' the body till CID gets here." Harcourt's color had darkened to a nervous shade of pale.

" 'United States Military Police School—class of nineteen hundred and sixty-six.' "

"What?"

"You heard me—" Ramsey was losing patience with his partner. He examined the inside of the ring then let it fall back into the shallow pool of blood collecting in the valley between the woman's breasts. He jotted three initials down in his pocket notebook, frowned at the smeared blood his fingers left across the pages, then slipped it back in his flak jacket and snapped the flap shut.

"An MP's girlfriend?" Harcourt's feet were practically dancing with terror and he didn't even notice it. "Do you mean to tell me—"

"That's not where I was thinking I saw her before." Ramsey's eyes were scrunched up in thought again. "For the life of me, though, I cannot fucking place her face, Benny." He stepped away from the table and went down on one knee to examine some strange tripodlike

87

marks in the dusty floor of the warehouse.

A floorboard creaked an instant later, and both men whirled around to face the doorway, their .45's out at arm's length.

"Whoa-whoa-whoa-*wait a minute*!" Murphy's own hands shot up in the air as his feet scurried backward. "Don't shoot, you guys!"

"PMO wanted us to check on ya." Smitty stood his ground, hands on his hips, not in the least intimidated—the two MPs had reacted exactly as he would have wanted them to.

"WACO's been tryin' to contact you over the air!" Murphy said defensively, moving back into the doorway. He had decided it was safe to reappear after hearing his partner's confident voice.

"Whatta ya two clowns got going here, anyway." Smitty moved closer to the body spread out on the table. "A goddamned orgy?"

"We *found* her that way!" Harcourt was the one sounding offended now, but his tense features relaxed when he spotted the gleam in Ramsey's eyes.

"Been dead coupla hours now." His partner smiled up at Smitty. In the background, Murphy was lighting up a cigarette. He took one puff then dropped it on the floor, walked across it, and moved to the staff sergeant's side. At the sight of the woman's split skull, he clutched his stomach, and, bent over, fled from the room again.

Frowning, Smitty listened to the man vomit outside before asking, "Have either of you called it in—or tried to? Nobody's heard you over the radio at all."

"I figured—what with Saigon burning down out there," Ramsey said, biting his lower lip hesitantly,

"WACO didn't have time for just another cunt killing, sarge." He didn't mention the MP Academy ring.

"*Jesus Christ!*" Smitty rushed away from the two privates and headed for a smoke-laced doorway. Flames crackled in the wood shavings on the floor where Murphy had discarded his cigarette. Smitty tried to stomp out the fire, but it quickly spread to the cracked and fading wallpaper spread across one work area. The room was soon engulfed in thick smoke.

"Goofy Murph," Ramsey muttered as he raced past Smitty and disappeared through the doorway. Seconds later, he had returned and was dousing the area with a fire extinguisher from one of the patrol units.

"There goes the physical evidence." Harcourt shook his head from side to side in resignation as he stood in the middle of the room, sucking in the thick fumes. "Looks like Article Fifteen time for you know who again."

"Shut the fuck up," yelled Smitty. "Gimme a hand here and I'll show you my scars later—nobody's gettin' no disciplinary action in their file, okay?"

Harcourt cleared his throat defiantly. "I already seen your fucking scars, sarge—in the locker room. Not interested."

Confident the fire was out, all three men moved outside. Between the jeeps, Murphy was still tossing oats at the night breeze.

Ramsey snuck an admiring look at Smitty. The NCO had weathered a million bar fights, or so the legend went. His motto was: *So long as I wear the armband, I don't lose no brawls*. And he had the scars crisscrossing his back to prove it. There wasn't a sergeant in the company who hadn't seen the man charge into a bar against overwhelming odds, quell the disturbance, and bring out the troublemaker who started it all—in handcuffs. But the encounters had cost him a quart or two of blood and more than a couple visits to the hospital. At the choir practices, where off-duty MPs got together at cop bars or the watch commander's hootch, the rooks were all treated to the show: a private viewing of the back that sported two bullet-hole scars and enough purple lines to flatter a gallows whipman. The newbies ate it up.

A trash can toppled over three blocks down the nearest street, on the other side of the compound fence line, and a body followed it into the gutter.

"What the—" Ramsey started to ask a question they all already knew the answer to: Some drunk was just trying to stumble home before another barrage of rockets descended on Saigon.

But then a shadowy form was standing over a man, and someone began kicking him in the face. "A strong-arm goin' down—" The words out of Smitty's mouth were unnecessary. All four MPs automatically headed for the compound gate, ignoring their vehicles.

Exiting warehouse row forced them into a time-wasting detour, however, and for a few seconds they lost sight of the alley down which the robbery was taking place.

When the four Americans had silently cut the distance between themselves and the assault victim in half, a third figure leaped from the roof above the scene of the disturbance—directly onto the person kicking the man at his feet. Both tumbled onto the victim, with the four MPs still a good hundred yards away, pistols drawn now.

"You gotta be jerkin' my pud!" Ramsey's words to Smitty were soaked in disbelief: The subject who had leaped from the rooftop was wearing a red cape, gas mask, combat boots. And nothing else!

He pummeled the side street hoodlum with his fists, then vanished in the dark moments before the MPs arrived.

"Follow his ass!" Harcourt, out of breath already and chest heaving, pointed after the stranger as Ramsey twisted the thief's arm back and snapped on the iron bracelets. Murphy was down on one knee, searching the victim for a pulse. He quickly found a weak heartbeat against his throat.

"Naw." Smitty holstered his pistol, placed his hands against the small of his back and arched his shoulders backward. "The goofyfuck—whoever he was—is long gone."

"He looked like a goddamned round-eye to me, sarge." Ramsey roughly dragged the arrestee to his feet, then slammed him promptly back down onto the blacktop.

"How could you see his face with that gasmask on?" Smitty was skeptical.

"Well, he *ran* like an American!"

"*Christ!*" Smitty spat into the polluted gutter and sat down on the edge of the upended garbage can.

Across the street from the four American military policemen, a slender Oriental man silently watched from the shadows of a brick doorway. He had thought the sight of the naked Westerner with the combat boots on was the most hilarious thing he had ever seen. But now his eyes narrowed cautiously and his smile disappeared. In his early twenties, the way in which the man concentrated on the arrest procedures taking place across the street made him look ten years older. His eyes rarely blinked as he patiently chewed on a strip of green bamboo. A swirl of breeze swept through the maze of tenements rising up all around him, and when he brushed some long strands of jet-black hair off his forehead, a tiny scar the shape of a unicorn's head appeared in the light of secondary explosions still erupting where rockets had fallen onto Tu Do Street.

Long after additional Military Police vehicles had arrived and left, the young man remained in the shadows, quietly staring at the Americans with his cold, somber eyes while a totally different scene replayed itself over and over again in his troubled mind.

3. The Vulnerable Years

"'Reilly, get that goddamned Aussie bush hat off!'" Sergeant Stryker waved his nightstick in the MP's direction, midway across the briefing-room full of seated patrolmen. Jeff wiggled his thick sun-bleached mustache slightly, ordered his nostrils into the now notorious Bugs Bunny imitation, then sheepishly removed the cowboylike camouflaged hat, its left flap bent up and held against the side with a metal snap. One of the housegirls had sewn velvet MP letters to the front of it.

Stryker's frown melted quick enough: Reilly was a good man he could always count on, and the infrequent assaults on military uniformity were often overlooked. But then the husky sergeant's gaze drifted above and beyond the helmets of the fifty or so soldiers waiting silently, and the frown returned.

In the back of the cavernous, dimly lit room, a half dozen MPs were clustered around an old, black and white TV set that the desk sergeants claimed hadn't worked in years. Stryker squinted through the dense cigarette smoke drifting slowly above all the helmets until he recognized the starship shooting through a galactic backdrop at warp seven. *They were watching "Star Trek" again!* Stryker cleared his throat loudly. "I hereby call this guardmount briefing to order!" he announced sarcastically, tapping his nightstick against the beloved teakwood podium. But the men seemed to be ignoring him.

Stryker gritted his teeth but kept his lips together, hiding the irritation. Ever since the Armed Forces Television Network had started piping in the popular science fiction series, his night watch briefings had gone to the dogs—the first thirty minutes anyway. The stocky MP tapped the podium again as he thought about sending a hollow-point through the tube. *On phaser-stun.* He grinned to himself. *Naw, they'd have my pension—for what it's worth.*

The show had just started—was coming on late this evening because another of the unpredictable Saigon power outages had delayed programming again. Capt. James T. Kirk of the U.S.S. Enterprise was opening the episode with the usual inspiring log entry, and muffled laughter filtered through the room as the MPs, all loyal trekkies since "The Man Trap" came out the previous September, ignored Stryker and repeated William Shatner's dialogue, word for word, precisely and without error:

*"Space . . . the final frontier. . . . These are the voyages of the Starship Enterprise . . . its five year mission: to explore strange new worlds . . . to seek out new life, and new civilizations . . . TO BOLDLY GO WHERE NO MAN HAS GONE BEFORE!"** *

*Used with permission of Paramount Pictures Corporation, the Owner of Star Trek® Properties.

A piercing traffic whistle sliced through the reverent silence that followed the show's heart-grabbing theme music. The six MPs around the TV set whirled their heads around to face the big man behind the podium.

"May I have your attention now?" Stryker feigned boredom as mock patience coated his soft tone. His heavy fingertips rattled against the edge of a clipboard.

"Aw, sarge," a youthful voice complained as the opening credits began to flash across the grey tube. "It's just starting. Relief shift'll cover for us. They'd understand: This one's got France Nuyen in it."

"The streets of Saigon do not roll up and O.D. into deep sleep just'cause you jokers wanna watch the boob tube," Stryker grumbled, always annoyed at the thought television had even found its way into a combat zone. "Crime in Sin City don't go on vacation just-'cause—"

"But sarge!" another rookie cut in respectfully. "This one's got *France Nuyen* in it!"

Stryker's anger instantly cooled. "France Nuyen?" he asked softly, lowering his nightstick as if he had just entered a nightclub, expecting a brawl, and found a basket of flowers on the counter instead.

"That's a Ten two-four, bossman," a third newbie added. "The one and only."

Stryker had been a loyal fan of the beautiful actress ever since she had starred as Liat in the smash movie *South Pacific*. Nuyen seemed, to Stryker, a simplification of the common yet complex Vietnamese family name, Nguyen, but the lady led such a private life he was not sure. She was the most beautiful woman he had ever seen, Asian or otherwise, and he was mesmerized by her sensuous voice. To think that a woman from his most beloved city in the world could succeed in the jungle that was Hollyweird motivated the Military Police sergeant more than he ever let on. *The lady brings charm and sophistication to the silver screen*, Stryker decided, everytime he watched one of her movies. *Maybe this war is worth fighting after all.*

"All right." He folded his arms across his chest. "You can leave the set on, but turn the volume down a little. And keep one of your ears perked my way, okay? I got a lotta info to dissimulate here and zero minutes left on my Rolex."

"What the hell's he talkin' about?" Anthony Thomas leaned to the side and whispered in Tim Bryant's ear.

"Aw, the Stryk's in another galaxy again. Happens everytime he sees France Nuyen on the tube." Bryant allowed a short giggle to escape him.

"Maybe we can score some workman's comp for him. Arrange an R and R to Singapore to duel with a shrink or something."

"This is the *army*, fool."

"Oh right." Thomas scratched at the stubble on his chin. "Forgot again."

Bryant resisted the urge to ask how anyone could forget they were working for the Green Machine. Besides, it appeared Sergeant Stryker was returning to reality. His eyes were losing their bottomless, misty glaze.

"Okay— awright." Stryker slowly focused on the numbered sentences across his clipboard. "First off, for those of you who don't know—"

"Those of you who been chasin' falling stars." One of the buck sergeants standing in the doorway motioned toward the MPs gathered around the TV with his jutting jawbone.

"Bravo and Charlie Companies of the Fifty-second got zapped by Victor Charlie again last week — so there'll be a lot of'em sharing your billets the next few weeks while the satchel-charge holes get patched up over at the Capitol," Stryker continued.

"Most o' my troopers are shackin' downtown anyway," muttered the same NCO again, his disgust growing heavier.

"Now you gentlemen show them a good time. After all, they provide the Hog gunners when the Alert sirens go off. Also, the Ninetieth Detachment lost ten more men to rotation yesterday." Stryker tugged at the bullet hole scar across his left earlobe. "And Jake Drake's takin' requests for MP station duty."

A few hands shot up, but Stryker ignored them.

He squinted at the second number on his agenda. "I've noticed a lot of you are practically overdosing on Vitamin A capsules." A slight grin curved the edges of his lips. "Ever since The Brick started the rumor Vitamin A increases your purple vision capabilities."

"What the hell is purple vision?" A rook turned to Bryant questioningly.

"Night sight, doofus."

"How *is* Sergeant Brickmann, anyway?" An anonymous voice filtered up through the nodding helmets.

"Still in Tokyo." Stryker's smile faded.

"Will he lose the arm?" Thomas's eyes flashed concern.

"Negative." A shiver shot down Stryker's back. "He's got nurses sittin' on his face day and night, and I heard he's already arm-wrestling the jarheads. It was a bitchin' wound, but —"

"He'll be back." Farthing's helmet dipped solemnly.

"He'll be back," Stryker affirmed. "Anyway, Vitamin A's fine for all you night watch supercops."

"Supercops." The sergeant in the doorway dropped a cigarette butt on the floor and slowly smothered the embers with the bottom of his jungle boot. "Where?"

"But take my advice: pig-out on fish. You'll get twice as much Vitamin A that way, and I won't get no complaints from Mr. Citizen that my MPs are poppin' pills on their beat.

"Now, as you know, we had another chase a couple nights ago. First watch stacked up two units, and Geoghan is in the hospital. More free advice: Aim high when you're chasing the bad guys through downtown Saigon. Have a big picture when driving—check the roadway for blocks ahead of you. If you're on Plantation Road or Thunder Highway, make that a mile or two—anticipate anything that might go wrong ahead of time—monitor all oncoming traffic—plan on the unexpected. If you're bustin' a red light, slow down for Christsake—"

"Unless it's an MP-Needs-Help." Thomas folded his arms across his chest and nodded smugly to Bryant.

"Make eyeball to eyeball contact with the civilians out there—remember: this *is* the Nam. Some of them motorists out there don't even know what a fucking siren is, much less how to react to it. When you run hot," Stryker said, striking out at a huge mosquito that had been buzzing him, "when you roll Ten-Thirty-nine, don't assume the right-of-way. Your red lights and siren are only *requesting* it." The stocky sergeant ran a thumb along the edge of his mustache and shifted his boots slightly before flexing his shoulder muscles.

"And I don't wanna see no more of you clowns taggin' behind Code-Three runs hopin' to write up a failure-to-yield on some half-blind papa-san dragging his water buffalo down Le Loi. I will not have chickenshit MPs in my battalion. Is that understood?"

The room had grown silent except for photon torpedoes blasting away on the television tube.

Stryker's eyes scanned the men sitting in a vast semicircle in front of him, then slowly blinked exhausted eyelids and glanced back down at the clipboard. "Smelled something uncomfortably similar to an alcoholic beverage on the breath of some of you guys during the uniform inspection last night." He was not amused. "Do us all a favor and use peanut butter or peanut oil to coat your stomachs if you wanna attend choir practice but are due on the six A.M. shift—that's what the boys in Decoy do, okay?" Choir practice was the universal term cops used to describe booze sessions held at a private location after a particularly tense shift on the street.

"Goes a lot easier on the pre-dawn hangover, too," mumbled the buck sergeant in the doorway.

"The heat of the tropics doesn't help much, I know," Stryker added, his eyes softening with compassion but his features remaining firm. "In warm weather like this you get less oxygen to your head. In cold weather, like back in the The World, you get *more* oxygen to your brain. That's why you feel more energetic—hell, feel better all around when it's not so hot."

"But you newbies fresh over from the winter wonderland will adjust quick enough," said the man in the doorway chuckling to himself under his breath.

"Special patrols." Stryker pulled a black pen from his

fatigue shirt and checked off another number. "Been getting a lot of disturbances lately at the Quick Draw Bar on Tu Do. Lotsa Man-With-A-Gun calls—most all of them *have* involved weapons of one sort or another. Tuesday we found a fatality under the piano after the gun smoke cleared.

"Precinct One units team up and make three or four walk-throughs per shift, starting tonight. And note it on your log— we'll be monitoring all activity in the nightclub districts particularly. The PM's on top of this one personally. *That* should tell you all you need to know.

"At the Bali Hai Lounge on Le Loi—manager complaining Madame Kwok's girls are saturating the joint again—especially Saturday nights. Roust'em every chance you get—"

"That's a *canh-sat* matter." A corporal in the back of the room all but snickered.

"Kwok's the best snitch we got." Stryker did not sound offended. "At least the most reliable. Humor her. If the *canh-sats* see us cardin' the cunts, they'll work another block. One hand washes the other.

"Number three five seven Nguyen Hue—the Blue Moon Saloon. Party in a black-over-blue Renault four-door selling stolen property from the trunk: ration cards, GI junk and the like. If you catch him dirty, toss his ass. There's a five day R and R to Cockbang Thailand for the first bust that don't fall apart in Saigon municipal court.

"Curly's Liquorbox on Mac Dinh Chi got hit again Thursday." Stryker reached over and handed a packet of BOLO flyers to the closest MP. "Pass'em around. The *canh-sats* know we cruise down that street a half dozen times an hour when running routine embassy checks. They'd appreciate we eyeball the place and smoke the appropriate hairballs should we encounter same."

Scattered applause filled the room. From back near the TV set, muffled whispers: ". . . And I got this fanfuckintastic tapestry down on Tu Do yesterday. Multihued blues in oil on velvet. Kirk, Spock, Bones, and Scotty beamin' up, with the Enterprise floatin' in the background. Couldn't believe it myself when I spotted it among the nudies at that stall across from the Miramar. A "Star Trek" tapestry, painted by a Vietnamese! *In the Nam!*"

"Speaking of *velvet*." Stryker's voice rose with the rest of his muscular form as he pushed up on his toes, cleared his throat, and leaned out over the men in the first row. His eyes locked onto the trekkies gathered around the TV set. "Got a complaint from the proprietor of the Velvet Turtle over on Phan Dinh Phung." He slowly shook his head from side to side in mock resignation, as if he'd just caught a kid with his hand in the cookie jar again. "States my Mike Papa patrols are congregating outside his lounge again, blocking the entrance while they flirt with the dancers taking their breaks. States he was told to perform an impossible function with his sex organ when he politely requested those same Mike Papas disperse. Stated next time he goes to the PM, *Mikey*."

Broox refused to look up at Stryker and instead continued rapidly writing in his pocket notebook, as if trying desperately to keep up with the briefing.

Stryker glanced at his watch and decided not to press the matter. Enough had been said. The men

101

would switch to another nightclub down the street. The bars and the broads were everywhere in Precinct One, like flies on a body bag.

"Any of you guys remember Patterson?" Stryker glanced around the room again. A few heads nodded in response. "For those of you who don't, he retired from the MP Corps couple years ago. Stayed on in the Nam as a fucking civilian. Goofy as they come. Opened up a furniture store down on Pasteur, if you can believe that. Called The Rattan Man."

"Bought me a damned good love chair there last rainy season," muttered the sergeant in the doorway. "Damned good. Ten bucks. Ten lousy bucks. Same crap goes for fifty minimum back in The World, if you can find it."

"A rattan love chair?" Thomas shot Bryant a quizzical grin.

"What would Monster Man want with a love chair?" Bryant whispered back.

"Anyway," Stryker continued, "Patterson's requesting special patrol if you guys are in the area. He got hit five times in the last month. Burgs. Through the roof every time. *Canh-sats* don't give a fuck,'cause he refuses to pay protection money."

"Probably the damn white mice pullin' the jobs." Someone in the back of the room was not joking as he spoke matter-of- factly.

"Those of you taking your short-sevens at the U-Brew-It on Le Loi, take note: An MPI snitch revealed some Victor Charlies from Gia Dinh have been bragging they're gonna snipe out the round-eyed coppers who take their coffee breaks there on night watch. Could happen — the front wall is wide open, like a goddamned picture window without the glass. You might consider switchin' to one of the dives on a more quiet side street, away from all the action. Deterrence while walking your beat or cruising the boulevards is one thing, but none of us gets paid enough to stop a round while downing Saigon tea. 'Nough said?

"Downpour hot runs."

"Downpour hot runs?"

"Rainfall." Stryker nodded seriously, and more than one rook wondered if his briefing sergeant had stepped off the cliff into that mental void all line cops know about but seldom worry themselves over. "Wet streets and speeding jeeps."

Thomas glanced over uneasily at his best friend. Both he and Bryant knew Mark had been going through a lot of stress lately, both on the street and in his personal life. But they also knew he was a proud man who didn't talk about his problems at the choir practices like a lot of the other NCOs. Bryant felt Thomas staring at him, but he did not move his eyes from the podium in front of him.

"When these crazy monsoon downpours sweep through the city," Stryker continued, "the first five or ten minutes of the storm are the most dangerous. Madison stacked it up last week racing to a Shots-Fired call down in Cholon because he flew balls to the wind without any regard to conditions on the street. This is *Saigon*, gentlemen. Not Friendly Lane, U.S.A. We got us a dirty, grimy, greasy, oily, polluted metropolis all around us, populated by three or four million Viets who must all own lorries or deuce-and-a-halfs that need an oil filter. I know for a fact many of you have near enough slipped out of your jungle boots chasin' a suspect down the back alleys 'cause the pavement is so slick.

"Then down comes the surprise rain, and it mixes with all that oil, grease, and grime, and it's almost like trying to brake on an ice rink with bald tires. So watch your ass when the storms roll in. Especially those first ten minutes. The water God so graciously dumps on us from heaven soaks into the blacktop's pores, forces the oil up to the surface not unlike water level in a straw riding above the lip of a glass—"

"It's called 'capulary action.'" The sergeant in the doorway smiled. "If you wanna get scientific, for Christsake—"

"And watch those puddles in the intersections, too," said Stryker. "Especially the dips along Pasteur. Madison lost it 'cause he hydroplaned his ass through a storefront that, so he claims, just happened to leap out into his way. Cars hydroplane at fifty-five miles an hour when the tire pressure is twenty-seven p.s.i.—to give you an example. Raise the pressure to thirty-two, and you can fly sixty-five miles an hour before you lose it. And that's *cars* I'm talkin' now, not jeeps, so you can figure out the difference on your own."

Stryker's eyes narrowed as he spotted something on the back of one of the MP helmets gathered around the television set. "Uhernik!" He raised his voice only slightly. "Tomorrow at this time you'll have that Ruck Fussia graffiti off your helmet liner—*or else*—" He paused to allow The Uke launch the usual casual salute in reply and acknowledgement, then he added, "I liked Peace Hell, Nuke Hanoi better."

Someone in the back of the room pressed his lips against the flesh of his bicep and blew as hard as he could. The sergeants weren't sure if he was imitating a nuclear blast or merely a bored MP passing gas and the time.

"Armbands," Stryker continued. "Some of you have been wearing black sashes over them because of the recent deaths of our men last month. Fine. In fact, I encourage it. But let's maintain some semblance of uniformity: Sashes will be no wider than one-half inch and run diagonally, front to back.

"Now comes the duties I dislike the most, gentlemen: giving sermons on the evils of the flesh and other things. But once again me and Richards had to bail a cherry-boy out of Chi Hoa jail because he forgot the golden rule: Booze, broads, and bets." Stryker seemed to moan in actual pain behind the podium.

"Booze, broads, and—*bets*?" Thomas cast Bryant his most innocent expression.

"I tell you guys, and I tell you guys—those three things are the root of all your problems. Stay away from the track, keep a cork in the bottle, and don't let the women screw up your perspective. Otherwise, none of you are gonna see your twentieth year on the street, be it in Saigon or Seattle." Stryker's head bobbed slowly from side to side, as if he was guarding a personal secret no one else was really curious about—*and he knew it*. "Booze, broads, and bets."

Broox leaned the other way and whispered into Sgt. Gary Richards's ear. "Booze, broads, and bets. What else is there in life, sarge?"

"I suspect there's lots of you out there whose job performance is suffering due to one or more of these factors," Stryker continued. "Needless to say, if anyone needs to talk to me or any of the other NCOs, don't hesitate to approach us. It'll all be kept off the books, gentlemen. Just one on one. And boy, can we keep secrets around here." His eyes scanned the blank faces without bothering to home in on anyone in particular.

"We're a little short on jeeps this month. Brigade came down with a reinspect directive after a couple troopers up in Danang were killed when their jeeps shot them."

"Their jeeps shot them?"

Stryker's frown hardened. "Seems some scrote pipes back in Detroit or wherever they assemble MP jeeps taped some shotgun shells to the transmission shield. After they heat up, the rounds discharge, sending buckshot up into the legs of the driver and passenger."

"That's the last time I ride *shotgun*." A whisper was exchanged in the rear of the room.

"MPI located a half dozen additional units with similar boobytraps. All the vehicles were recent arrivals from The World. The safety inspections should be completed by Friday. It doesn't affect the older jeeps— the ones that have been in the Nam awhile."

"They're ready to blow up on their own," another comedian seated along the back wall remarked loud enough to rate a couple claps.

"How many days in a jeep's RVN tour before it becomes a single-digit midget eligible for Deros, sarge?" The Uke's face was emotionless, as if he hadn't said a humorous word. As if he was dead serious. Stryker ignored him.

"Apparently the battalion is blessed with a dastardly do-gooder." The briefing sergeant's shoulders rose slightly as he grasped the edge of the podium and let his head sink. Several laughs answered his body language. "Captain Condom struck again last night," he said somberly.

"Captain *Condom*?" Bryant all but fell out of his chair as he held onto his stomach.

"For those of you coming off break," Stryker said, running his tongue along the edge of his lower lip, "an unknown Caucasian wearing only a gas mask, cherry-red cape, and combat boots—"

"A streaker?" Thomas's eyes lit up as he scanned the fifty odd patrolmen cluttering up the room with their gear.

"—has been drop-kicking unsuspecting robbery suspects before we can get to them. Then he flees the scene after rescuing the stick-up victim. He leaves an army-issue rubber tied around the ear of the unconscious cowboy—a different color every time. Last night it was green."

"Green?" Bryant was incredulous and practically on the floor now.

"This is not a laughing matter." Stryker rose his hands to silence the uproar. "Sooner or later, the goofyfuck is gonna get his whanger blown off. Maybe a simple strong-armed robbery victim'll bite the dust along with him, and it'll all make the Seven-sixteenth look bad in the eyes of the public. I want you men to hustle out there and scarf his ass up for his own safety. The PM or even the president of South Vietnam can give him a citizen's medal if he wants, but for now, I want this caped crusader off my streets. Any of you got a problem with that?"

"What if he's one of us?" Another MP in the back of the room offered a twist to the mystery.

"I've never once worried about such a possibility."

107

Stryker smiled for the first time. "Trigger-happy as you all are, I just can't see one of my Saigon Commandos passin' up the chance to smoke a back-alley scumbag, once provided the opportunity."

"Who let him get away this time?" the NCO leaning in the doorway shadows asked Stryker. Smitty, Murphy, Ramsey, and Harcourt all turned in their seats to direct an unforgiving scowl at him. Their expressions were all the answer anyone needed and Stryker did not comment. A paper airplane sailed through the humid, emotion-thick air. Near the doorway, bubbles rising in the water cooler made the only noise until the airplane impacted against the wall.

"Heard a little excitement entered *your* life without warning, sarge." Thomas allowed himself a guarded snicker. "Last night, in fact. Something along the lines of a Russian-made one-twenty-two twirler."

"Slammed through the rooftop of the Miramar," Bryant affirmed. "Tore through the top two floors. Came to fucking rest right over his bed, according to Jon Toi!"

A murmur of excitement and suppressed awe fluttered through the room as rooks and vets alike went wide-eyed with surprise. "Nothin' to get your hemorrhoids in an uproar over," Stryker said, suddenly wondering about the obscene phone caller who had been pestering him the last few weeks. Wann had recognized her voice, yet in all the commotion that followed their hectic departure from his room at the Miramar, he had neglected to pin her down on the matter.

"Speakin' o' weirdos," he continued, "got a real psychotic-type loose on the streets, men." Stryker ignored the repeated requests to elaborate on his misadventure the night before, except to say that one of Egor Johnson's gunships had routed a squad of Cong at the suspected rocket launch sight, killing ten of them. "A maniac who cottons to splitting bargirls' heads down the middle with a buzz saw."

"I'm impressed," an *un*impressed short-timer in the rear of the room muttered.

"So keep your eyes open, especially in the warehouse districts."

"I heard the victim was on the rag when she got raped." Broox, always one for gross particulars, pressed Stryker on the subject.

"Like I said, the dude's a definite psycho ward candidate. Any *other* questions? If not, maybe we can get this show on the road."

"What have you heard on the rings, sarge?"

Stryker frowned at the interruption. He rolled his eyes in resignation but maintained an unperturbed cool when he said, "Right. Sergeant Schultz is taking orders for MP rings. Those of you who passed up the opportunity to purchase one at The School—"

"MP rings?" A newbie in the front row sat up straight in his seat. "They were out of stock when *I* was back in Georgia."

"Well now you can order one through Raunchy Raul, made in Saigon, no less, complete with Vietnam dragon if you want, and of course year of graduation from The School, Military Police cross pistols—the whole nine yards. Got mine back in the old days." He held his hand up. "Come to think of it, maybe a bit o' gold jewelry'll go a long ways in motivatin' those of you with a poor attitude." He grinned ruefully.

"Tomorrow prior to swing shift some skates from

MPI will be showing a training reel on officer survival, civilian style." Stryker placed another checkmark midway down his clipboard. "Now I realize all you hotdogs are immortal and have never lost a minute's sleep worrying about gettin' KIA, but it might do some of you a lotta good to watch the experts back in The World knockin' down silhouettes of old ladies on the Shoot-Don't-Shoot range."

"Shit, sarge, you know we is all inde*struct*able!" A private in the center of the room lit up a Vietnamese Blue Ruby cigarette.

Stryker locked eyes with the eighteen-year-old but did not smile again. Visions of bodies littering the scene of the ambushed payroll convoy the month before were sending shivers down his spine. He forced himself back to the present, but the scene in front of him was just as sad.

The newbies—especially the youngbloods fresh out of the MP Academy—made him moody, reflective. He sincerely felt for them. Stryker's eyes scanned the room again. Easily half the law enforcers gathered before his podium had yet to reach legal drinking age at most bars stateside. And now here they were thrust into a steaming metropolis at war—probably straight from some modest farming community deep in America's heartland—and forced to deal with life and death matters on a day-to-day basis, in an exotic land where it was eternally difficult to tell the good guys from the bad.

For Stryker, life dragged on. Saigon, though it was the most intense city in which he had ever lived and worked, was really just another duty station as far as most NCOs were concerned. It was not his first, and it probably would not be his last (though he had prayed for that good fortune countless times in the past). Stryker feared his life — his usefulness — his purpose in life might crumble around his soul were he ever forced to leave his precious City of Sorrows. He could not imagine life without the girls of Tu Do strolling by, or the two giant soldier statues rising from the mist in Le Loi Park, or the bumper-to-bumper traffic harboring the VC weekend warriors extending out as far as the eye could see at Checkpoint 6-Alpha.

These rookies, on the other hand — these wide-eyed, attentive supercops polishing their customized belt buckles and chrome pistol clips — were susceptible to the worst Vietnam had to dump on them.

They were so young, he realized sadly. These were their vulnerable years. The period of time when their safety was most endangered, emotionally. When Lady Saigon would leave her biggest impression on them — her deepest wounds.

Not one of them would hesitate to throw himself in front of Stryker if they saw a satchel-charge coming. Not one of them would think twice about racing eighty klicks an hour down Tu Do with the sun in their eyes, enroute to an MP-Down radio broadcast. Danger was the farthest thing from their minds (or so they professed), though the *thirst* for danger was all they talked about at the choir practices, after twelve hours on their back-alley beats. They were young and immortal — thrillseekers. Saigon could never kill them.

Stryker remembered when he was that way. He tried to decide at which birthday drunk his attitude changed. Had it been his twenty-fifth? His second tour in the Nam?

Though it seemed he still lived for the chase, and pursuing cat burglars on foot across moonlit rooftops still brought immeasurable job satisfaction, he found more joy now in watching his men reach that adrenaline rush—discover the comraderie and brotherhood of the badge. When had the family disturbances, loud party complaints, bar fights, and cold crime reports become just another migraine?

At countless briefings past, the rooks with their know-it-all attitudes and do- gooder approach to police work had provided him with many a laugh. He'd give his near famous sermon about how they needed to approach law enforcement more realistically than from a bleeding heart liberal's viewpoint because *Even Christ couldn't save the world, could he*?

He felt for these American boys. They were still, many of them, driving around the city in circles, dazzled by the menacing intensity of the Pearl of the Orient. Here they found their manhood. They found women who behaved like slaves and treated them like masters. And they found an off-duty atmosphere that existed nowhere else in the world, except perhaps a few side streets off Patpong Road in the Venice of the East—Bangkok. Even on a buck private's salary, they could live like kings.

They would plow awkwardly through the human refuse lining the city's gutters; they would party with each other till dawn after scraping up the dead bodies night watch unloaded on them; they would sit together in this very briefing room, elbow to elbow, struggling through the MP reports. Stryker would watch them live and grow and suffer and learn, and he would see some of them die before he could lift a gun to save

112

them.

He would joke with them, bleed with them, even cry with them if that was what the situation called for. And before they knew it, their Tour Three hundred sixty-five would be up and they'd be on their freedom bird back to The World. Alone.

Returning to a small town or impersonal city with none of the Saigon flare. A grim, concrete graveyard where it snowed half the year. Where the people could be just as cold and impersonal. (He hated the winters stateside — snow on the sidewalks and that crispness in the air reminded him of those agonizing days when he returned stateside from his first Vietnam tour.) Where some of his ex- MPs found the time to send Stryker a postcard or even a short note after they returned to the drudgery and routine of the factories or the stores, and spent their coffee breaks reminiscing about the legendary Stryk and his boys back in the Nam. Where the others spent their sleepless evenings thinking about the magic of Saigon nights and the women they left behind.

The women.

Stryker hoped none of them found their first loves here in the Orient. He hoped none of them fell in love with the streets, either. Like he had. Cops became easily cursed under these conditions, when so young — so inexperienced. So impressionable. So vulnerable.

The impressions would flash back at them for years to come, when they least desired the reminders — both good memories and bad. And Stryker didn't wish a life-altering spell like that on even his enemies.

A white blur sailing before his eyes nudged the man back to reality. He watched the giant paper airplane,

113

fashioned from a blank Form-Sixty-eight accident report, slam into the VNP Wanted Posters hanging above the precinct maps. It fluttered to the polished teakwood floor, nose crimped, and he rested his right hand on the pistol butt protruding from the black laminated rainflap of his holster. Stryker enjoyed the cool feel of the automatic compared with the stale mugginess of the briefing room. He reveled in the confidence and *situation-control* it sent coursing through his veins, though he also repeatedly cautioned himself not to place too much reliance on his service weapon — *that* could leave you more dead than second place in a quickdraw gunfight.

"Now." The tall watch commander paused for dramatic effect. "What you've all been waiting for with baited breath," Stryker said sarcastically, taking a second to straighten out the RVN service ribbons across his chest without disturbing the layer of smog coating them. (The MP sergeant often judged a man's street experience by the amount of big-city pollution clinging to the multicolored decorations.) "The lovely, succulent, scrumptious, and dazzling dreamboat Kiwi Kolana is making her debut appearance in Sin City this week, a guest of the MACV hierarchy —"

An immediate chorus of whistles and wolf howls greeted the announcement.

"Kiwi Kolana?" A man fresh off injury leave was genuinely *and pleasantly* surprised.

"She is generously donating her time for a USO tour, but I've also heard from Rumor Control that her agent is scouting terrain for an on-location cinemascopic-type war epic for the silver screen. And Miss Kolana will be needing some trustworthy bodyguards,

114

courtesy of the Seven sixteenth. Any volunteers?"

Practically every hand in the room shot up, though many of the men were not really that impressed with plastic products from Tinsel Town. Even a goodwill gesture like a USO tour often meant nothing more than publicity stunts in a combat zone. But the duty beat manning a sweltering bunker at Fort Hustler, butt-stroking dragon lizards that hung from the concertina wire pretending they were dead branches. The ear-to-ear grins flashing before him were contagious: Stryker's grim face cracked slightly in response.

"It could mean a lot of overtime with no comp logged on the rosters. And you *know* Uncle Sammy don't *pay* for overtime in this here Green Machine."

The hands remained in the thick, sticky cloud of cigar and cigarette smoke drifting a few feet below the ceiling.

"I'm gonna need ten good men." Stryker's smile broadened. "*Young bucks* capable of keeping up with the Kolana entourage." A few NCOs in the crowd sighed in mock resignation and slowly lowered their fists.

Stryker leaned over against the podium and started pointing at helmets. "Ramsey—you and Harcourt. And Smitty, I'll put you temporarily in charge. Take the Murph with you, and I—"

"What about us?" Thomas stood up. Bryant grabbed onto his web belt and promptly pulled him back down onto his seat.

"Okay—awright." Stryker made a production out of buttoning the pocket containing his voice-activated mini-recorder. "Makes sense. Decoy's in—if you can get the C.O.'s clearance."

"No sweat!" Thomas slammed his fist against an

open palm.

"How'bout it, Gary?" Bryant stalled for time as Stryker continued scanning eager faces. "We're not on any stakeouts or narc games this week, right? Tell 'im!"

Richards slowly stood up. His words did not sound enthusiastic. "We'll probably put a Code-Five on this buzz saw bullshit," he muttered, "but so far the crap hasn't flowed downhill."

"Then Decoy's in on it." Stryker made it official as he scribbled away on his clipboard. "You and Smitty can coordinate supervision between yourselves. Just make sure your troopers keep their minds on business and not the factory line of boobs that are sure to accompany Miss Kolana into our territory.

"Now, that adds Richards, Bryant, Thomas, and Broox to the clusterfuck. I need two more men—"

"*Attention!*" a voice called out from the back of the room.

A few men gathered around the doorway slowly rose to their feet.

"At ease—at ease." Lt. Tony Slipka bounded down the aisle between rows of seated MPs. Five newbies in shiny green fatigues followed behind him, apprehensive looks on all their faces. The officer folded his blue-tint prescription sunglasses, slid them into a shirt pocket, and slicked his thick blond hair back with his fingers. Beads of perspiration collected along the tops of his furrowed eyebrows.

As Stryker's favorite lieutenant reached the podium, three more soldiers slowly sauntered into the room.

"Got a busload of FNGs in tonight." Slipka smiled as if in relief. "Just picked'em up at Camp Alpha."

"What's an FNG?" one rook in the front row asked

116

the man beside him.

"A Fucking New Guy."

"Bunch o' F.O.B.s." Slipka was not being insulting.

"F.O.B.s?" the private asked again.

"Fresh Off the Boats, clown."

Stryker's eyes narrowed as he examined the three men in the doorway. The hairs along the back of his neck rose slightly, and he felt himself drifting into phase yellow — caution. There was an almost animal presence invading the briefing room. These men were definitely not newbies. They were in no way cherry. They looked like they had just emerged from six months in the Cambodian jungle.

Two were black. The third might have been white at one time. Now, towering above his two friends, he was dark bronze, with light brown hair cropped close to the scalp and a thin layer of sweat coating the exposed muscles of his chest. His forearms looked like tightly wound cables wrapped around steel. But the tropical tan seemed to have the opposite affect, visually, that it should have had: The soldier looked powerful but not healthy. He looked like walking death. Only his eyes displayed any sign of life. Sunk deep inside dark sockets, the orbs, a bright rain forest green — like the topmost layer of jungle canopy blocking out the sun — darted about the room, almost throwing slivers of sparks against the fowl cloud that seemed to surround the man, until they came to rest on Stryker.

The soldier was a Spec4, one rank below sergeant. His combat patch was tattered, faded, and torn along one corner. He nodded slightly to Stryker then glanced away, and shook his head slowly side to side when one of the newbies tripped on a stray boot as Slipka led the group of replacements to the front of the squad room.

Stryker felt an inner glow of relief. The man, maybe twenty-five at most, was obviously a vet. Most probably combat tested. He already knew the ropes. He wouldn't be hanging onto the back of Stryker's web belt — would probably be avoiding the NCOs in fact. Stryker thought he might promote the man right now and put him in charge of the newbies, and the impulse made him smile again. His nametag read Zane. Stryker chuckled to himself: The man looked almost *insane*. But you didn't need all your marbles to do this job. You went *dinky-dau* quick enough anyway after the first couple rocket attacks.

But Stryker's inner smile faded when he visually inspected the black man in the middle. He was underweight but not skinny. He wore fatigue trousers but no shirt — only an open flak jacket. His skin, with smooth muscles running beneath it like an anatomy chart, was jet black. He wore a necklace of human teeth and a camouflage-pattern silk scarf. Stryker felt a gold ring hanging from his nose was all the private would have needed to make him look like a Zulu warrior straight off the African plains. The man's wristwatch was what made Stryker frown. A black velcro flap covered its face, so the VC couldn't spot the luminous dial by night, (so the theory went), but the actual desired visual effect was easily achieved, deceiving no one: It was a black power sign. An MP wearing a *white* band around his arm would bring the NAACP and ACLU right to Saigon on the next flight, Stryker thought to himself, but nobody ever said anything about black bands or the tri-colored patches of the Black Liberation Army. He chalked *that* one off to ignorance among

118

social crusaders from his own ethnic background category. Racial charts sucked, he decided.

Stryker'd be the first to admit he had a few rednecks in his battalion—it came with the police psyche sometimes; he didn't need this kind of friction in the ranks. The soldier seemed to snarl at him before looking away.

The third man reminded Stryker of a nervous ostrich, being stalked by a playful tiger. His head bobbed up and down, back and forth while his eyes skimmed about in the opposite directions, as if he was afraid some enemy was about to pounce on him without warning.

The man was in his late teens and appeared neatly groomed except for a medical-waiver beard that was patchy and full of short tangles. He stayed close to the soldier with the molar necklace. If they didn't look so tough, Stryker might have suspected they were lovers.

The three men ignored Lieutenant Slipka and moved through the rows in the back of the room, toward two vacant seats. The bronze soldier and the black private with the beard sat down. The African wildman with the mean streak across his features glared down at a young rookie who was listening attentively to the lieutenant mutter something about an upcoming uniform inspection. "Move yo ass, newbie!" the Zulu warrior growled like a lion whose tail had just been stepped on by a passing elephant.

The recruit glanced up at the stranger without saying anything, then returned his attention to the officer behind the podium. A few helmets turned back to take in the one-sided flurry of hostile words, but nobody said anything—the directive sounded little different than a thousand similar outbursts that always pre-ceeded one form of horseplay or another.

The soldier with VC teeth clacking about his throat latched onto the recruit's arm with lightning speed and jerked him to his feet.

"Hey —" A few men from Charlie Company began a murmur of mild protest. One rose to his feet but he was three rows away.

Smitty was not so slow. He leaped across the metal folding chairs, knocking one over, and was in front of the Zulu warrior instantly.

His hands, palms out, slammed against the stran-ger's chest, knocking him back off balance. But the newcomer quickly regained his footing and flew to a nose-to-nose position with Smitty, fists raised.

"Go ahead, mother-fucker," Smitty growled. "Gimme a reason to split your jive monkey face!"

"Hey — *hey*!" Stryker abandoned his podium and started toward the disturbance, casually.

"What the fuck's going on?" Lieutenant Slipka was genuinely shocked. He had never seen two MPs fight-ing *each other* before.

"Up yo ass, honky lifer!" the Zulu warrior muttered under his breath so only Smitty could hear. Then, louder, "I'll have yo stripes, sarge! You just *ass*aulted an enlisted man!"

Smitty slammed his palms against the soldier's chest again, knocking him back from the side.

"Hey!" The Murph rushed to his partner's assist-ance, but his help wasn't needed. The bronzed warrior with the bright green eyes reached out and calmly re-strained the wildman's friend.

"*Attention!*" Lieutenant Slipka yelled above the com-

120

motion. Everyone except Smitty and the newcomers—and Stryker, of course—shot to their feet and locked their heels.

"Who the fuck are these punk jungle bunnies, anyway?" Smitty grumbled, loud enough for every MP in the room to hear.

"Cool it, Big S," Stryker whispered as the no-nonsense lieutenant rushed down the aisle toward them. The room had fallen deathly silent except for the sound of his jump boots against the teakwood planks and Captain Kirk beaming back up to the Enterprise on the TV set.

Slipka cast an irritated scowl at the men gathered in a ringing semicircle around the television, then locked eyes with Smitty. "I wanna see you men in my office in zero five, *got that*?"

The collage of different colored faces nodded, the briefing slowly dissolved without being dismissed, and the other MPs filed out into the dust toward their patrol jeeps.

"So what's the goddamned problem?" Slipka had spent a full minute pacing back and forth in front of the men before finally speaking. "I mean, personality conflicts are one thing, but fisticuffs between my line sergeants and EM just don't hack it, gentlemen."

Smitty, the recruit who had been grabbed, and the three newcomers stood at semi-parade rest in front of the officer's makeshift desk, a plywood strip covering some empty C rat cases. A plaster buffy atop one corner kept the warping wood somewhat level, and Smitty leaned an elbow on the white elephant's back.

Stryker sat on a stool on the other side of the room, a formal and mandatory witness for the lieutenant. His face was troubled but neutral. There were already enough Adam-Henries* out there willing to kill a cop—he didn't need his own men at each other's throats. They were acting like rabid dogs of the same breed challenging a new mutt on the block merely because they didn't recognize it.

"This coooool chimpanzee with the dentist's correspondence course around his neck was givin' my man Palance here a hard time, Lou." Smitty's jaw moved about like he was chewing gum, even though his mouth was dry and empty.

"There's no need for racial slurs, sergeant." Slipka frowned.

"Okay." Smitty shifted his stance. "I apologize for the remark about the dentist."

"Jesus." Slipka turned and stared at a black and white photo enlargement of his Military Police officers' graduating class hanging on the wall in a bamboo frame.

Stryker grinned across the room at Smitty, though he was not condoning the NCO's behavior. Then both sergeants glanced up at the lieutenant, waiting for his verdict. Both men trusted his impartial fairness, and, off the record, Smitty knew he had run off with his mouth beyond a supervisor's privileged grace period.

Slipka would not back off just because the two accused were black. He had spent his time on the street, pounding his beat. He refused to be intimidated by

---

*Police slang (phonetic spelling) for Asshole.

pressure from minorities, their close-knit groups, or even their lawyers and bleeding-heart buddies.

He was disgusted with white people who buckled under to fist-waving fanatics, or who found it fashionable to befriend or humor blacks simply because of their race. Some Caucasians, he believed, were just afraid to stand up and talk loud to dark skin and *deserved* to be called white bread.

Smitty stared at the man with the molars on a silver chain, but he was seeing a scene totally removed from reality: the man roped to a burned KKK cross. Stryker stared at the militant also, but what he saw in his mind's eye was Craig Davis, one of his men who had perished in a VC mortar attack less than a month earlier. Davis, too, was black. But he was as close to Stryker as a brother, and one of the best damned cops he had ever known. Stryker had never really thought of him as being a Negro. And when the recent Bronze Star winner had lost his skull during the surprise attack, Stryker was almost shocked the man's blood did not flow P.D. blue.

Smitty, in contrast, was a laugh a minute. Stryker rarely took him seriously. He was the kind of MP who felt suspects were guilty until proven innocent (or else he wouldn't have arrested them in the first place). Men in Decoy up in Kon Tum, (where they spelled it Con Tomb in their police reports), still told the story about how he had ripped the heart from a VC sapper during hand-to-hand combat, tore a piece of it off with his teeth, then swallowed it with a satisfied grin before belching loudly and radioing the line Lou for permission to take his lunch break at the MASH morgue again.

"So you want one o' my stripes, or what, Lou?" Smitty turned his ire on Slipka. "You gonna buckle under to this pussy-faced radical like all them panty-waste been doing?"

"Now slow down a minute, sergeant—"

"I won't!" Smitty drew his pistol and slammed it down on the lieutenant's desk. Stryker's hand instinctively went to his own gun butt, but then Smitty plopped his MP helmet liner down on top of the automatic. "You want my heater, too? You want my whole fuckin' pension? *Fine!* You can take it and—"

"Calm down, Smitty." Stryker spoke for the first time with a hint of anxiety in his tone.

"I won't!" Smitty exploded, glaring at Mark now. The ex-Green Beret refused to lock eyes and glanced down at his boots, smiling. "I've had it with these cry-baby jigaboos! Always bitchin'—never satisfied with anything—always complainin' it's the white man's fault—never content unless they're dribblin' a basketball down—"

" 'Cause all us *black boys* are doin' the dirty work in this lousy war!" The soldier with the beard spoke up defensively, cutting Smitty off.

Stryker shook his head in resignation. There Smitty went again with his anti-minority speech, yet he was making the same mythical errors he was so intent upon attacking. *Basketball dribblers*, for Christsake! Stryker wanted to pass gas at everyone in the room, but his bowels were in unusually good spirits this evening. The common stereotype: blacks were superior in sports to whites. He wished he had an hour and the patience to explain to Smitty race was not a factor in physical development. It was just that when a large

124

percentage of black youths had nothing to do but shoot baskets twelve hours a day or chase each other through the ghettos, or hurtle chain-link fences for kicks, it was obvious many would go on to careers in physical education. A disproportionatley *large* number.

But that was life in the big city. Stryker had heard the stories. About how Smitty had been a boxer for so many years. About how he fancied himself the next great white hope. About how he chased the titles not so much for his pride or people but mostly because he enjoyed breaking black faces with his fists. About how a sniper's bullet in Seoul had nearly torn off his right arm and prematurely ended his golden gloves career. The army had given him a Purple Heart — his seventh — but the price was worth a million times the face value of the decoration itself. Not to mention that slice of sanity the incident claimed.

"We sacrificed three black brothers so far for every lilly-white KIA in this farce of a war!" The soldier with the beard said.

"Now let's not get into that crap!" Slipka held up a hand. He pulled a sheet of statistics off his desk and handed it to the private. It showed the number of black casualties far lower than their percentage of the national population.*

"This whole fucking country's going to hell!" Smitty continued, referring to America. "When the news me-

---

*Post-war statistics showed that, of the 58,479 Americans killed in Vietnam, 50,478 were white, 7,273 were black, 254 were Malayan, 225 were American Indian, 121 were Mongolian, and 128 were of unknown ethnic division. All but eight were male. (SOURCE: *The Vietnam Veteran* newsletter, Gastonia North Carolina) Sept. 1984.

dia ain't gangin' up on cops, they—and the wimpo politicians—are too chickenshit to stand up to the blacks. *They* are the ignorant ones. They get rich and pampered and feeling guilty about their white collar position in life and 'look at the poor, impoverished Negroes,' they say at their royal butt-fuck parties. *They* never had to live among these jive fuck-heads like I have or they'd really know what assholes they are—the young bucks anyway."

"Come on, Smitty," Stryker muttered without looking up. "Mellow out." He sounded bored.

"No, let me have my say, Stryker! I been puttin' up with this crap long enough. Right now's a prime example of their bitchin' and moanin', trying to claim unfair treatment on war-zone assignments—*but do you hear them defending arrest statistics?*

Stryker slowly pulled off his helmet and clutched it to his stomach as though he had suffered a sudden attack of indigestion. None of them could see him smirking: *Smitty was going too far again!*

"Do you hear them callin' me a liar when I tell you ninety-five percent of my arrests involve blacks—*have* involved blacks ever since I put on the armband an eon ago! Explain that one to me!" He threw his lower jaw out at the Zulu warrior. "Lou." He turned to the lieutenant. "I never experienced no damn racism till I joined the army and became a *victim* of it! This black power crap turns my stomach! I've tried to put myself in their place, but I can't 'cause something deep in my guts says *hate*! Hell, I even went to Africa on vacation once! How many of *them* been to fuckin' Africa before?" He faced the newcomers again.

"Did you get it *all* out of your system, Smitty?" The

lieutenant produced a weary grin that said it all. One of the black soldiers was shifting his feet about, mouth open, trying to produce a verbal protest, but no sound came from it.

"Yah." Smitty sighed, slowly reholstering his pistol. "Fuck it, sir. Can I get out on the street where I feel at home with all the low-life back-alley scum?"

"You got anything to add, Mark?"

Stryker checked his clipboard, feigning memory lapse. His smile slowly grew until it extended ear-to-ear. "Well, I *do* have two positions on my executive protection detail to be filled."

"The Kolana thing?"

"That's a rog."

"You can't be telling me you want anybody in *this* room!" Slipka asked incredulously.

"I was thinking about Zane here." He pointed to the bronze man, then checked the Zulu warrior's nametag. "And Biggs here." The bronze man grinned. The Zulu warrior bared his teeth dramatically.

"Any objections, Smitty?"

"Fuck it." The sergeant stomped out of the room without being dismissed. "So long as they do their job and stay outta my way."

Slipka chuckled and turned to look at Stryker. "You believe in using dynamite instead of logs in your fireplace, don't you, sergeant?"

"Gotta keep the place hoppin', Lou. Gotta keep the place hoppin'."

"You men are dismissed," Slipka told the MPs standing against the front of his desk. "Check the bulletin boards outside every twelve hours, and sooner or later you'll see yourself on an assignment

127

roster. Until then, your time's your own."

They all walked out onto the Orderly Room reviewing stand in the rear of the International complex, overlooking the endless line of parked patrol jeeps extending to the high perimeter wall. "You might consider acquainting yourself with the customs and traditions of the local culture." The lieutenant motioned toward a group of female employees strolling in the direction of the ID gate.

A honking MP jeep pulled up to the veranda railing.

"Sounds like you got a personal problem." Stryker winced at the noise as he stared down at Pvt. Carl Nilmes. "And I suggest —"

"Hey, sarge." Nilmes ignored the pleasantries. "You comin' to our choir practice tonight — at the Queen Bee? Heard your hootch took a direct hit last night. You can crash in the back room after closing. They got some new waitresses workin' there this week — and you know how easy it is to get in *their* pants!"

Stryker hesitated in making an immediate reply. His men loved him, he knew, and he feared not participating in their after-watch parties might ostracize him from the Brotherhood, but he wanted to go home to Wann's apartment and sack out. He envied them — their energy to stay up till all hours of the night, relieving their stress and frustrations by telling the war stories over and over again and tossing a beer bottle or two against the Jane Fonda photo on the wall. He remembered when sleep was an inconvenience. When he always woke at sunrise, or predawn, eager to face the challenge of a new day on the street—when even nights spent beside a woman were restless: You always fought off sleep so you could experience the sensation of her body against yours—drink in her fragrance—melt against her warm curves—rest your ear against her racing heart. And gently kiss her eyelids—those half-open eyelids Asian women slept inside—hoping to somehow join her in her dreams.

"Got a lotta paperwork, buddy," he finally said. "Thanks to those friends of yours in Bravo Company who still don't know how to properly write a Form-Thirty-two. But I might make it there."

Zane, the bronze man, was already sauntering down to what every MP affectionately called the meat market, where women of questionable virtue gathered to meet off-duty Americans. He spent all of thirty seconds inspecting the bulging halter tops propped up against the wire, then pointed to a woman with so much red lipstick on her lips they appeared twice their normal size.

"Looks like he chose Little Oral Annie."

A second jeep had coasted up. Inside, Harcourt and Ramsey giggled at the scene unfolding down at the main gate.

"He knows a good set of lips when he sees one," Stryker said with a grin, rubbing his crotch.

"Well, his whanger's gonna fall off in a couple days, according to Ramsey." Harcourt sounded like a kid ratting on his big brother.

Ramsey just nodded and continued laughing.

Zane did not sign the girl on-post but met her outside the perimeter fence line and flagged down a taxi. He slid in without holding the door open for

129

Little Oral Annie, and the blue and gold Renault vanished in a swirl of dust and smoking rubber.

"Hope she bites it off," muttered Lieutenant Slipka. "I hate to say it, but I don't like the looks of that character. Why they got reassigned to the Seven sixteenth, I'll never know. I'd feel much better if he were aboard one of Egor's dustoffs on its way out to a hospital ship in the South China Sea. I've seen his kind before. The look of defiance in his eyes spells trouble, Stryker. Nothing but trouble."

Sgt. Mark Stryker made no reply to the lieutenant's remark but merely nodded, then started down toward his patrol unit parked a few feet away. "Let's hit the bricks!" he told the men within hearing distance. "First MP to smoke me a cat burglar on Pasteur Street gets a six-pack of Vietnamese Thirty-three!"

"Make it Bud and you got a deal!" Nilmes called back.

"Okay." Stryker twisted the starter toggle and a powerful engine rumbled to life under the hood of his unit. "You're on. But you gotta call it in by twenty-four hundred hours. And that doesn't leave you much time."

Nilmes laughed as if the victim of a practical joke. "What's the rush?"

"No rush," Stryker said. "Just a challenge." And as the MP sergeant started off down the gravel access road toward the jungle of blinking neon, Nilmes felt a strange inner warmth taking hold of him. He wasn't sure if it was just admiration for the ex-Green Beret or love for the streets, but he didn't waste time pondering the feeling.

The MP private sent a short burst of siren after Stryker, then gunned his motor and set out in search of that brand of adventure which was indigenous only to sweet Saigon.

4. Double Delight

The bright blue parrot cocked its head to one side, stopped chewing on the cashew nut clutched in its talons, and peered down at the two figures on the bed.

The soles of a woman's feet pointed up at the bird, and they dipped up and down slightly as the man between her legs pumped her pelvis repeatedly into the plush mattress.

The parrot's head bobbed to the other side as the woman began groaning. She ran her fingernails along the man's slick back, leaving a thin scratch behind. A few drops of blood appeared, and the bird's beak cocked farther to the side as his bulging eye zoomed in on the couple. The woman's fingers came to rest on her partner's buttocks as they rose up and down, and she squeezed with all her might, drawing him deeper inside her.

The man brought his arms up and took hold of her calves the moment the woman's legs shifted vertical to the bed, pointing straight up, and when he forced her thighs forward to their limits—so that her knees were practically touching her breasts—the

132

drawn-out moan that left the woman sent the parrot's feathers to ruffling wildly again.

The bird considered dropping from its perch inside the open cage and gliding for the window, but the woman with her legs spread wide was the food provider, and this memory made the bird hesitate, though it rocked back and forth on its perch during the entire sex act, suffering an anxiety attack.

And then the woman's muffled screams trailed off to an exhausted sigh. Her legs dropped back to the mattress, and the ivory-white haunches between them shuddered slightly then rolled away, off to the side.

For several moments, the only sound in the room was the ceiling fan sluggishly dispersing the heart that closed in on the bed.

The parrot silently watched the two forms — unmoving, except for the wild thumping of their heats — but its attention was quickly diverted to a small ladybug climbing up the mosquito netting that was suspended from ceiling wires over the bed.

Harcourt stared up at the blue ceiling of the bedroom. His head was still swimming, and he seemed to flashback to a murder scene he and Ramsey had rolled up on a couple months earlier:

The victims' apartment was like Neptune's underwater kingdom. Stuffed "fish," made of multihued aquamarine silks and filled with fluffy feathers, hung from the ceiling on invisible threads. More were scattered about the floor's carpet. Blue-green crepe streamers of varying lengths fluttered between the fish. And the bodies tangled on the bed looked like a hungry shark had torn into them. Someone had stitched the lovers straight up their spines with a submachine gun. The man had been an agent with the American Criminal Investigations Division. The crime was still unsolved in the police books.

"So when do we do it?" The woman lying naked across Harcourt's chest asked him for the fifth time that night.

"Soon." He didn't look her in the eyes but glanced up at the parrot staring back at him.

"Soon? How soon?"

"What's *his* problem?" Harcourt was referring to the disapproving parrot in the bamboo cage sitting atop a tall stereo speaker.

The woman slugged his arm harshly. "Talk to me! How are we doing to do it?"

"We're undermanned." Harcourt sounded like he was planning the caper for the first time. "Code-Zeroes every night — guys callin' for help left and right — assistance a few minutes away at best. Could be we might run into an ambush or encounter some cowboys on a rooftop somewhere, and I might not save ol' Derek like I always have in the past.

"Or I could skid sideways into an Arvin tank. They're always rumblin' down Phan Dinh Phung in excess of fifty klicks."

"That sounds so — gory, Benny."

"*You're* the one who came up with the idea, baby."

"Yes, well —"

"You're sure his life insurance policy is still in affect, right?"

"Yes." Her voice trailed off as her lips moved slowly down his chest toward his crotch. He watched

134

her long, black hair fan out below him.

"Yes, there you go." Harcourt guided Mrs. Derek Ramsey's mouth to its most pleasurable position. He lightly grasped her ears with his fingers and began moving her head up and down to remind her *he* was in charge tonight.

Then he lay back on the pillow and stared at the ceiling, listening to the sirens crisscrossing the city below the window of their secret hideaway on quiet Thanh Mau Street.

The parrot squawked down at them in irritation as the woman began to groan loudly again with each jerking plunge of her lips, exaggerating her enjoyment.

Harcourt made a pistol with his fingers and sent an imaginary round up at the overweight bird, causing it to ruffle its feathers violently as it turned its back to him.

"Was that shadow movement, or am I starting to see things?" Thomas whispered across the jeep to Broox. In the back seat, Bryant slept soundly across several flak jackets, abruptly snoring now and then.

Broox sat up in his seat and brought Richards's folding binoculars up to his eyes. "Yah." He licked his lips. "I think we're on the verge of havin' somethin' go down, Ants baby."

Down the street, partially hidden in the shadows of a looming tenement, Decoy Squad Sgt. Gary Richards lay on his back in the gutter, a bottle of Vietnamese beer in his hand, feigning an advanced stage of intoxication.

The four Americans were in civilian clothing, and their vehicle, a souped-up jeep painted totally black, was devoid of any emergency equipment or police markings. They were working undercover, and they were volunteering their time.

Decoy duty was always voluntary. An MP had to first complete his regular duty tour in uniform before his squad sergeant could recommend him for the after-hours assignment. And a regular duty tour was already a twelve-hour shift. Most of the men avoided the squad. The team almost always consisted of Broox, Thomas, and Bryant, with Richards leading them. There had been substitutes and temporary replacements in the past, but the original four glory-tunes characters had always returned in their staring roles, though Bryant was exhibiting considerably less enthusiasm on the street since he had gotten married several months earlier.

Tonight Richards himself had volunteered to take the back-alley drunk role. Broox had worked it the night before, and after a large tomcat urinated on him and tried to rip his ear off, he swore they'd never catch him out of the jeep again. A wad of laundered money hung out of Richards's pocket. The men had doused him with enough alcohol it could be smelled a block away. The squad had been used for everything from robbery stakeouts to nabbing murder suspects, but when the extraordinary crimes in Sin City tapered off, the men always returned to their favorite strong-arm takedowns.

The town was swarming with cowboys after midnight curfew: Vietnamese hoodlums who prowled the side streets looking for trouble and an easy victim, usually drunk GIs booted out of the bordello after they became uncontrollable.

In its first few months of operation, the Decoy Squad had been an unqualified success. Richards's men had collared over a thousand felony arrests and dusted a dozen undesirables with their arsenal of sterile weapons. But then the Saigon Press had gotten hold of the story, and after numerous front page series stories about the secret squad in the *Saipan Post* and *Vietnam Guardian*, the back-alley hoods became more wary about stalking drunk GIs, and the glory busts tapered off. But now several weeks had passed since the four friends had hunted the hunters, and the dark boulevards of the Pearl of the Orient appeared stocked again with defiant sharks, eager to do battle.

"Yep, I got movement." Broox slowly focused the binoculars with his forefinger. "Better wake Tim up back there." His free hand started to reach for the mike clipped to the dashboard. "I'll radio it in—"

A huge form rushed from an alleyway and grabbed Gary Richards by the ankles, jerking him partially off the ground.

"Let's go!" Thomas yelled as Richards abandoned his drunk act and began yelling at the top of his lungs for backup, fearing his men had missed what was happening.

Broox hit the jeep starter, but before the engine even turned over, Bryant and Thomas were leaping out of the vehicle and sprinting toward their leader.

Broox threw on the headlights of the "Black Beast" and let the clutch pop out. Rear tires spun and the unit raced forward, rapidly gaining on the two MPs as the headlights drenched the intersection with brilliant light.

The man who had grabbed Richards stood nearly seven feet tall! His back was to the Americans as he swung the army sergeant into a brick wall, over and over again.

Broox reached for the sawed-off shotgun in a bracket beside the gearbox as the jeep rapidly overtook Thomas and Bryant, but before the headlight beams swept across the giant assaulting Richards, another intruder entered the eerie scene. Clad in a cherry-red cape, gas mask, combat boots, *and nothing else*, he dropped from the nearest rooftop, knocking both Richards and his assailant to the ground. All three tumbled off the sidewalk into a gutter, groaning.

"Captain Condom!" Broox was laughing, not awed, but the scene unfolding in front of his eyes was anything but comical. The man who had originally accosted the Decoy sergeant was now slowly rising back to his feet — the caped crusader riding his houlders from behind, trying to get the behemoth n a throat lock.

Broox hit the three wrestling men with a spotight. Richards had tackled his attacker now, and hey all crashed back to the ground again, but he could not make out the features of either stranger. There was no way the tall guy could be a Vietnamese — not at nearly seven feet — but he might be Japanese, or even Korean. A lot of ROKs were fighting in Vietnam, too, and Seoul grew 'em big!

As he pulled up to within a few feet of the three fighters, Broox let fly a round of double aught buckshot from the shotgun, and glass from a streetlight that hadn't worked in years sprinkled down across the intersection.

Upon hearing the unexpected blast, the dark giant sprung to his feet again, whirled around, and threw Captain Condom through the plate glass window of a nearby shop before booting Richards in the face and fleeing down the closest corridor between buildings.

"Get him! *Get him!* Get his ass!" Thomas yelled as he caught up to Broox's skidding jeep. Tim Bryant had slid up to Richards and was now down on one knee, checking on his dazed and battered boss.

"I'm fine!" Richards snapped, both hands clamped across his temples as if he were trying to hold his head together. "Snarf up that rubberhead streaker in the storefront window over there!" He pointed to the plate glass window with the huge hole in it, where Captain Condom's combat boots hung out, polished toes in the air, soles facing the angry MPs. "Forget the monster just tried to roll me — *I want the faggot in the cape!*"

"Right, sarge!" Bryant holstered his automatic as he watched Broox leap from the jeep and follow Thomas into the gloomy crevice between two leaning tenements. Then he hustled across the street to the damaged shop, a burglar alarm already clanging against the silence of the night.

"I'll take the lead position!" Thomas was already out of breath as they left the relative safety of the wide-open intersection and entered the tense darkness of the unknown. But Broox was laced with energy, and he quickly overtook his friend, pistol

139

raised in the air, and ran down the corridor until the first doorway came into view several dozen yards away.

Broox slowed to a cautious walk, weapon extended at arm's length now, and dropped into a combat crouch as he reached the doorway, but it was empty — the entrance to a noodle cafe was still securely bolted from the inside.

Broox routinely waved Thomas up to his position, but before the other MP could make his way through the debris littering the corridor, a trash can off in the distance was slammed onto its side.

A trio of cats cried in response, and Broox felt an uncontrollable chill race down his spine — the barrel had been flung against a brick wall with unmistakable force. They were chasing a man of incredible strength: someone who was running from them but not fleeing in panic. Broox got the feeling the man was toying with them. Visions of the monster's huge hands waiting down the corridor to reach out without warning and clamp across his throat filled Broox's mind. And he hesitated an instant longer than was acceptable.

"*Come on!*" Thomas, though still not fully recovered from his initial sprint, brushed past his partner and vanished in the gloom. "The sonofabitch is getting away, Mikey!"

Broox swallowed hard. The look in Thomas's eyes had been unmistakable: shame. He was ashamed of the way Broox was reacting. He was hesitating longer than warranted. He was exhibiting fear. Exhibiting it in his hand movements, the way his feet froze, his icy facial expression — not just his eyes.

It was okay to let your eyes light up with uncertainty during the chase — that was accepted, even expected. You could not mask the eyes or camouflage the emotions displayed involuntarily during the pursuit, but hesitate at the wrong moment and you were doomed. And worse than that, worse than death, your actions could kill your partner, too.

Broox willed his feet to move, to chase after Thomas into the dark, the unknown that awaited both MPs. He mentally commanded his legs to pump the rest of his body down that narrow corridor, but he could not move — was frozen to the spot. He could not understand any of this!

This was not Michael Broox's body he was inside!

He had always been so daring in the past, so unafraid of injury, death, or the consequences of charging down dark alleys in pursuit of suspects.

Then the shot rang out.

Fifty yards in the distance — in the blackness that had swallowed up his partner.

"Anthony!" he called weakly. "*Anthony!* You all right?"

"Mike! Get your ass down here!" Thomas's voice cracked. He sounded hurt, shaken.

Broox found himself running. Sprinting. Faster than his feet had ever taken him in his life.

When he came upon Thomas, it was abruptly. The MP was down on his hands and knees, bleeding from the nose. He couldn't see anybody, but off in the dark, he could feel it — somebody was running away. Escaping.

"Sonofabitch got me in the face with a two-by-four," Thomas muttered, slowly wiping his nose with the back of his hand. The board lay on the ground beside him, smeared with blood.

Broox went down on one knee beside the man. "You okay, Anthony?" He sounded shocked, bewildered. "You all right?"

Thomas slowly looked up and stared at him, an incredulous expression on his face. "What the hell you wastin' time for jawin' for Christsake?" Thomas pointed into the black void before them. "The mother-fucker's gettin' away!"

Broox remained where he was, though he raised his pistol up to ward off the evil feeling closing in on them. "But are you—*okay?*"

Thomas reached out and grabbed him by the collar, dragging him down closer to the blacktop. "*What's the matter with you, Mikey?* Go get his ass!" And he flung his brother MP away, propelling him down the corridor several feet. "I ain't ever seen you act this way before. Now move it! I'll cover you. I'm all right—I'll cover you."

Broox swallowed hard and wiped the sweat from his brow, then continued down the narrow passageway between the two towering buildings.

Anthony was right, he thought, as he cautiously checked each doorway and shadow. *I'm not myself lately—haven't been myself since I met her*. Slowly, he began to feel the controls returning. His street sense was back, the fear had left him. But the thoughts remained. *Ever since I found someone more important to me than the street*.

Suddenly darkness engulfing him lightened several shades of black, and he discovered a gorilla of a

142

man was standing mere inches from him. Cornered. His back to the wall. An instant later the steel plank slammed into his belly, doubling him over. On his way down, Broox jerked the trigger in repeatedly, over and over, filling the narrow corridor with splashes of light and sound—until the slide of his pistol locked back down on an empty chamber and the seven foot monster man toppled over on top of him.

For a moment he blacked out, but then the overcast sky above was swimming with stars, and Thomas was struggling to pull the behemoth off, slamming him with a nightstick in between each tug. "Off him, asshole! You're under apprehension! You hear me? You're under fucking—"

"He's dead, Ants!" Broox was laughing now, though his voice was muffled by the huge bulk crushing him against the blacktop. "Lay off the guy, will ya?" He tried pushing the dead man off from underneath, but the torso refused to budge, and he laughed all the harder—*he was feeling great!* With the giant's blood soaking his uniform now, he was back on the mountaintop! Experiencing that high that only comes after gunplay.

"You're okay, Mikey?" Thomas screamed, nearly hysterical. "You're all right?" The shoe was on the other foot now, and Broox ate it up.

"I'm fine, Ants, I'm fine! Just get this elephant off of me, okay?" And his lungs laughed their hardest now that he had a hand clamped across the monster's throat and there was no pulse whatsoever.

"He's fine!" Thomas grabbed the dead man's wrist and, after planting a boot against the armpit below

143

it, pulled fruitlessly as he stared up at the startled faces filling the windows above the almost comical scene. Lights came on, illuminating the pool of blood gathering beneath Broox and causing the dead man's eyes to glow slightly. "He's all right!" Thomas stared down at his partner as more lights came on. "I always knew you still had it in you, Mikey! I don't know what happened back there tonight. Hell, I know that wasn't you, brother! I know it won't happen again!"

Broox's smile faded slightly, but his chuckle lingered on, and he shook his head in agreement with Thomas as the dead man finally rolled off. But deep inside, MP Michael Broox knew he was finished. The street was not his anymore. Not to toy with the way he had these last two years while one of Stryker's boys.

A new priority had entered his life. And you couldn't fool Lady Saigon. Not for long. You had fallen from her graces, and it wouldn't be long now before she canceled your ticket. It was a one-way trip, and once you chose your sleeping partner, you couldn't change your mind. Sin City was worse than a Vietnamese woman scorned. She rarely forgave. And she never forgot.

"Sergeant Richards is doing fine," Stryker announced at the guardmount briefing the following evening. "A couple stitches on the chin, so I wimped out and gave him a comp day to recuperate. He's probably got one of them damn Third Field Hospital nurses sittin' on his face this very moment," he complained, through his tone feigned intense jealousy. "His ward number and visiting hours are posted on the bulletin boards. Try to pay the man a visit on your way down to the whorehouses, okay?" Several MP helmets bobbed up and down obediently. "And you clowns on town patrol are authorized a short-seven at his room, so long as you code out with WACO and don't try smuggling any liquor to him. Gary needs his rest, and I need *him* back on the street!" Stryker glanced down at the podium, but his clipboard was gone. Someone had hidden it again. He visually checked his stool. It appeared intact, but he remained standing anyway.

"No way he's gonna recover with some army nurses sittin' on his snout," an anonymous voice called from the back of the room.

"I think that's illegal!" another MP declared. "A man could suffocate."

"But what a way to go!" Thomas added with a contemplative smile.

"Our hero, Tim Bryant, who you see seated in the last row back there," Stryker said, pointing the blushing soldier out, "is also recovering, gentlemen: from a case of bruised ego." The men in the room were all close enough that they could pick on each other without anybody's taking it personally. "Seems he allowed Captain Condom to escape last night—"

"Captain Condom?" Several voices sounded aghast. "Not *Captain Condom!*"

"I was checkin' on Gary!" Bryant rose to his feet defensively. "I didn't figure the caped idiot with the gas mask was going anywhere. I could see the bottoms of his boots the whole time!"

"But the rest of him wasn't lying inside the broken plate glass window like everyone thought!" Stryker explained. "Just his lousy combat boots. The dude managed to slip them off and make good his escape while Timmy was kissin' his squad sergeant's ass."

The room erupted into jeers and catcalls, and paper airplanes by the dozens crashed into one another inches above Bryant's head. Stryker instantly wished he hadn't made the impulsive wisecrack, but it was too late. There'd be no way to salvage the briefing now.

And then the men in the rear of the room, near the doorway, grew suddenly quiet, and the hush quickly spread throughout the rest of the room. Every helmet turned back toward a muscular black MP with a submachine gun cradled in his arms and hostility in his eyes.

"Well, *awright*!" A cheer went up and a chorus of whistles chased out the silence. Flanked by two PR men, Kiwi Kolana sauntered into the room, her wavy blond hair brushed over a shoulder so all the men could see her dazzling smile.

"Hi, guys!" She tightroped down the center aisle atop precarious high heels that only served to accent her sleek, flaring thighs.

Stryker doubted any of his men were looking at the flash of teeth, *except perhaps the Zulu warrior with the molars on a chain around his neck*. He chuckled to himself. They were all checking out the size forty chest swinging from side to side and up and down with each sensuous footfall.

"Well aren't you guys gonna welcome me to your roll call?" She giggled and feigned hurt feelings with the same expression.

A dozen MPs vacated their seats and offered them to the starlet, but Kiwi Kolana locked eyes with Mark Stryker, and, like an air-to-air rocket homing in on its target, she pranced directly for the man behind the podium.

"Well aren't *you* one hunk of *man*!" She swooned a few seconds later, tangling her fingers in his chest hair as she draped an arm over his shoulder and molded her body against his.

The room exploded into applause and whispered suggestions, and Stryker struggled to rebutton the top of his shirt again.

"*Ohhhhhh!*" Her voice rose an octave as if someone had just pinched her from behind. "And so modest, too!"

Gentlemen! Gentlemen!" One of the PR men had expertly moved up to the podium microphone while the big MP sergeant had his hands full. "Miss Kolana just wanted to drop by to let you know she appreciates your unselfish sacrifices as far as all the overtime you're providing to insure her stay here in Saigon is a safe one." Additional cheers and modest nods of dismissal answered him.

"My people are setting up some coffee and donuts in the—what do you soldiers call it? The Orderly Room? Well, we're trucking in refreshments, and we're gonna have one hell of an autograph party! Am I right, boys?"

The rafters almost shook loose from all the applause.

"I think we've disrupted your briefing enough for tonight, sergeant." The short, balding public relations man slapped Stryker on the back and tried to lead Kiwi away from the podium, but she clung to Mark's thick biceps.

"He's hard as *rock!*" She flashed her teeth at the MPs gathering closer to the podium. *"Feel him!"* She challenged the agent with the perpetual grin.

Her words were met with another wave of laughter, and Stryker pulled away, attempting to straighten out his uniform.

"Feel him!" Thomas motioned Broox forward playfully. "Feel those big, bulging biceps!" Broox balked. Stryker blushed and busied himself with paperwork.

"Until I see you all again!" Kiwi bared her teeth in a broad, photogenic smile and blew kisses to all sides of the room, apparently forgetting she'd be meeting the men again right after the briefing.

Like Secret Service agents ushering a presidential candidate out of a convention center, the MPs Stryker had assigned to Miss Kolana's bodyguard entourage split up, just as they had been drilled a hundred times prior to the starlet's arrival in Vietnam. Unsmiling, half of the squad preceded the woman into the hallway, searching for potential dangers or suspicious persons. The other half followed her bouncing bottom out. One man gave Stryker the thumbs-up.

"Okay." Stryker's fingertips rattled loudly against the edge of the podium as Kiwi Kolana's high heels click-clacked down the hallway. "I've got some good news—and I've got some bad news."

None of the sarcastic remarks he had half expected materialized. The room fell silent. "The good news is that we're temporarily back on eight hour shifts—" A single pair of hands began clapping slowly. "But that could change anytime, as it has in the past. Depends on what the PM does with the newbies we just got in.

"The bad news is that I found some disturbing paperwork in my box this afternoon." His eyes burned into Michael Broox, who was staring at the KIA plaques on the far wall and smiling. "Tell me it ain't true, Mikey."

"Tell you *what* ain't true?" a voice called out from the far corner of the room.

"It seems our beloved Mike Broox is leaving us—"

"What?" Thomas shot to his feet and cast Broox a betrayed glare.

"P.C.S.," Stryker muttered in mock disgust. Permanent Change of Station. "To some MP detachment at a chickenshit army med center in Colorado. For a couple months. Then E.T.S. Mikey's leaving the corps, gentlemen."

"Leaving the cops?" Bryant glanced over at Broox but remained seated.

"Well *on your feet*, trooper!" Stryker growled. "Explain yourself!"

Still grinning smugly, Broox slowly rose and removed his helmet liner. "Getting married, brothers," he said loudly, pride and a sense of accomplishment in his tone.

"What!" Several men protested with boos and hisses. Someone dropped a nightstick in shock, and it rolled under several rows of chairs before bouncing off the toe of Stryker's boot.

"Just so long as she's not a national," a tower rat in

149

the back of the room shouted.

"Her name is Miss Ky."

"Fi Fi Ky, the Hong Kong movie star?" Thomas fell back heavily in his seat, mouth agape.

"She's Vietnamese," Broox replied calmly. "Just happens to speak Chinese. And French, too, as a matter of fact — not to mention fluent English. How many of your dumb blondes back in Brooklyn can boast *that*?"

"I can imagine." Thomas stared at his buddy, eyes unblinking.

Stryker's brows came together in mock bewilderment. *Fi Fi Ky? Kiwi Kolana? What could be next?*

"You're gonna catch it in the ass, cherry-boy." Someone giggled from the last row, as if from experience. "All she really wants is a Pan Am ticket back to the big PX stateside."

"Sucker!" another man yelled, but the remarks were all given in a friendly vein.

"She makes bookoo bucks." Broox defended his choice. "More, in one month, probably, than I could make in a whole career with the military police. Besides, she walks on my back all night, cooks for me, bathes me, and you-know-what's me, and never asks for anything in return, except *this*." He cupped his crotch affectionately. "And a bit of understanding when it comes to her eighteen-plus hour days on the movie set downtown."

"The guys might be right, though," Stryker worried aloud.

"Not you too, sarge." A hurt look glassed over his eyes.

"What would she want with an ugly street cop?"

150

Bryant was more honest.

Broox's grin dropped into a slight frown. "She likes the length of my whanger, dildo-breath." He was serious.

"How long you known her?"

Broox felt like he was being interrogated by his parents. *Fifty* of them. "Long enough." He sat back down. "What you bums worried about anyway?" he asked. "Like I said, she's already loaded."

"But that visa back to The World is priceless," Bryant argued. "Some of these cunts would kill for it."

"She's not a—cunt." Broox looked away. "And who are you to talk? What about your Hue Chean?"

"Plus marriage means instant citizenship."

"Bullshit." An armchair lawyer corrected Tim. "Only permanent residency."

"Well, citizenship for the dozen baby-sans that'll eventually come along—" An echo of laughter bounced about the room.

"Then you'll be sponsoring her whole family."

"Brothers, sisters, fathers, mothers—"

"Grandmother-san! Grandfather-san!"

"Third and fourth cousins—*hundreds* of them!"

"Christ!" Broox stood back up and locked eyes with Stryker. "Is this briefing over yet?"

"Yah, we'd like to get out on the streets." Thomas cast a disapproving glare at his best friend. "We got *things* to talk about."

"Does she give good head?" an anonymous NCO called from the dark doorway. He was flanked by several other smirking E-5s.

"Yah." Someone close by agreed. "That's all that

151

really matters."

"No, the briefing's not over," Stryker said. "Have any of you psycho ward outpatients seen Zane?"

"Zane?"

"One of the new guys from up north. The one that looks like a Doc Savage poster."

"Last I saw of him," a sergeant in the doorway said, "he was getting into a cab with a claptrap of questionable virtue."

"Yah, that's the last time I saw him, too." Stryker checked his clipboard. "Well, as of now, his ass is AWOL. If any of you are pals with him get the word to him. Show up in front of my desk tomorrow at six sharp and all'll be forgiven. I don't want none of my Mike Papas on the coward roster.

"If you guys on town patrol see him, scarf him up pronto. Be sure and note this on your hot sheets. I want his heels locked in front of me before thirty days elapse and the PM jumps him to Deserter status.

"Sergeant Schultz, who also miraculously avoided the jaws of death couple nights ago when a pissed-off projectile slammed into his—" Stryker paused dramatically and gave Raunch Raul a contemptible smirk. "Fifth floor flat, has requested me to advise you to keep an eyeball on the complex at nine two nine Nguyen Van Thoai. Had a murder-suicide there the same night as the rocket attack. A slightly dinky-dau female found out her baby-san was leaving the Nam without her, so she pulled the pin on them both."

"Gross out." Carl Nilmes pretended he was throwing up in his helmet. "Another grenade-under-the-mattress while they were el-fucko-in-progress?"

"Correctamundo!"

"Ain't that the rage these days."

"Yah."

"Anyway. I guess the dude *bought* the lousy apartment, or thought he did, and the chaplain is asking we make sure no squatters move in before he can take care of the legal crap."

"Who gives a fu—"

"Yah, but do it for the holy man, okay, if nothing else."

"Was the guy an MP?"

"No, but—"

"Then screw him, sarge."

"He already got screwed, son. He already got the ultimate shaft."

"I guess he did, didn't he."

"And if you see any suspicious types limpin' down Le Van Duyet with a chain saw, dust his drapes and FI 'im for Smitty. MPI found another victim in the warehouse sector with her skull split down the middle."

"Sexually assaulted?"

"Yah—appears so. That's S.O.P. around here, ain't it?"

"I guess it is, sarge."

"So what are you waitin' for?" Stryker stepped away from the podium. "Let's hit the bricks. Let's go out and *get some*! Now you all know I'm not a stat man, but I hate skaters when there's carloads of crime waitin' out there for ya. And I haven't seen a good Frank sheet come across my desk since The Uke pasted that burg suspect comin' out of the

153

Queen Bee Friday night."

Something tugged at Stryker's memory when he said the name of the bar, but the notion only lingered a moment before vanishing and, unable to grasp it, he dismissed the whole feeling. "And check your damn dipsticks before you get into your units out there," he added. "Next guy that blows his motor during a chase pays for repairs."

"Well *fuck me*," Jeff Reilly muttered to himself. He was on his seventh MP jeep.

Somebody laughed in rebuttal, then the men began filing out of the room.

Across the street from the International, a young Vietnamese man stood beside a sugarcane vendor's stand, his features shadowed by the brightly colored umbrella overhead. He patiently chewed on a strip of green bamboo for several minutes, watching the half-hundred American policemen splitting up into pairs before the long line of MP jeeps. When he spotted Sgt. Mark Stryker, his eyes lit up briefly.

He watched the tall, stocky NCO lift the hood of his jeep and begin inspecting the engine.

A beautiful woman in a pink, flowered *ao dai* joined the Vietnamese man, and they spent several more minutes watching the big American silently.

Once they exchanged a knowing glance but never smiled.

Back across the street, at the MP static post where a long line of vehicles was being slowly, routinely inspected for hidden bombs and contraband, a young private was in turn watching the pair.

A long, doubledecker bus, belching thick blue clouds of smoke, slowly rolled between the MP and the Vietnamese couple, and after it passed, he found that they had vanished in the smoggy haze. Their sudden disappearance sent alarm bells ringing in his gut, but he merely shrugged his shoulders, attempting to imitate his heroes, Stryker and Richards, and shifted his attention to a civilian van waiting to enter the International compound. *Fucking correspondents*, he decided, the words in his thoughts taking on Raunchy Raul's accent.

After he routinely checked the gas cap and found a tube of heroin suspended on fishing wire, he arrested the driver, basked in the elusive rush of job satisfaction, then field-phoned for a prisoner transport, logged his five hundredth felony arrest in his pocket notebook, and completely forgot about the Vietnamese couple across the street.

5. Don't Mention the Moon

"My name Miss Lee." The bargirl leaned up against the soldier and ran her fingers through the hair on his arm. "But you can call me what you like most." She batted dark eyes up at him and pressed her swollen halter top against the edge of the counter.

The American glanced down at her, his expression noncommittal. "I like call you cocksucker," he replied in pidgin English without emotion, unaroused.

The bargirl frowned, whipped her long black hair over the opposite shoulder, then tried a different approach.

She slid her hand down his chest and gently grabbed his crotch. "If that's what you like." She winked up at the tall man with the Finance patch on his left shoulder. The soldier was a slick-sleeve. "But first you buy me Saigon tea?"

The man grinned for the first time, picked up the wadded piaster currency next to his drink, and stuffed it down her halter top. He took his time pulling the fingers free.

"Let's go." He rose from his bar stool and grabbed

the woman's wrist. "No time for another watered-down drink." He led her toward the swinging front doors of the Queen Bee, roughly pushing a path through the patrons on the dance floor.

"Where?" She feigned total innocence.

"There's an alley right out back, honey." His uniform was lined with perspiration from the humidity in the air, even though it was night.

"We go my room," the girl stated coldly.

"No, I no go your room." He was adamant. "We go alley."

"I no like do it alley." She skidded to a stop, but he pulled her off balance through the front doors.

"No sweat, *manoi*," he said. "All you gotta do is drop to your lovely knees and swallow it up. You don't need no fuckin' springs under your ass. I been workin' graves and savin' it up—won't take long at all."

"Working—*graves*?" Her almond eyes went wide with worry.

"Never mind, sweet thing—"

"We go your barracks then." She pouted. "You take me go cinema—you take me go bowl alley—then I make you feel reeeeal good, GI."

The soldier grinned down at her. His expression said, *You gotta be kidding*.

"It's nearly curfew, honeybuns," he said. "MP bastards won't let me sign you into my hootch, much as I'd like to use your snatch as a pillow tonight."

"MP bastards." She agreed bitterly, speaking the words under her breath.

He escorted her down the steps of the Queen Bee and led her toward a dark alley running off busy

Nguyen Hue Boulevard. An MP jeep cruised slowly by, its driver cautiously making his way through the throng of pedestrians spilling over into the streets from the crumbling sidewalk. A teenager riding shotgun, his helmet tilted against the bridge of his nose at just the right angle, inspected every person within an arm's length of the vehicle. In the back seat, a third patrolman stood behind a mounted M-60. He leaned against the stock of the black machine gun, popping bubblegum loudly as he made intimidating faces at the curbside prostitutes. None of the MPs seemed to notice the tall skinny American with the Finance patch, but they all eyeballed Miss Lee — for purely professional reasons, of course.

The soldier glanced over his shoulder as darkness closed in on them, and the noisy activity of the street fell off in the background.

They started across a canal that snaked down through the tenements behind the Queen Bee, and Miss Lee stared at the buttocks of the man walking along the narrow planks in front of her. The fatigue trousers were baggy, and he needed some meat on his bones, but she could tell he otherwise kept in shape. Perhaps he wasn't really so brusque. Maybe, if she really showed him a good time — gave this trick that all-out effort — he'd move in with her, if only for a year, and she wouldn't have to walk the streets to support herself anymore. Until next year. When his Tour Three hundred sixty-five was up. If only they could —

Suddenly the American was being propelled back into her with brutal force. He groaned and toppled to the ground, a board with protruding nails stuck

158

to his forehead and eyes.

Miss Lee tried to scream, but a huge dark shape was rushing up through the dark — was upon her without sound, without warning. Something slammed against her face, and she felt herself tumbling back into the canal. Then the thing in the dark was hoisting her up over his shoulder, had caught her, saved her from the murky water, though she feared she was headed for hell worse than death, and he clutched tightly at her thighs as he bolted across the narrow plank and started down a black sliver of alley with no streetlights. The stars overhead became a numbing swirl of silver just before she lost consciousness.

She awoke strapped to a metal table, a sharp whining noise in her ears. She felt naked, *violated*, though she knew her miniskirt was still riding her waist. She lifted her head, and before the pain overwhelmed her like riptides, she saw the skirt had been hiked up over her hips. She could feel that the insides of her thighs were moist and sticky, though the bindings had her legs spread apart. A warm breeze rustled through the vast building, tickling her nipples. Her halter top had been torn off.

She waited a moment for her vision to clear, then glanced about, inspecting her surroundings, painfully aware of a throbbing between her temples.

An empty warehouse rose up on all sides. A few feet away, an indistinguishable form was setting up a tripod.

With a fancy camera on it!

Finally making her movie debut! She laughed to herself sarcastically, but the relentless pain kept her lips in a downcast crescent.

"Smile, bitch," a deep voice muttered from behind the tripod, in Vietnamese.

When the flash went off, a searing pain exloded across the top of her head and blood sprayed across her vision. The front page stories of the grizzly murders the police were investigating flashed in front of her mind's eye, and as the grinding blade bit into her skull, slowly splitting her head open, she knew she had become the latest victim of the buzz saw killer.

Long before the hungry steel sliced through the bone into brain matter, Miss Lee lost consciousness from the intense pain. She fell backward into a dark pit of screaming nightmares where sheets of pain engulfed and consumed every cell of her body. It was the Deep Sleep—one she would never wake from.

"Okay, cut the siren," Ramsey muttered across the jeep to Harcourt. "It's only a couple blocks away now."

Their roof lights sending beams of crimson through the midnight mist, the two MPs coasted in silence the last half mile to the deserted warehouse behind the Queen Bee. The streets were nearly deserted because of the rapidly approaching curfew, but a siren would bring spectators to their balconies and brave juveniles right up on the scene, and Investigators would play hell trying to canvass the neighborhood for legit witnesses.

"How'd he get here so quick?" Harcourt's eye narroed when he saw another unit already parked in front of the building, its motor off but red roof light splashing rays against the high tin walls. "He was assigned to work way over in—"

"Smitty never works his own sector." Ramsey grinned. "The entire city's his playground, and tonight he took over someone else's sandbox."

"Then he can handle the paperwork that goes with it," Harcourt complained. One of the most thrilling aspects of policework is being the first unit on scene at a violent crime. The unknown is staring you straight in the face, daring you to jump in, watching how you'll react. The first few moments provide the potential for some real gunplay, and that adrenaline high that can last for hours afterward. If you make a mistake, it could mean cold steel through your throat. Smitty was an expert at "jumping calls." He had the fastest jeep in the battalion, next to Stryker's. Slipka was always threatening to take it away from the man, but he never did. A lot of the troopers didn't care one way or the other. Most of their time was centered around marking another X across their short-timer's calendar. But it mattered to Ramsey and Harcourt. They were in the Nam to stay. And their patrol sector was sovereign territory.

"Well, call us on scene." Ramsey padlocked the mandatory chain around the brake pedal and steering wheel, and stepped out of the jeep. He unsnapped the rain flap of his holster but did not draw his weapon.

"Smitty didn't radio his arrival," Harcourt protested softly.

"He never does." Ramsey started for the open

door in front of the sergeant's unit. "He's got one of those pak-sets on his hip. He's always—*available*, which is all that really matters. Catch my drift?" Harcourt was becoming a real pain lately, Ramsey decided. But the man *was* his partner, and that made their on-duty relationship sacred. Even his wife had complained about the long hours they spent working the street together, but women were always bitching about this or that, he also decided, and she had known what his job was all about before they got married anyway.

"Ah yes." Ramsey used his best Lon Chaney accent after sneaking up behind Murphy. "Sleeping beauty!" He ran a forefinger along the dead woman's scalp, tracing the deep gash that had exposed the top half of her brain. "And has the brave prince kissed her yet?"

The Murph had nearly somersaulted off his feet. He and Smitty were both crouching beside some strange tripodlike marks in the dusty floor. Neither man had heard Ramsey walk up, though he suspected Smitty did not miss the sound of their jeep arriving outside. A few seconds later the portable radio on the sergeant's web belt came alive, and Harcourt's metallic voice could be heard coding them on scene.

"Tripod marks again?" Ramsey went down on one knee beside the MP sergeant and imitated Smitty's intense concentration.

"Yah—looks like it."

"A camera perhaps?" He glanced over at Smitty's partner. The Murph had drawn his pistol when the two MPs entered unannounced. He was now trying

162

to reholster it while staring at the dead woman's terrified expression.

"Probably something kinky," Smitty finally muttered. "A body hoist for a deviate pervert who wanted to dangle over her bod while dining or something."

"Like Raunchy Raul." Ramsey chuckled lightly.

"Or Stryker."

The room filled with an ear-splitting concussion as a .45 automatic discharged a few feet from Smitty's ear.

The corpse on the table shuddered slightly as a hollow-point round slammed into her hip.

"Jesus Christ!" Ramsey and Harcourt had instinctively flattened out on the floor, but Smitty was still calmly in a crouch, inspecting the marks on the floor. Ears ringing, he glanced over at Murphy.

"You dumb fuck," the sergeant muttered softly at his partner.

The Murph was staring down at the smoking barrel of his pistol, then over at the gaping hole on the woman's exposed hip, then back at this weapon. "It was an accident." It looked like tears were about to well up in his eyes.

"At least you didn't hit her in the goddamned head." Smitty rose to his feet with a sigh.

"Or the love muscles," Ramsey said with a laugh. He did a couple push-ups before getting back on his feet.

Harcourt rose next to Ramsey, an angry expression on his face. "What the *fuck* happened, Murphy?"

"*It was an accident!*" Murphy repeated, his weapon

still in his hand unholstered.

Ramsey glanced at the crescent moon hanging in the hazy sky beyond the open doorway, laughing down at them. *And it's not even full.* He slowly shook his head from side to side.

Smitty walked up, took The Murph's gunhand, and slowly directed the .45 back into its holster. Then he leaned over and examined the woman's bloody head wound. The sparkling blade from the buzz saw was imbedded clear to the base of her neck, her head split completely open like a pineapple.

"It was an accidental discharge, guys!" Murphy said again.

"Don't worry." Smitty frowned. "I'd say she was already dead, Murph."

"But what about—"

"What about the bullet wound?" Harcourt finished Murphy's question. "Doesn't that screw up the physical evidence?"

"CID's gonna be pissed," Ramsey said.

Static crackled on Smitty's pak-set, then the second half of an excited transmission filled the warehouse. ". . . needs help! On top of the Continental! Ten-Two! On top of the Continental—MP needs help!"

"Did you recognize who that was?" Harcourt's heart began racing laps around the room while he stood there wide-eyed.

"What the fuck's he doin' on top of the Continental?" Ramsey countered.

"Let's roll!" Smitty yelled, ending the discussion as he whirled around and started for the door.

"Murph! You stay here and maintain custody of the evidence chain. And don't burn the place to the ground!"

"What?" Murphy demanded. "By myself? In here?" He glanced down at the woman's mangled head, her right eye bulging out slightly and staring up at him. "*With her?*"

But they were gone.

Outside, a young Vietnamese couple stood in the shadows of a tenement doorway, silently watching the MPs sprint out to their patrol units. Both were slowly chewing on strips of green bamboo. The woman, a slender lady with long shimmering hair that almost glittered like stardust beneath the moonlight, held a disappointed look in her eyes—like someone she had expected was late in arriving.

The man beside her did not exhibit any outward emotion whatsoever, until a helicopter gunship cruised past low overhead, rotors slapping at the hot sticky air. The Huey, soldiers' jungle boots dangling out the open hatch with M-16 rifles balanced haphazardly across their thighs, banked sharply to the left after passing over Nguyen Hue, and disappeared between two leaning tenements. The delapidated structures rose nearly ten stories above the bustling crowds on flower boulevard, racing against the clock, and tenants on their balconies pointed up at the aircraft, some in awe of the pilot's flying expertise, others disturbed by the rotor noise, and still others telling friends and relatives they knew this and that soldier, when in fact they couldn't recognize anybody at that distance.

The young man stared at the sky for several moments after the sound of flapping rotors faded, then he tightly closed his eyes, lost in an old but recurring memory. He didn't hear the MP jeeps screaming past, lights and sirens in operation — only the faint echo of a man screaming as he plummeted from a helicopter to the uncaring ocean, thousands of feet below.

A roaring black jeep swerved in front of Smitty's unit as he turned onto Tu Do Street. Normally he would have chased down the driver and broke an old nightstick, but two things made him keep his cool: He recognized the Decoy Squad's undercover vehicle; and he wanted to be the first unit on scene. A slugfest at the Continental Hotel this late at night meant drunk reporters, specifically foreign correspondents — totally arrogant bastards, in Smitty's book, who would most likely need their jaws broken or noses flattened prior to being "subdued with the minimum amount of force necessary."

Smitty hated journalists. He despised anyone who made their living with a pen — excluding cops, who were bogged down with paperwork the globe over (mainly because of jerks like journalists) and had no choice. But it wasn't that Smitty hated only news media people. He hated cabbies and ice cream vendors and little old ladies who drove slow in the fast lane and fast in the slow lane. He hated everyone who didn't wear an MP armband or its equivalent, a police shield. Everyone believed he even hated his mother.

Stryker claimed the man didn't *have* a mother.

Both jeeps skidded up to the hotel entrance, and as the men all jumped out, six more units screeched in off the street, loaded down with eager, sap-wielding single digit midgets, who knew they'd be long gone back to The World before the goofy reporters could lodge a citizen's complaint for excessive force. It would take them a week just to wake up in their hospital beds.

Smitty bolted between two uniformed privates, clamping his hands on their shoulders so he could propel himself past them. "I'm the N.C.O.I.C. here!" He kept the laugh in. "So I'll go in first!" It was the first time he had willingly claimed to be *in charge* of anything.

But Richards and his Decoy Squad were already halfway up the stairs. "Dream on!" Thomas called down to him.

The doors at the top of the stairs burst open and three men yelling in French accents flew out backwards and tumbled down onto Broox and Bryant.

A nightstick cracked sharply, someone groaned, and the civilians were thrown out of the way. A dozen sets of boots raced up the steps.

Richards and Smitty reached the doorway at the same time, and inside the smoke-clogged establishment a shot from a large caliber handgun exploded.

Richards dropped to an automatic crouch out of reflex, ever ready to spring back to a fighting stance, but Smitty burst through the heavy teakwood doors, his pistol pointed at the ceiling.

Two more shots rang out, and a lazy lance of silver smoke spiraled out over Smitty's head, chasing the slug of lead. The MP sergeant emptied all eight rounds from his pistol, and after he ejected his magazine, the men outside could hear him yell above the noise of lobby patrons rushing for the exits. "Somebody get to the ground-floor rear exit—two armed suspects headed that direction! One man down in here!"

Ramsey and Harcourt, still lingering at the foot of the stairs, (*let the rooks have all the fun and all the bruises*), automatically pivoted on their heels and darted for the back alley.

Short of breath but ready for contact, they arrived behind the hotel just in time to see two large men with western features ducking into a narrow corridor that ran between a laundry and a fish market—both closed at this hour.

The moment they entered the pitch-black corridor, bright flashes of light erupted thirty feet away. Thunderous discharges, amplified by the close proximity of the high brick walls, rushed out at them, and bullets whizzed by their heads.

Ramsey fired a shot in reply, and both MPs pressed their bodies flat against either side of the corridor entrance. "I'll take the lead tonight." Harcourt flashed his teeth eagerly, but Ramsey failed to catch the conniving gleam in his partner's eye.

"No sweat—I'm due. I'll take it."

"It's yours." Harcourt did not argue. His tone sounded unemotional, routine. But his grin brightened perceptibly.

Ramsey did not notice any of it. Out of habit, he tapped the palm of his hand against the butt of his pistol, checking the magazine seal, then he ducked around the corner of the wall and charged into the

168

corridor, squeezing off three rounds in a fanning motion, from left to right.

When he noticed a doorway in his peripheral vision — it was only an outline in the dark — he rammed his body into it, nearly crashing through the bolted door within. An instant later, two bullets tore through the muggy air inches from his nose, and he pressed his body flatter against the smooth bricks.

He hoped Harcourt didn't make his move yet. There was too much lead bouncing about. But his partner had a reputation for heroics whenever there was gunplay, and Ramsey started to sweat profusely. He didn't want to pay Benny's girlfriend a visit in the morning to notify her her man had bought it — got his ticket canceled for a one-way trip. Another bullet zinged by, ricocheting off the bricks with a Hollywood whistle, and after firing off two more rounds in reply, he caught himself giggling. Dehb, Harcourt's girlfriend, was one of the most beautiful women in Saigon, but she was unfalteringly dedicated to her man and had yet to even look Ramsey in the eye when they stopped by Harcourt's hootch on a Short-7. Ramsey's wife had been giving him the cold shoulder these last few months, it seemed, and those evenings when he had coaxed her to spread her legs, she'd have been shocked to learn her husband was fantasizing about Benny Harcourt's girlfriend and her firm, muscular thighs that just wouldn't quit.

Another slug impacted against the doorway abutment, sending chips in Ramsey's face. Then the night went abruptly silent. A hush seemed to swirl in over the neighborhood, except for a stereo high above the alley, playing a soft, barely audible Vietnamese love song. Few if any people had flocked to their balconies to see what all the shooting was about. But a thousand eyes peeked through cracks in bamboo shades all up and down the block.

Ramsey carefully edged his face along the end of the bricks until he could see down the alley. His eyes were adjusting to the intense darkness after all the discharge flashes, but the far end of the corridor was pitch black and he could detect absolutely nothing.

Back where Harcourt waited, there was a soft glow of light from the rear of the hotel, but his partner was nowhere in sight. *Well?* Ramsey thought. Where is he? Now was the time to move up.

A noise high above caught Ramsey's attention, and he glanced up at a third-floor balcony. Their frames silhouetted by the glow from a lantern behind them, several youths stared down at the American. They were in their late teens and professed allegiance to no one — communist or anticommunist. They were street toughs, and someone was intruding upon their turf.

But for now they seemed content at silently standing above the confrontation developing in the street, sizing up the situation. After all, these were not just punks from another block, challenging their authority, but one of those crazy military policemen from the International, trading high-caliber slugs with two bonafide adults. It would be better to just observe at this point. The way their luck was running these last few weeks, the MPs — usually outnumbered and outgunned — might just lose the gunfight, and while their assailants fled through the night, the boys on the balcony could send the youngest gang member down to scarf up the American's pistol before help arrived.

Ramsey glanced up at the youths on the balcony repeatedly as he waited for his partner to make his move. They represented that seamier side of Saigon that sent a shiver through his gut even when he was patrolling the streets on day shift: that element that was always lurking in the shadows, forever watching, waiting for a weakness—ready to strike. Even during the worst of times, the city could be a peaceful place, but the young hoodlums were always lurking in the background, careful to smile at you when they were alone, but ready to pounce when in their roaming groups, like a pack of wild dogs on the prowl. This was a city that held much intrigue and beauty, but you could never relax, even out of uniform, for the streets and back alleys were a concrete jungle, and the rules of the rain forest more than applied here too.

Several rounds struck the blacktop in front of Ramsey, ricocheting off in the direction of his partner, and he realized what the two gunmen were trying to do: bounce bullets off the ground into the MP's legs. It was commonly known to both hoodlums and cops that slugs aimed at the pavement rarely bounced more than a foot or two off the earth as they continued their short-lived flight, regardless of the angle from which they were fired. Ramsey could cope with that, and the fact the two gunmen had not vanished altogether was something else that didn't particularly bother him. But what made the hairs on the back of his neck rise — after another flurry of shots whistled by — was that the discharges were getting closer. The gunmen were slowly doubling back, deciding to stay and fight it out rather than run!

Ramsey fired off his last two rounds then slammed his final clip into the pistol. Eight bullets left — *No!* He felt sweat break out against the small of his back. *Seven! Only seven slugs per magazine!*

And Harcourt! *Where the hell was Harcourt?* He knew he should have brought his M-16 along, but it was still back at the jeep, chained to the radio support bar. It was policy they left the heavy firepower behind when responding to a simple brawl, though a lot of the men charged in with Ithicas when a Ten-2 went down. A twelve-gauge shotgun spoke whole chapters when it came to quelling a disturbance downtown.

"Kiss your ass good-bye, copper!" One of the gunmen sounded only twenty feet away now, but he had to be low on ammo, too. Ramsey fired a single shot around the doorway, then ducked back in moments before three rapid discharges answered him — *the barrel flash told him they were closer than even that!*

Where the hell were all the rooks who had charged up the stairway back at the Continental? he wondered as he gripped his .45 with both hands now, aware he might just be standing in the doorway where fate decreed he would die this night. Suddenly Saigon did not seem so important. Suddenly he realized he was American, through and through. So why was he in the middle of a shoot-out deep in the heart of a foreign city that didn't care if he lived

172

or died? *Why?*

And Smitty's words flashed back at him: *"I've got a man down in here!"* And he envisioned an MP lying on his stomach, dead from a gunshot wound, his black and white helmet liner rocking upside down beside him.

And he thought of Benny. Maybe Harcourt had been shot also! Maybe his partner had stopped one of those wild rounds and was back there bleeding to death right then!

"Benny!" he called out, half ignoring the two Frenchmen creeping up on his position through the shadows. "Benny! You all right?"

And then his world exploded.

Two pistol barrels were barking fire and hot lead inches from the back of his head, and chunks of brick and wood were flying about, slicing into him. A man the size of a gorilla was upon him, pistol-whipping the back of his head, slamming him to the ground with a flying elbow.

Ramsey rolled to the side after crashing against the blacktop. He fired off three rounds, aiming high yet not aiming at all, and two slugs caught the Frenchman in the chest, throwing him back off his feet. He landed against a line of garbage cans, up-ending several of them, and unexpected applause filtered down from some of the balconies, followed by scattered catcalls and hisses.

A loud torrent of French profanity drowned out the spectators however, and Ramsey rolled to the other side just as the second gunman fired down at the ground. The bullet ate blacktop inches from the MP's leg, and he brought up his gunhand, centered

173

the end of the barrel in the middle of the shadow taking shape beyond the bright flash of discharges, and jerked in the trigger. But nothing happened.

A misfire!

On the edge of panic now, his lungs sucking in the hot air of the corridor and the licorice taste of gunfire clinging to his throat, Ramsey tried to chamber another round.

The dud ejected quickly enough, but the fresh round failed to seat properly in the chamber, and the slide rammed against the lopsided brass cartridge, jamming it firmly in place. In less than a second, the weapon had been rendered inoperable.

Frantically, Ramsey brought the pistol back like a hammer. He knew the odds were against him — that it was likely he was now lying at the scene of his murder, but he would throw the heavy weapon as hard as he could, hoping to inflict some kind of damage before he died. The Frenchman towered above him, only a foot away now, seething with anger. His teeth flashed white against the darkness, and he bellowed out a roaring laugh as he slowly brought his pistol to bear down on the military policeman.

Ramsey threw with all his might, aiming at the gleam above the shoulders that was the man's face. He tossed his pistol so hard that he wrenched his shoulder, but he did not notice the pain.

For the instant he threw his .45, the gunman standing over him appeared to explode in front of his eyes.

Flat on his back, Ramsey's eyes flinched as bright red laserlike lances of light appeared in the air above him, and another burst of M-60 tracers tore into the Frenchman, opening his chest further, like a powerful firecracker taped to a watermelon. Wet body matter sprayed across Ramsey as the gunman's upper frame, split apart horizontally at the navel clear to the spinal column, flopped back, and the lower torso crumpled to the ground.

As the numbing echo of machine gun fire bounced back and forth between the tenements and finally fled across the rooftops, the only sound left was the Frenchman's pistol as it clattered against the blacktop.

Ramsey stared at the dead man lying in a mangled heap a few feet from him for several dazed seconds, then he leaned back on his elbows and glanced over his shoulder to where the two bursts of M-60 fire had come from.

Standing in a gun jeep at the other end of the corridor, Sgt. Mark Stryker was leaning against the support bar that held the smoking Hog inches above the vehicle's windshield. Patting the warm barrel of the machine gun affectionately, he stared back at Ramsey, his grin illuminated by the dual red lights revolving lazily on the jeep's hood. As the crimson beams cut shafts through the mist creeping up from the river, a stunned Derek Ramsey managed to wave weakly and show his teeth, but the two veteran street cops were not smiling about the same things.

6. While Saigon Danced

"And I'm still accepting applications for Air Traffic Controller." Stryker joked without smiling as another paper airplane sailed by, inches in front of his podium. It struck Sergeant Schultz in the back of the head, but he merely lifted an obscure gesture above his helmet without looking behind him.

"Okay—awright," Stryker raised his voice slightly to quell the minor disturbance that followed. "We're runnin' this briefing late as it is, and the Lou tells me some of Kiwi Kolana's people are about to show up to talk to you about something or other, so let's cut the crap.

"I'm gonna dispense with the usual bull and carve into the meat of the matter—"

"The sarge *do* have a way with words." Smitty chuckled across the tow to Richards, loud enough for the Zulu warrior from up north to overhear him. The black MP knew the jive accent was directed at him all along, but neither he nor Richards looked back at Smitty.

"Now I wanna thank all you who rolled in on that Ten-Two, Ten-One hundred last night. CID informs me the whole thing was a drug deal gone bad—and we happened to get in on the tail end of it and smoke a couple big-time Frenchmen who represent an H Ring across the pond, in Paris. Could be repercussions, but I doubt it. They were big dudes but small-time — musclemen only, sent to make a delivery.

"Whatta ya mean 'we,' sarge?" Thomas stood up like he always did. "You dusted the creeps. You and Ramsey. Don't be spreadin' the glory among the battalion like you always do. I'm gettin' tired of it. Take the fucking credit when it's due you, okay?"

"Sit the fuck down, Anthony," Tim Bryant called out loudly.

"Well it's true." Ants slowly took his seat again.

Stryker frowned at the interruption and made to scratch at his forehead, attempting to hide the blush he felt flooding his face. "As I was about to say, *teamwork* on our part did those punks in. If they had any brains, they'd have kept running when they had the chance. But no, they were nothing but small-time street toughs, who couldn't resist the chance to snatch a couple MP armbands for souvenirs."

"So they wouldn't leave Saigon emtpy-handed." Richards made reference to the huge shipment of recovered heroin.

"Anyway," Stryker continued, his smile back now, "Ramsey here owes his life to many of you gentlemen. And he tells me he and his old lady are throwing a party tomorrow to celebrate Buddha's decision to grant Derek a second life — "

"My third," Ramsey cut in softly, so only Stryker and a few MPs in the front row could hear. "Don't forget that cowboy behind the Xin Loi last month who took a bead on me only to have his carbine blow

177

up in his face."

"Yah," Stryker muttered in an even lower tone. "And you *still* let him get away!"

Ramsey forced a smile as Stryker went on to tell about how the MP who originally called for assistance at the Continental was all right, and that the dead man inside the hotel had turned out to be one of the porters who got caught in the crossfire, but he was far from being in a jovial mood as he stared across the room at his partner with cold, narrow eyes.

Harcourt had arrived at the briefing late. By that time, the seats around Ramsey had filled up, so Benny had claimed a folding chair near the doorway. After a faint wave at his partner, he never looked Ramsey's way again. *And they were partners, damnit!*

Ramsey felt a twitch in his gut when his wife's face flashed in front of his mind's eye for no reason at all. He remembered now that she said she'd be gone all day — to visit relatives in Gia Dinh, or something, up by the airport — and he fought off the unforgivable suspicions that were bouncing in on his blind side without warning.

He forced himself to pay attention to the briefing, but his concentration only took him back to the shoot-out last night.

After Stryker pulled him up off the ground by his web belt, they had raced back to where Harcourt was last seen. And they found him facedown on the pavement, a slight bruise under one eye.

Ramsey thought his heart had stopped! He reached down and turned his partner over, searched his body for nonexistent wounds, then lightly slapped him awake. "Tripped on something in the dark when I was running up to cover ya," he told them later. "Rammed my puss into that brick wall there — knocked me out cold! I'm sorry, Derek."

Stryker had checked the corner edge of the wall after they took Harcourt to Third Field Hospital for a checkup. He found blood smears and a patch of skin, and he seemed satisfied. Shaking his head all the way back to the gun jeep, he just seemed happy the right people had died that night.

"We had another buzz saw murder last night, too." Stryker continued the briefing whether all the men were listening to him or not — it seemed a quarter of the MPs were off in their own dreamscape a hundred percent of the time, so he worked on keeping the attention of the other seventy-five percent. And it was a job worthy of sergeant's pay. "No clues to speak of. Apparently the dipshit's taking pictures of his bizarre behavior-in-progress, so like I said before: If you notice a suspicious type walking around Tu Do with a buzz saw over his shoulder or a tripod under his arm, take a few minutes from gawkin' at the whores and F.I. his ass, okay?"

"You oughta get Captain Condom on the line, sarge." Thomas did not stand up this time. "I'm sure he could solve this mysterious caper!" A few laughs followed, but not near as many as the MP had hoped for.

"I half suspect he's the one behind these killings," Stryker responded.

"Where the hell was he last night?" another man asked. "When we needed him. At the Continental, you know?"

"I wondered about that one myself," Stryker admitted. "Like I said before: Better not be one of you clowns runnin' around town in that cherry-red cape!"

"Hell sarge." One MP ducked behind a row of bobbing helmets. "You know none of us would be smart enough to wear the gas mask."

"Can't you put a trace on those combat boots he left at his last encounter with the authorities?"

"And how do you propose we trace a pair of jump boots?" Stryker braced an elbow on the podium and rested his chin in the palm of his hand. "Huh?"

Nobody answered him directly, but in the back of the room a rookie asked the veteran sitting beside him, "Can they take toe prints?"

The Uke's eyeballs rolled up toward the ceiling, but he didn't say anything.

"Uh, by the way," Stryker said, as an afterthought. "Should any of you supercops luck out and come across our buzz saw killer, exercise Code-Zero, okay? CID tells me they found a forty-five slug in the latest victim's hip." His eyes passed briefly over a reddening Murphy but did not stop on the MP. "So consider our friendly little murderer armed and dangerous—he don't have to plug in no forty-five automatic."

Stryker's eyes *did* stop on Broox however. "How many, Mikey?" he asked. "How short you gettin', brother?"

Broox had maintained a suspicious smile the entire evening. He paused for the mandatory moment, then said, "Sarge, I'm so short I'd have to climb a ladder to see an ant's ass! Three days and a wake up."

"A single digit midget." "Ants" Thomas stared straight ahead, mock disgust in his tone. Broox thought he was really angry.

"You want me to stick you on turn-key duty?" Stryker's eyes looked sad suddenly. He was thinking about how rowdy the holding cells at PMO got sometimes when he said, "Or someplace else where you won't break a leg or lose your nose—"

"Ship his ass out to Fort Hustler," Thomas muttered, still refusing to look his longtime partner in the eye. "Where the dragon lizards and Victor Charlie sappers can eat his worthless head for breakfast."

Broox frowned at the last comment, then looked up at Mark. "I'd just as soon stay on the street, sarge, if you don't mind. As long as I got you guys around me, I'm safer than the gold in Fort Knox."

Several sighs of mock affection filled the room, and Raunchy Raul blew him a loud kiss.

"Okay." Stryker began folding his fatigue sleeves up above his rock-hard biceps. "Any of you boy scouts seen Zane yet? I'm gettin' awful impatient waitin' for his young ass to show up in front of my desk."

The room fell silent, and several men's eyes fell as they stared down at their boots or fingers.

"I expected as much." The ex-Green Beret's disposition was rapidly changing. "Well, it seems this epidemic of freedom from the Green Machine is spreading. Don Mallory from Charlie Company didn't show up for day watch briefing this morning. Don't seem to me he's the kind that would have anything in common with that Zane character, but who knows—maybe they were friends from way back. Anybody wanna confess their sins to me? Anybody wanna snitch in private even? If so, I'll be at my desk for a couple hours after *uniform inspection*," he said dryly. Several groans answered the announcement. "Correcting—in *red ink*, I might add—the endless errors some of you geniuses continue to make on your Form Thirty-twos even after I've sent them back to you repeatedly. *And circled in pencil*, no less! Well, no Mister Nice Guy." He exaggerated.

"I saw Mallory and Writter over at Tan Son Nhut yesterday," said Nilmes. "Egor Johnson was gonna take 'em up on his chopper to see Saigon from the air."

"Writter's out of the hospital?" Stryker's brow hiked up slightly.

"You didn't think a lousy claymore could keep one of my men down and out, did you?" Sgt. Raul Schultz bellowed from the back of the room

"That was about fourteen or fifteen hundred hours," Nilmes added.

"I saw them after *that*," said Richards. "At least Mallory, anyway. He was down at the meat market, checking out the leg o' lamb and chicken breasts."

Stryker spread his boots slightly in a defensive stance and folded his massive arms across his chest, waiting for the punch line. "Well?"

"No joke, Mark. That's it." Richards feigned bewilderment. "He got into a Bluebird taxi with one of the regulars, and—"

"Did you see which bitch?" Stryker asked.

"No, not really. But I did get an eyeball on the cabbie." Richards shifted around in the uncomfortable metal folding chair. He hated it when briefings lasted longer than the thirty minutes they were supposed to go. "And she was a real looker, boy. Definitely somethin' I wouldn't mind burying my nose in. But then again, you never know—only got a look at her from the shoulders up. She might be a real hippo—who knows?"

Stryker pointed at a young private sitting next to the doorway. "Beat feet over to Gate Four, okay son? Tell the MP working the meat market I wanna know if he shows Writter or Mallory—or Zane, for that matter—on his sign-out roster. If those guys are doing their job, we'll have not only the name of the cunt they left with, but also her National ID number and the exact time they left post."

"Come on, Mark," Richards spoke under his breath. "You know most of the guys out at the meat market look the other way when MPs come and go. I do it myself. A lot of these guys are married, and they don't want their names written down on a permanent log when they're arm-in-arm with a almond-eyed girl of questionable virtue who's all leg and no morals."

"Well it's not right," Stryker countered, motioning for the private to carry out his directive.

"I never said it was right," Richards replied. "I just said that's the way it is in Sin City."

Attention!" The private who had darted out the doorway rushed right back in and called out.

Even before the men could rise to their feet, Lieutenant Slipka bounded into the room, a stocky sergeant right behind him. "At ease—at ease!" the officer waved the MPs back into their seats. "As you

183

were — as you were — "

Stryker wondered why they even bothered to get up. Somebody always yelled "Attention!" and Slipka always told them to disregard formalities. The other officers were the same way. After all, this *was* the Nam.

Schultz slid noticeably down in his seat as the officer rushed by, and Stryker wondered what Raunchy Raul had done *recently* to raise the lieutenant's ire. They were constantly going at it — and it had all started back in The World, many moons ago, when Raunchy Raul streaked through Fort Carson on a snowmobile, leading Slipka's troopers on a high-speed chase through ten foot drifts and blizzard conditions. *Schultz had mooned him!* Wearing only combat boots and —

Naw. Stryker shook his head. Sergeant Schultz had an alibi. He had been working the desk or riding patrol with another NCO both times Captain Condom had been spotted. And Stryker knew where Slipka had been also — he wasn't taking any chances; he was keeping tabs on everyone! After all, not only was this the Nam, it was Saigon. Pearl of the Orient. City of Sorrows. Land of Lost Loves. Tour of duty assignment every MP opted for just once, so he could leave his name carved on the bedposts of the Tu Do Street hotels, or make a legend of himself in the streets. Some men left their lives behind. Others left only their hearts.

Stryker examined the man who was easily keeping up with the high-strung MP officer. In his early twenties, he stood an inch or two taller than the lieutenant, weighed in at around a hundred and eighty,

184

and was clean shaven. He had dark, wavy hair and a perpetual grin, but he had that special look about him—that aura that told you the face was only a mask: This soldier could spring like a tiger and tear your throat out. He wouldn't think twice about devouring your heart while others watched, cowering behind the bamboo. His skin looked pale, however, almost like death itself, and this contrasted with the sense of power that radiated from him.

Stryker glanced at his uniform: Back-in-The-World fatigues, without the numerous pockets. His shirt was tucked in, while with jungle fatigues, the blouse was kept outside the trousers. The patch on his left shoulder was a Military Police command in Korea—either the 728th in Pusan, or the 55th in Bupyeong. His nametag read: PRUETT.

"Mark, meet Sgt. John Pruett." Slipka waved a hand toward the grinning NCO.

"Greetings from the Land of the Morning Calm." Pruett extended his own hand, and the ex-Green Beret shook it. Alabama accent, decided Stryker.

"Didn't mean to barge in your briefings," Slipka said, "but John here's got some info from back in the ROK that can't wait." Slipka checked his watch. "Looks like your men oughta be out on the street by now anyway." His forefinger tapped the face of the watch a dozen times in two seconds. Stryker wanted to tell him to mellow out—he was going to get high blood pressure and vapor lock right in front of the whole crew, but he remained silent—Raunchy Raul would cause him a medical early-out soon enough.

"What kind of information?" Stryker asked, turning to dismiss the guardmount, but a commotion at

185

the door to the briefing room caught everyone's attention. The air soon filled with whistles: Kiwi Kolana was back on base.

"Hi guys!" She swooned as she floated through the wide double doors, throwing kisses with both hands. Tonight she was dressed in a billowing tank top and hot pants — both an eye-dazzling pink. Every eye in the room was locked on the firm canteloupes pressing out against the sheer fabric. Her fluffy blond hair (it was a different color every time Stryker saw it) looked like heavenly clouds clinging to her ears. Her high heels tightened her calf muscles, and her thighs flared with radiant energy. Raunchy Raul envisioned himself strangled by them.

Today she was wearing a black beauty mark on her right cheek. "I'll be with you in a minute." Stryker smiled over at Pruett. "Duty calls." The sergeant from Korea replied with a knowing grin and leaned back against the sacred podium to watch the proceedings.

"Good news, guys!" Kiwi Kolana swayed her hips from side to side as she glided to the front row. A half dozen MPs offered their chairs, but she tangled her arms around Stryker and snuggled up against his chest. The men howled!

"We're going to make a movie in Saigon!" she announced, releasing Mark and flashing her hands back and forth in the air, as if trying to attract Hollywood ground-to-air spotlights. 'And Uncle Sammy wants *YOU* to star in it!" She thrust out her finger and slowly pointed from one end of the room to the other, dropping to a sensuous crouch as she imitated the famous recruiting poster.

"What?" Lieutentant Slipka stepped forward. In the doorway, Miss Kolana's entourage of Military Police bodyguards crowded the entrance protectively. Stryker glanced over at Smitty standing beside the Zulu warrior — the two seemed to have reached a temporary truce. Biggs was even wearing an army-green shirt instead of just the flak jacket. VC molars still hung around his neck.

"We've decided to film some spots in one of Miss Kolana's upcoming movies right here in South Vietnam." A short, balding overweight man with an ugly cigar dangling from his mouth rushed up to the lieutenant and patted him on the back.

"Meet my new agent." Kiwi frowned slightly, as if she were not totally happy with the forty-year-old's abilities.

Stryker frowned, too. He had never been impressed by an American movie star. Especially a dumb blonde — or whatever she was. *What you need, honey, is a few hours in the submissive position,* Stryker thought to himself, *with an erection spreading those Venice Beach thighs all the way to your midsection!*

"Well, I don't know." Lieutentant Slipka's chin dropped to his palm in contemplation. "Nobody briefed me on any of this."

"How long do you think it would take to get clearance from higher-up?" The agent was walking circles around Slipka, and Kiwi Kolana had drifted from Stryker to the lieutenant — was now running her fingers through his blond hair and removing his blue-tint glasses. "All we need is a dozen or so MPs for the bank robbery scene."

"The bank robbery scene?" Slipka's eyes went wide

and he broke out in a sweat. He slowly broke free of Kolana and moved behind Stryker for protection.

"I thought you meant you were gonna do some jungle fightin' scenes." Richards stepped forward, mildly protesting. "After all, this is Vietnam. But a bank robbery?"

"The MPs up in Danang already helped us film the rain forest sequence we needed," the agent explained. "And the plot has Miss Kolana being chased down to the big city by international jewel thieves. We've even got some anticommunist freedom fighters. *They've* got to rob the bank of Saigon so they can finance their jungle operations against the North Vietnamese."

"It's going to be Big Time!" Kiwi Kolana's voice rose an octave halfway through the sentence. "And we're all going to get Oscars from John Wayne and ride around in our own limousines."

"*You* are, *you* are." The agent ushered Kiwi back toward the exits. "You're the star, honey. All we need here are some extras."

The little man seemed very nervous about Miss Kolana's promises of fame and fortune. He wasn't about to break out his checkbook for a bunch of unknown talent.

"You had no problem clearing it with the Brass up in Danang?" Lieutenant Slipka had his O.D. green handkerchef out and was wiping Kiwi's fingerprints off the lenses of his glasses.

"None whatsoever, major." The agent's grin was ear to ear.

"It's lieutentant," Slipka corrected him bashfully. "Well, in that case—"

188

"I'll run it through channels anyway, Lou," Stryker said, "before I hit the bricks tonight." He turned to the men still frozen in front of Kiwi Kolana. "Well, what are *you* guys waiting for?" He motioned them all toward the exit.

"Very well," said Slipka, folding his glasses and sliding them into his pocket instead of replacing them on his nose.

"Wanna see my bongos bounce?" Kiwi shook her tank top for him. Her full, ample breasts jiggled about wildly inside the tissue-thin fabric. Slipka swallowed hard as Stryker began playfully pushing his men out onto the street, and he was glad he had kept the glasses off.

They would have fogged up.

Outside, Stryker and Richards got together and leaned against the wooden railing at the edge of the Orderly Room balcony, watching the MPs group up and file out to their assigned units.

"Quite a place you've got here." A voice behind them made both MPs turn around.

"Oh, sorry Pruett." Stryker made room for the man at the railing. "Forgot you had something to brief me about."

"Yah, quite a place." He glanced up at the golden flares already drifting along the edge of the city. Two Phantom jet fighters cruised past low overhead and vanished just as quickly. The railing and some glassless windowpanes rattled slightly as the sonic boom rolled through the city. Other planes raced their engines miles away, at the airport, and there seemed to be a constant electricity humming in the air.

"Damn flyboys," Richards muttered as he chewed on a cinnamon-coated toothpick. He continued to stare out at the dark sky long after the Phantoms had disappeared.

The courtyard of the International compound came alive with flashing red lights as fifty MPs began checking their unit's equipment. One siren, then another, then more than forty filled the air at the same time, and as they died down after the short toggle switch bursts, Stryker cocked an ear in the direction of the Saigon Zoo.

As if answering the metallic cries, the mournful wail of two caged tigers could barely be heard now if one listened carefully, and Stryker smiled with satisfaction. "Yes, John Pruett from Korea," he said. "This *is* quite a place. You might just get to like it yourself. You might *fall in love* with Lady Saigon if you're not careful." Stryker reached over and felt the man's upper arm. It was hard as stone. "Yes, tougher men than you have fallen under her spell—and never recovered."

"Speaking from personal experience?" Richards goaded him.

"Yep, you oughta re-up for the Seven sixteenth," Stryker suggested, ignoring Gary. "You could use the tan."

"Three feet of snow in Korea right now," Pruett admitted. "But I love the place, anyway. Don't ever wanna leave, if I can help it." Stryker glanced over at Pruett, really checking him out closely for the first time. Could the man be serious? Could another country affect someone the way Vietnam had affected him?" "Got me a yobo back there and everything, with a little one on the way, maybe. The duty's all right, and in ten I can retire on fifty percent pension. If we stay in Pusan, we got it dicked, fellas."

"What's a yobo?" Richards asked.

"A girlfriend," Stryker explained. "A *close* girlfriend."

"You must be in CID." Richards examined the newcomer out of the corner of his eye.

"On loan to MPI," the Alabaman replied. His accent made Richards homesick for those southern nights spent at forest woodsies outside The School, when he was still a raw recruit.

"So what have you got to tell me that's so important the provost marshal in Korea would send you clear to Saigon to do it in person?"

Pruett started to explain, but Richards pointed down to the meat market and interrupted.

"Hey, ain't that Phipps getting into a cab over there?"

"It's all right." Stryker didn't seem interested. "He's not on the roster tonight — it's his day off. We get six and one, remember Oh-Dedicated One?"

"But that's the same cabbie who picked up Mallory and his whore, Mark. I'm sure of it!"

"Maybe she can tell you where she took them," Pruett offered. "Then you can snarf up their young EM asses." He spat a wad of chewing tobacco down onto the black and silver stones covering the compound. "I *hate* AWOLs."

But Stryker had already jumped the railing and was sprinting toward the meat market.

"Wait a minute!" he yelled out, but the taxi was

pulling away from the gate—its driver didn't seem to hear him. *"Wait a minute!"* he repeated, raising a hand to wave them down as he cut across between Gate Four and the north guard tower.

A windshield on one of the parked MP jeeps exploded as he passed it, and then he heard three more rifle rounds slam against the rocks near his feet. All tracers, they ricocheted off into traffic beyond the compound walls.

"Sniper!" The MPs at the meat market called into their field phones, exchanging helmet liners for steel pots. "We got a Signal-Three hundred at the International!"

From his position lying prone across the hard rocks, Stryker watched one of the tracers smash through a car windshield. The driver, killed instantly, swerved into the oncoming lane of traffic. The night filled with a dozen skidding, screeching tires, and a terrible head-on crash followed. All the streets surrounding the Military Police Headquarters compound became instantly clogged with screaming motorists and blaring horns.

Stryker watched two men on the roof of the hotel direct powerful spotlights at the treeline on nearby Nguyen Gu Trinh, where it was suspected the sniper was holed up.

A muzzle flash erupted in reply to the brilliant beams of glowing silver, and one of the lamps exploded in a spray of glass and went out. Clouds of mosquitoes and gnats drifted in and out of the other light's white shaft, driven into a swirling frenzy by its brightness.

Several MP jeeps roared past Stryker's prone

frame, sliding out the compound gate on two wheels, their red roof lights throwing bloody beams across the faces of startled women pressed against the chickenwire at the meat market.

Stryker glanced back over at the access road where the accident had occurred. Hubcaps were still spinning in the gutter, but somehow the taxi had managed to make it onto Tran Hung Dao before the collision blocked off the road. It was now nowhere in sight.

7. Cinnamon Skin

"I'm home!"

Mike Broox held his arms out after swinging the front door of his bungalow open. He bowed like a veteran ring fighter: slowly, and without taking his eyes off his opponent. In the distance, a slender woman wrapped in silk was approaching from the dark interior of the dwelling.

Fi Fi hit him on the nose with her tiny, clenched fist, and the tall MP flew backward, landing hard on his haunches against the teakwood steps. Total shock registered in his eyes as he rubbed his bloody nose.

"How dare you!" The beautiful woman reached down and helped him back to his feet, then dragged him into the bungalow and slammed the door shut.

She was wearing one of the latest French designs: a combination pants suit and shawl that was loose fitting and fashioned from a single piece of shimmering silver silk that began at her throat and spiraled down to her hips, then split to cover the legs to just under the knees. Her breasts, large for her size and filling the top of the blouse tightly, swayed back and forth in front of his nose, bringing the smile back to his face. Her hair, dark as midnight and cut straight along the bottom, fell to her shapely hips.

Broox wrapped his arms around her waist and lifted Fi Fi off the ground. He pressed his lips against the breast over her racing heart and sucked hard, making the silk wet and the woman even madder. She kicked him in the shins with a high heel.

"Put me down!" She slapped at his shoulders with open palms but the flurry became playful and she quickly tired out.

"Not until they pop out!" Broox continued to suck, breathing heavily against her chest at the same time, heating her up like he always did.

"Put me down!" She repeated, grabbing his ears this time.

"Not until I get a standing ovation from the nipple between my lips," he mumbled with his mouth full, sucking in more silk until her breasts were pulled tightly together.

"Put me down, *Michael*!" She grabbed his chin and tried to make him look her in the eyes, but he merely started for the bedroom, bringing one hand down under her bottom to caress her thighs and the spot where they came together while he moved. "Ohhhh Michael!" Her tone changed dramatically. "Put me dooooownnnn."

They passed quickly through the short hallway between the kitchen and backyard veranda, and he knocked over a lamp as they flopped onto the bed. But they didn't need the light. They knew each other's body, inside and out.

Broox tugged at her outfit, and a seam started to rip.

"Don't tear it!" she yelled, throwing off his web

belt. It clattered against the bamboo shades besides the bureau and crumpled onto the teakwood floor. She pulled angrily at his fatigue shirt, ripping several buttons loose.

He still couldn't find the hasp or zipper or whatever it was that kept the silk sheet around her body, and he began tugging again. Another seam split loudly, and again she screamed, "Don't tear it!"

He kicked off his trousers and, totally naked now, untangled himself from her and slid his lips down the silk covering her stomach until his mouth was against the fabric guarding her crotch.

"*Michael!*" she sighed loudly, ripping her own blouse off now as his lips took hold of her and began to tease.

He could feel the bush beneath the silk, coarse and rough, summoning him as she moved it up and down against his mouth, rapidly growing moist along the bottom.

She was soon pulling the fabric free. Silk slid along under his lips, against his tongue, and then he was pressing against warm, nearly steaming flesh, and she was spreading her legs as far as she could for him.

He wrapped his arms around her haunches, pulling her so tightly against him that she yelped mildly in between the groans, and then she was wrapping her legs up around his shoulders and drawing him in deeper until the room filled with her whimpers, and her body began to shudder and tremble. "Okay," she finally cried out. "Stop—*please stop!*"

He shook his head no, exaggerating the movement so that it drove her even further beyond control, but she grabbed his ears and pulled him up, and she was sliding over to the center of the bed, pulling him along.

Her legs opened for him again, and as he lowered himself onto her, she guided him in with gentle fingers. Her entire body was already drenched with perspiration for the ceiling fan was off, and the tropical heat saturated every corner of the dwelling and everyone inside it. It was strange how they both tasted and smelled like sugarcane, she thought.

His lips and his tongue and all his other little tricks had loosened her up like a sponge, and he entered her easily, plunging to his full length with the first stroke. Her thighs automatically went up as he pressed her down into the mattress, and the sensations that wracked her body made her mind go blank, and her eyes filled with white light that did not fade until they were finished, several minutes later.

She opened her eyes and darkness closed in on her from all sides. Michael was beside her — she could feel his presence. They lay there silently for an hour, he breathing smoothly, dozing, she trying to remember her climax and why she couldn't stop smiling.

"I love you."

He wasn't asleep at all but lay on his side, up on one elbow, his chin braced in an open palm, and he stared down at her, a dreamy look in his eyes.

"You asshole!" She lashed out and slapped him hard, knocking him back off the bed. "How dare you!" She repeated the same accusation that had greeted him upon his arrival home from work.

"Jesus!" He stumbled about on the floor slowly

and playfully peered back over the edge of the bed. "What the hell did I do to deserve *that*?"

He flicked his tongue at her, snakelike, and her angry scowl disolved into a tense smile.

She grabbed his ears and dragged him back onto the bed, ignoring his painful groans. "I watched the TV tonight!" she said, pointing to the small black and white set on the dresser.

"Good for you!" He wrestled her hands free and rubbed at his stinging ears. "I hope you were watching Captain Kirk and his boys and not one of those porno flicks on the VHF channel." They both sat up on the bed a safe distance from each other.

"Michael!" She raised her voice at him, clenching her hands into tiny fists as she shook the upper part of her body in frustration. Her breasts swayed from side to side as they jutted out at him. He found himself becoming aroused again, as if for the first time. That was how she always affected him.

"They had a story about MPs at International," she said, shaking her fist at him. "Some goddamned mother-fucking VC sniper tried to kill you!"

"Knock off the profanity, okay? It doesn't become you. You're a lady."

"I *Sac Mau* Victor Charlie, you hear me?" She shook her chest at him this time, the tips pointed straight out, accusingly. "I *Sac Mau* them back to their mothers, Michael!"

Broox grinned again. "Good for you," he said. "You can drop-kick every one of Ho Chi Minh's juvenile delinquents, Fi Fi, but just don't bruise these beautiful breasts." He bent forward and lightly licked the tips of her nipples, sending them erect

198

again.

"Stop that!" She pushed him away. "Listen to me! This is important."

But he loved the way they tasted, especially just after lovemaking: *like cinnamon!* He just couldn't resist.

"Stop it, Michael!" She locked her arms in front of him, but he gently knocked them apart with a routine police technique and sprung back on top of her.

They were soon a tangle of arms and legs again, and the room quickly filled with her groans as he expertly brought her to multiple orgasms.

"I love you, Michael," she whispered later, kissing him about the forehead and cheeks. "I love you, I love you, I love you."

"I love you too, honey." He slid his hand in between her legs and began massaging her the way she liked it. "So does that mean you're going to slap me silly again?"

Her body went rigid and she grabbed his chin so that their eyes met. "You have two nights left as an MP," she said. "I refuse to let you out on the streets so you can play cops and robbers with your buddies. I will *not* leave Vietnam with grey hairs!"

He laughed out loud, amused by what she had just said and the way she said it.

"I'm serious, Michael." Her hand slid down across his stomach and took hold of him. "My bags are already packed. Our flight leaves Thursday morning at eight sharp. *Both* of us shall be aboard it—and you will *not* be lying in a casket; do I make myself clear, mister?"

This time he did not laugh but merely formed an

innocent expression with his eyebrows. "I didn't think you cared so much," he said after several moments of silence. "The guys at the battalion say you just want a ticket stateside, but I'm beginning to think you really love me."

"You know I don't need your support." She waved her hand around the room as she began kissing his chest. The bungalow was expensively adorned—all bought by her paychecks from the studio. "I only need your love."

"We could stay here," he replied softly, as she began running her tongue along his Adam's apple. "In Saigon. I'm rather attached to the place, actually."

"I'm dedicated to you, Michael. To the death. And I'm all psyched up to play the obedient American housewife role. We are *going* home to the stateside."

The obedient American housewife? He chuckled to himself. Boy, does she got things twisted around. Well, what she doesn't know won't hurt her.

"You'll miss the movie studio," he said, stroking her long hair. It was so dark—jet black. And smooth, yet it felt strangely like tinsel in his fingers. "You'll miss all the excitement, all the fans. You'll miss your friends—and fam—" He bit his tongue, remembering too late her family had been killed by the communists in the north twenty years earlier. A maid had hidden her in a basket and dropped her in the Perfume River.

She had floated south to safety. And Saigon.

"From this day forward," she said, "my only role will be standing by your side." She ran her tongue down to his stomach again. "And I will not be

200

acting."

"I can not call in sick these last two nights," he said reluctantly. "I do not want Mark and the others to remember me for that."

"You have no choice in the matter," she said. "You are my prisoner. You are not leaving this bed until Thursday morning, and that's final!"

"But I still have to out-process—to turn in my gear—my service weapon." His eyes went suddenly moist with sadness at the thought of surrendering his MP armbands with their Eighteenth Brigade combat patches sewn inside the laminated cover. Somehow, he decided then and there, he would manage to keep just one—for a souvenir.

And then he laughed at himself as his body began to tingle all over. What was he so worried about? The best Saigon souvenir he could want was between his legs just then, working hard to please him.

He reached out to touch her head as it came up, and he ran his fingers under the long, silky hair, massaging the base of her skull as she engulfed him.

Michael Broox lay back on the pillow and breathed in the collage of fragrances swirling about the bedroom. The veranda window was open, and the sounds of Saigon drifted in to mix with the smooth, sucking noise. His nostrils tingled suddenly. Someone was cooking his favorite shrimp soup and rice meal down the street.

He reached back over his head and flicked the switch that sent the cassette stereo rolling. A moment later, a lady named Thai Hien was singing about lost love in a city at war. He sighed as the words and music soothed his soul like no American songs had ever done.

Saigon. He would surely miss her.

Benny Harcourt stared at the woman in the flowered *ao dai*, sitting across the room next to his partner. She glanced at him a couple times, but except for the slight gleam of recognition, never really acknowledged his presence at the party.

"Can I get you something, Benny?" The slender woman on his arm must have noticed him staring at the girl across the room. The slightest spark of jealousy could be seen in her expression as she looked up at him. "A drink from the bar or some egg roll? One of the girls brought a huge platter of Vietnamese eggroll."

"No thanks, baby." He ran his eyes along Vo Dehb's figure — she was a knockout. They had fought last week after she cut her hair into a shorter style without checking with him, but you couldn't change the curves beneath the western-style peasant dress she was wearing tonight.

Times like this, when she so aroused him in public, made Harcourt wonder why he was having an affair with his partner's wife.

Ramsey's wife was younger, but her body could not compare with Dehb's. There was no contest.

But her lips. Her mouth. She did magic with it. And that was why Benny Harcourt risked discovery, death at the hands of Derek, and the wrath of Vo Dehb: The woman sitting across the room was irresistible. And he would have her. Derek Ramsey would not get in the way. And they would have a nice insurance settlement to pad their honeymoon suite in Singapore too, though Harcourt hadn't really thought about marrying any widows on short notice. They had to be allowed a respectable period of mourning. One or two years at the least.

He wasn't sure what would come of Dehb. But he didn't lose sleep worrying about her either. With a body like hers, she wouldn't face much grief rebounding in Sin City.

"A toast!" A sergeant from Delta Company had climbed up on a table and was raising a beer mug and losing his balance at the same time. "To Derek Ramsey! May he have countless extensions on his Tour 365!"

The small private room in the bar filled with the mandatory applause, then somebody slipped a few coins into the jukebox, and mixed couples flocked to the cramped dance floor.

"Check that chick out," Thomas whispered over to Bryant, motioning toward the woman standing next to Harcourt. "Does her face bang a gong, ol' chap?"

"Kinda," admitted Bryant. "But I can't place it. Probably just some chippie off the street. You know how that goofy Harcourt is—can't keep his cock out of the chicken coop."

"Well, she's givin' me the heebie-jeebies, Tim. I seen that face somewhere before—maybe on a VNP wanted poster or something—"

"Don't get your tush all worked up into an uproar." Bryant sucked the straw of his Singapore Sling. "Just enjoy all the thigh prancin' around, okay. Look—check out the cunt in that *cheong-sam* over there. Now *she's* got a set of legs that won't

203

quit!"

Thomas grinned, noticing that Bryant's wife, Hue Chean, was not at the party. She stayed home a lot lately. He would not be talking so brave if the woman was standing beside him. And then memories of the shooting flooded back to haunt him, and he forced his mind to change the subject. "Where's that goddamned Mikey, anyway?"

"I didn't think he'd show, Ants. He's gotta work tonight, you know."

"So do we!" Thomas focused on Ramsey and his wife in the middle of the dance floor.

"That's different." Bryant laughed. "*We're* different!"

Both off-duty MPs watched Benny Harcourt leave his girlfriend and walk over to the dance floor. He tapped Ramsey on the shoulder from behind, and, after some smiles were exchanged, moved in to dance with the other man's wife.

Still smiling, but with a tint of hesitation in his eyes, Ramsey left the dance floor and joined a group of men from Fort Hustler. They slapped him on the back, yelled some rowdy congratulations at having cheated Lady Death again, then tossed him a mug and filled it with beer.

"Derek better keep an eye on Harcourt." Thomas laughed softly but he was dead serious. "I wouldn't want the dude around *my* wife."

"You're not even married." Bryant wiped foam from his upper lip.

"Then I wouldn't want him around my mother even!"

"We're all cops here, Anthony. For Christsake! If

we can't trust each other, who else can we trust?"

Thomas scanned the room until he found the girl Harcourt had just been with. She was standing alone, by the doorway, an irritated look in her eyes. "Yah, I guess you're right." He patted Bryant on the shoulder and started moving away, toward the doorway. "I guess you're right, Timmy."

Bryant shook his head from side to side as he watched Thomas glide up to the woman in the peasant dress and bow an introduction. *When did it end? When did the love merry-go-round ever stop?*

Then he glanced over at Ramsey.

The man was still in the midst of the tower rats from Fort Hustler, but he was no longer smiling. His eyes were watching Benny Harcourt float across the dance floor with his wife in tow. Ramsey frowned — he had never been a very good dancer. But Harcourt was a regular gold digger.

Ramsey instinctively rested his hand on a gun butt that wasn't there when he saw Harcourt squeezing his wife's shapely bottom.

Mark Stryker glanced at his wristwatch.

If he didn't get these lousy reports done soon, he'd never make it to Ramsey's party on time.

And it wasn't like he would be able to just hop in a patrol jeep and cruise over there. First, he'd have to take a cyclo home to Wann's apartment, change into civvies, and shave. And Wann would be waiting for him. He had promised to take her, though he knew she wouldn't really be disappointed if they didn't go: She was still uncomfortable in public.

And Stryker felt perhaps she wasn't ready mentally to be around so many military policemen who'd be talking nothing but shop—just like her Johnny had so many months ago.

Jesus Christ! Stryker muttered to himself halfway through one of Broox's crime scene sketches. "I tell the guy and I tell the guy. Ya don't ever try and draw these damn things to fucking scale! It just won't work."

He dropped his pencil and leaned back in the chair as memories swirled down at him from everywhere.

Michael Broox.

It was hard to believe the kid was actually leaving the 716th. Broox was a damned good MP. Stryker had never written a bad efficiency report on him. He was a hotdog, to be sure, but that was why he'd assigned the kid to Decoy when he was still cherry, and now some almond-eyed enchantress from downtown had captured him in her tiger trap and was dragging him in for the kill.

Stryker bit his lower lip, remembering the numerous times Broox had saved him and Richards and all the others. Surely he could handle a skinny Saigon actress. He closed his eyes and bit on a pencil eraser, picturing Fi Fi—or whatever her real name was—in his mind. She was definitely no France Nuyen. Her acting was not polished, and, in Stryker's opinion, her presence on stage was not halting or inspirational like France Nuyen. But who was he to judge and compare?

If Broox was happy, then that was all that really mattered. Fi Fi claimed she was leaving the movie

206

business anyway. Perhaps Broox saw something in her besides beauty. At least she had not been a porno queen, (though he had seen a couple of *them* he wouldn't mind spending the rest of his life with). But Stryker couldn't shake the nagging suspicion this beautiful starlet had something up her sleeve. She always watched Stryker from the corner of her eye when he passed, and she had never smiled at him. Broox claimed she just didn't like sergeants and other persons in the position of authority. So where did cops fit in?

Well, all was not lost. He still had the man scheduled for a career counseling session tomorrow, and if *he* couldn't talk Mikey into remaining with the MPs, there were always the NCOs at his new duty station back in — where was he going? — cold, cold Colorado or someplace like that?

Yes, he only had a couple months left in the military, but maybe a few graveyard shifts on a blizzardy, windswept TCP box in the Rockies would remind him of warm, tropical Saigon. Maybe that's all it would take to get Broox to re-up for just one more Tour 365.

They could really hit the streets this time together — and the guys. They could really clean up the town, make a hell of a difference for a change, leave a legend or two behind. The girls of Tu Do Street and the cowboy in Chi Hoa jail would still be talking about the Saigon Commandos long after they had all retired from the Military Police Corps.

Dream on! The little invisible genie on Stryker's shoulder laughed at him. He opened his eyes, chasing her away, and focused on the pile of paperwork stacked precariously on the edge of his desk. And cover shift had not even turned in their reports yet!

He thought about Kim, his old girlfriend, and the temple curse she claimed to have put on him before they broke up. The threat of oriental magic no longer worried him. He had been in Saigon so long now he felt immune to the spells the city weaved over foreigners.

And he thought about Lai, his tribeswoman up in Pleiku. Would he never find her? When would—

There came a soft knocking at the door, and Stryker shot up off his seat, visions of a bare-chested Lai standing outside, in the rain, tears in her eyes, returning to him.

His arms reached out as he tried to embrace the vision.

Another knock came at the door, and he caught hold of himself. He rubbed his eyes, trying to shake the weariness away, and when he opened them again, the pile of reports were still there, mocking him.

"Yes—come in," he said softly, lowering his arms.

The door, which was always unlocked, slowly swung open, and a tall soldier in stateside fatigues appeared. "Afternoon, Sergeant Stryker."

Stryker let out a disappointed sigh. It was John Pruett, the MP from Korea.

Pruett spotted the depression in the ex-Green Beret's expression. It was written all over him, but especially in the lines along the edges of his eyes. *Jungle green* eyes, Pruett decided. "Expecting someone else?" he asked. "Perhaps I could come back a little later."

"No—no, John—have a seat." Stryker waved him over to a nearby chair. Then he sat back down himself and let the embarrassed laugh rumble from the depths of his gut. "I wasn't expecting anyone—nobody at all." He glanced at the small framed photograph of Wann on his desk. Who was he trying to fool—himself?

Always moody over the disappearance of Lai, up in Pleiku, so many lifetimes ago. Yet had he really loved her so much? Had he devoted himself to her? Only a matter of weeks had passed after he originally moved down to Saigon before he was shacking with a different woman—Kim. And now that Kim had left him, there was Wann, the war widow. Always another skirt to get him through the lonely nights, to distract him from pulling the pin.

Yet no matter who he was spending his nights with, his dreams were always of Lai. He thought of her every day since he had met her, but weeks could pass before something reminded him of Kim.

And hadn't he called Lai's name while making love to Wann the other night? She had accused him of whispering it enough from his dreams before, but this time he had heard it himself. And though Wann had pretended not to hear, acting as if she were caught up in their little sexual act while they both groaned and sighed, while flesh slapped against flesh, he knew she had heard, and that their relationship would never be the same again. *Never, ever.* He shuddered inside, hearing the voices of all three women. Such a coincidence that they all took to using that phrase when warning him never to butterfly on them: *never, ever.*

"About this information I've been trying to relay to you." Pruett pulled a small manila envelope out of his shirt pocket. "I think you'll be interested to know—"

One of the two phones on Stryker's desk began ringing.

Feigning intense irritation, he held up a hand to silence his fellow sergeant. "Sorry, John. Just a minute. Probably WACO. Let me see what animal's shit hit the fan now."

He slowly picked up the phone and waited a few seconds after placing it against his ear before saying, "Stryker."

"Mark?" A feminine voice on the other end of the line sounded troubled.

His eyes lit up. It was the obscene phone caller who had been pestering him for several weeks now. "Just a moment," he said.

Placing his hand over the mouthpiece, he told Pruett, "Go into the next office and pick up the extension. You gotta hear this chick. She'll make your day. All she can talk about is sucking cocks and licking assholes!"

"*Stryker!*" Her screaming voice could be heard despite his hand clamped against the receiver.

"Yes dear." He pretended to be the spineless husband as Pruett tiptoed out of the office.

"You haven't returned my calls!" She sounded hurt now.

"Returned your calls? You mean to tell me you're leaving call-back numbers now? Well, I haven't received any messages."

"You've trained your desk sergeants well," she said

sneering. "They're screening your calls, and you know it!"

Stryker didn't say anything. What was the use in arguing with her? He made another mental note to corner Wann and find out who she suspected the caller was. Then he'd put an end to this nonsense once and for all.

"I heard you were almost killed by a rocket crashing into your hotel room a couple nights ago." Her tone changed to a concerned hush.

"Yes," he admitted. "I had quite a close call." He heard a slight click on the line signal Pruett had picked up the extension and was listening in.

"You didn't injure your—*thing*, did you honey?" He could tell she was smiling wickedly.

Normally he would have hung up, but for Pruett's benefit he decided to see how dirty he could get her talking.

"My what?" he asked.

"Your shaft, stupid!" she yelled into the phone. "That ten pounds of meat that hangs down between your legs, you stallion, you! I can see it now, honey. I can feel you ramming it into me, spreading my legs so far apart while you do it that the skin splits and bleeds!"

"And after I make you feel so good," he said, baiting her. "What will you do for me, baby?"

There was a pause in her breathing, then a long silence on the line.

Finally, she said, "Are you taping this, Mark Stryker? Are you preserving this wicked little conversation of ours so you can send it back to the MP Museum in Georgia U.S.A.. Are you, *baby*?"

Stryker's enthusiasm drained from him. She was not so stupid after all. They would not get another suggestive phrase out of her. He decided to just break the connection and quit wasting time.

"Don't you hang up on me!" she screamed, sensing what he was about to do.

"Then get to the point, bitch." He regretted the last word the instant he tacked it on to the end of the sentence. He had no idea who this woman was. He only knew she was insane. Piss her off, and it could only make things worse. She'd be calling him in the middle of the night until the year 2000!

"Bitch?" She screamed so loud he had to jerk the receiver away from his ear. *"Bitch?* You call me a bitch? What about that whore you've been sleeping with the last few weeks: Johnny Power's wife!"

Stryker swallowed hard and his smile faded.

"You thought I didn't know, did you?" She laughed like a maniac. "Well I did! And I'll tell you what else I know, Mr. Macho-MP, super stud, well-hung hero!"

"Yes?" He challenged her after she paused to catch her breath.

"You know that crazy man who has been pretending he's a lumber jack and sawing pretty little girls' heads clean through? You know the sweetheart I'm talking about, Mark?"

Stryker's heart seemed to skip a beat at the mention of the buzz saw murderer. He had chopped up another Vietnamese woman just last night — and only two blocks from the MACV annex MP substation.

"Yes, you know which sonofabitch I'm talking

212

about!" She laughed like the witch from the *Wizard of Oz*, and as boyhood nightmares returned to haunt him, Stryker felt a chill race down his spine. "Well, he happens to be visiting a small apartment over on Bui Vien right now, lover—"

Wann's face flashed before his eyes. *Her apartment was on Bui Vien street!*

"And you know how he has this weakness for defenseless, little Vietnamese women."

"Did you send him over there?" Stryker yelled into the phone. "Do you actually *know* the bastard?"

But she just laughed and slammed the receiver down, breaking the connection.

"Don't hang up on me!" Stryker yelled. "Hello? Are you there?" He was answered with a buzzing dial tone.

"Shit!" He raced past the desk, knocking the pile of reports on the floor, and rushed out to his jeep, leaving the sergeant from Korea behind, in the adjoining office.

8. Quest of the Jade Lady

"Lights—camera—" The tall, skinny American with the Fu Manchu mustache and a floppy artist's hat covering his bald spot made an angry face and pointed to an overweight technician stuffing his face with a hotdog. "Soundman—*you!* Have we got sound?"

The technician jumped slightly, set down the hotdog, and raced over to an instrument board sticking out of the end of a long silver van. "Christ!" he muttered, wiping his hands on his pants. "Is this a take? I thought they were still rehearsing."

Smitty rested a heavy elbow on Murphy's shoulder. "Unbelievable." He was impressed. "Unfuckingbelievable. All this hardware and time just to shoot a ten second scene."

"No wonder it takes them two or three years to make a movie these days," the Zulu warrior added. He was elbow to elbow with Smitty, but the husky sergeant didn't seem to mind or notice. Things had changed. Attitudes had softened. They were a team, and things were running smoothly.

They were not white or black or purple but police blue, with a shade of soldier green. And they had a mission to accomplish. Protect Kiwi Kolana from the

214

crazies out there, and squeeze yourself into a frame or two of instant stardom while you were at it. After all, how often would an opportunity like this present itself? They could always go back to fighting each other after the movie makers went back to Hollyweird.

They were set up in an abandoned warehouse along the riverfront, and the scene had Miss Kolana meeting with some hardcore hoodlum types who were planning to rob the Bank of Saigon.

The last two hours had been spent just filming Kiwi as she walked into the safehouse, supposedly located in Saigon's sister city and Chinese suburb, Cholon.

"One more time." The director pointed his finger at the star, and she went outside, listened for the boards slapping together, then entered, wearing only a wraparound Thai-style sarong.

Smitty thought she looked ridiculous in it. Her billowing blond hair ruined the atmosphere of the scene, in his opinion.

Smitty and the ten other MPs in the room watched her enter through a smoke-laced archway of bamboo drapes, sit down at a table where some rough-looking characters were playing cards, then lean over and whisper something into the ringleader's ear.

"So heyyyyy — *okay!*" The director took off his hat and slipped on a pair of sunglasses. *"Cut!* That's a take!" He got up and whirled his hands about in a tight circle, a signal for the crew to wrap it up. "We're moving right along on schedule, gentlemen." He turned to face the MP extras. "Let's all trot on outside now and go through the chase and shoot-'em-up scene — one more time."

Most of the Americans began eagerly filing from the

warehouse, but Smitty paused, holding his arm out to stop Murphy as well.

"What is it, sarge?" The Murph rested his elbow on his holstered .45.

"Somethin' about this dude, Murph." He stared at the tall, lanky director. "Somethin' about his walk. He reminds me o' someone I seen on the street."

"He walks kinda like Gary Richards, if you ask me."

"Naw—someone else, but I just can't place the prance."

"How long's this going to take?" Some of the MPs' enthusiasm was waning. "I'm scheduled for Alert duty tonight. We been here five days now, and nobody's put this flawless face on film yet." He lifted his chin so they could check his profile, and the men around him laughed.

"Tha' 'cause they don' wanna break no mo-fuckin' cam'ras." The Zulu warrior put his hand out, palm up, and the black MP beside him slapped it to start the jig.

"Nor has this potential overnight success seen the twenty-five-a-day in extras' fees we were promised," another man complained.

"Just a few minutes—just a few minutes." The director laughed, waving the group outside. "All we're going to do today is a little—how do you say it? Dry-firing? Yes! We're going to do some dry-firing. *Tomorrow* we suit up and shoot the big scene, boys. Yes!" He sounded very excited. "Tomorrow we set off all the fireworks and rob the bank."

Murphy scurried up to Kiwi Kolana's short, balding agent and pointed to a second warehouse across the street. Several technicians on their lunchbreak were gathered around the doorway, peeking in. "What's that

216

all about?"

The agent frowned, and a worried crease warped his sweat-slick forehead. "That's just another sound stage," he said. "It's off limits to you over-sexed GIs, I'm afraid. That's where they're doing the skin shots."

"The skin shots?"

"Sure. You know: where Kiwi drops her drawers for the camera." The agent sounded bored now.

"Drops her — *drawers?*"

"Sure, sure, sure, sure." His manner was going impatient, but he was a man with nothing to do. "You don't think we can sell a war movie on action alone, do you? Gotta have sex, son. Sex and violence. That's what sells these days, you know. Sex and violence."

Someone was tugging on Smitty's elbow. A wave of pleasant perfume tickled his nose an instant later.

He was startled to find Miss Kolana herself looking up at him with large, sad, makeup-free eyes.

"Y-yes ma'am?" he stammered, shifting his boots about uneasily. Unexpected confrontations on the street were fine and dandy, but this was not in the FM 19-5, (the Military Police manual).

"You're in charge of security, am I correct, general?" She batted her eyelashes up at him innocently.

Smitty blushed. "It's sergeant, ma'am. Staff Sergeant Smithers. But you can call me Smitty. All my friends call me Smitty."

"Well thank you for considering me your friend, Smitty." She snuggled up to his stocky frame without really touching him. She sounded sincere. And frightened.

"What is it, ma'am?" He detected her hesitation. "What's the problem?"

217

"I received this today, Smitty." She handed him a blue envelope with plastic imitation alligator skin sealing the flap. "It's number four."

"Fan mail?" He smiled down at her.

"I get fan mail all the time," she said. "But I've never gotten anything quite like these before."

Smitty pulled out a small piece of paper that had been shaped into an intricately folded swan.

"May I?"

"Please do."

Smitty held the letter a foot from his eyes, proud he did not yet need spectacles to read like so many of the other NCOs his age.

My Dearest Kiwi,

You refuse to answer my letters, love. What can I do to prove my loyalty to you? My endless devotion? My everlasting love? You must think me a joke, but, my sweetheart, you could never be farther from the truth.

Would my suicide catch your attention? Of course not! How many broken hearts have you already cast by the wayside? But I must act! Soon the president of South Vietnam will fall victim to my sniper's bullet. Then you will know to what lengths I shall go to win your hand in marriage.

Forever yours,
the Sandman

"The sandman?" Smitty quickly reread the note. "Do you have any idea who this bozo might be?"

Kiwi Kolana shook her head in the negative and began to open her mouth when a shot rang out from the warehouse where the sex scenes were to be filmed.

Smitty's head turned in that direction, and an instant later, on the other side of the lot, two MP jeeps raced past, sirens screaming, heading in the direction of Bui Vien Street.

Behind the wheel of the lead jeep was Mark Stryker, his normally expressionless face grim and tense.

Stryker jumped out of his jeep even before the skidding wheels slid to a stop. His pistol was drawn as he was flying through the air. He sprinted up the long walkway to Wann's apartment and tested the doorknob.

Unlocked.

Take the back, his fingers spoke silently as he motioned an MP private to the rear of the building. A one-man town patrol unit had picked up on his Code-Three run from the International and followed him to the scene. He didn't know the teenager.

Shielding his eyes from the harsh, pre-dusk dawn, Stryker gave him thirty seconds to get into position, then slowly opened the door, careful to keep his body clear of the kill zone within the frame.

The apartment was dark.

Dust particles danced in the weak rays from the setting sun that lanced in through the doorway.

Stryker cautiously peered in, careful to remove his MP helmet liner first. (They made great souvenirs— but even better targets.)

A woman's leg protruded from behind the rattan loveseat near the center hallway. It was smeared with blood.

He rushed in, abandoning all caution now—his gut instincts, bewildered, shifting back and forth from phase red to yellow.

Visions of Wann flashed past him: the evenings they had spent picnicking on the banks of the Song Saigon; the restaurants and cinemas he had taken her to; the months she had spent reading the Vietnamese poetry and legends to him: the day the Russian KGB agent shot her down after killing her husband and daughter. But the instant he saw the body behind the couch he knew it did not belong to Wann.

That changed his reactions. He rose from being down on one knee and scanned the apartment, fanning his pistol right to left, with his line of sight.

Nothing.

He glided into the kitchen, then the bathroom. Empty.

He slowly moved to the back door and checked the bolt. Locked.

He raised it without making a sound, and the door swung open from outside. A .45 automatic appeared against his nose.

He backed up and turned away, unimpressed. "It's Code-Four," he told the rook. "Holster it. For now. Call me a Ten-Five. Got a foxtrot down in there." Foxtrot was MP talk for female.

"A foxtrot, sarge?"

"Never seen her before in my life." He suddenly felt the remark was somehow untrue.

He was back down beside her a moment later. And he found a pulse.

Stryker ran his fingers down her backbone. Then,

220

finding no obvious fractures, he slowly turned her over. She was clad in a form-hugging black and white *ao dai*.

Her lips were horribly cut, and her nose was broken. The impression stamped clearly across her face told him someone had struck her with the end of a board.

Stryker slipped the canteen from his web belt and unscrewed the top. He smelled the inside—water. (Sometimes Lai put Kool-Aid in there, and Kim often slipped him some vodka—but he forgot neither of them were in his life any longer. Wann always boiled tap water for him, then placed it in the small icebox overnight.

He poured a modest amount into the palm of his hand and rubbed it across the woman's bruised forehead.

As if she had never been unconscious, the woman's eyes popped open. She locked onto Stryker. A spark of recognition made them flash wider for a moment.

But Stryker himself was not surprised. To him, she was just another stranger in a city of over three million. He wondered what she was doing in Wann's apartment.

With much effort, the woman's lips slowly parted. A trickle of blood appeared at the corner of her mouth.

"Sergeant—Stryker—" she said weakly.

That she knew his name was no shock. Stryker and his crew were forever making front page headlines in exploit after exploit. They even had a following of sorts: a small, unofficial fan club of Vietnamese high school youths with a police monitor, (stolen from the VC themselves), who listened to his every on-duty move, his every misadventure and escapade. He had even gotten a fan letter or two, praising him and his squad, addressed only to "Car Niner," care of the Saigon MPs at the International Hotel.

"Sergeant—Mark—Stryker?"

"Yes," he replied softly, shifting her into his arms, comforting her, suddenly caring. Trying to make her feel at ease. Protected. Safe. "Do I know you?"

The woman tried to smile, but the attempt only produced more pain. "Mytho," her voice cracked, coming across as a dry whisper. "Mytho, sergeant. Nineteen sixty-two."

Stryker felt himself grow numb. Blood rushed to his head, and he thought he might pass out for a moment, but the sensation quickly passed. Visions of two small children watching their mother being raped and their father falling from a helicopter fluttered in front of him, then it was only her face—her eyes—the woman in his arms.

"We tried to stop him this time," she said. "We've only watched before, but we tried to stop him this time. He is so big."

"He?"

"My brother stole a gun. He took it yesterday, and today he pointed it at the man, but he never fired it. I knew my brother wouldn't be able to do it. I told him twice: *let me do it!*"

Wann." He glanced around the room again. "Where is Wann?"

"He took her. He took her away, Sergeant Stryker. My brother tried to stop him but since *it* happened my brother has been afraid of everything, including his own shadow. He can not help it. It is because in his

222

mind he failed that day—that day when he was only a child. He was unable to save them, and he feels now that he will always be a coward. My brother tried to stop the man, but he just hit my brother and dragged them both out the door."

"Do you know which they went?"

She shook her head from side to side, then lowered her eyes. "We knew he would come back. And now he is here."

The MP private at the back door walked up to Stryker, his flashlight out now, checking the ominous corner shadows that grew taller by the minute. "Ten-Five's en route," he said. "ETA ten to fifteen, sarge."

Stryker nodded his head and slowly laid the woman back down. "Don't move," he said. "Help is on the way."

"Don't leave me!" She clutched at his arm, eyes wide with terror now as they darted around the room, checking the doorways and windows.

Stryker went back down on one knee beside her. "Don't worry," he said in Vietnamese. "I won't leave you, dear. Not until he's dead and buried."

His eyes were locked on the round buzz saw blade sitting on the rattan loveseat.

The blue-green parrot's head bobbed up and down as its pink eyes squinted, trying to see down through the layers of incense floating above the bed.

They looked dead.

Two legs spread, toes pointing up. Two more legs in between the first set, toes down—pale buttocks mooning the bird in the bamboo cage.

The parrot shifted its head to the other side, keeping

its beak down. The pale buttocks were moving about now, in a slow circular motion.

The woman on the bottom groaned, exhausted, and the buttocks ground to a halt.

The parrot ruffled its feathers and buried its head under one wing.

"Enough," Benny Harcourt whispered when the woman brought her hands up and laced her fingers around his haunches from behind. She pulled down, forcing him deeper inside her. "Enough," he repeated.

"You're getting old, Benny," she said. "That was only twice. You used to be able to rock off in me four times before we called it a night."

Her growing fluency was beginning to annoy him. He liked it better when she just spoke pidgin English. "Such wishful thinking," he muttered. "That's when I was back on day shift. I get stressed—out on nights—you know that."

"You need a stimulant." She slid out from beneath him.

"You'd *best* not be talkin' drugs, woman." Harcourt's irritation was growing.

"I'm *talkin'* the sexiest, black, see-through nightie your cherry-red face ever laid eyes on, lover!" Harcourt rolled over, onto his stomach, half asleep, while Mrs. Derek Ramsey moved off the edge of the bed and walked over toward the closet's wide, double-doors.

"I just hope your husband's really workin' a double shift out at Fort Hustler, baby, and not—"

Her scream filled the bedroom, causing the parrot to emit an ear-splitting screech, trying to imitate her.

Harcourt rolled back over, bumping his nose on the headboard as he tried to see what had frightened his

224

partner's wife.

Sitting in the closet, in a pool of blood, was Derek Ramsey, his .45 pistol still in his mouth, blood from the back of his head splattered across the collection of fancy negligee hanging behind him.

9. Voices in the Storm

Smitty stared into the eyes of the black MP squatting across from him and grinned. The Zulu warrior smiled back, and as he shifted about on his sore feet, the molars around his neck clinked softly.

"Always did say one thing you jigabooes had goin' for you was at night no one can see you against the dark, *boy*."

Biggs's teeth flashed white, revealing he was closer to Smitty than the NCO had thought. Uncomfortably closer.

Biggs bent forward slightly and ran a finger through the layer of charcoal on Smitty's face. "Your mascara is running sergeant — *sir*."

There came a scurrying of footsteps across the rooftop, and soon Anthony Thomas was crouching beside the two. "Bryant's in position," he whispered. "He'll be leavin' that trailer there." He pointed to one of the small mobile dwellings on the makeshift movie lot. "And walking over to that Quonset hut about seventy-five yards down the way there. Richards is set up on the west side of the fence line there, in the Black Beast." Biggs's throat snarled like a caged panther. He considered him*self* the black beast. "Stryker is on the east side, in a gun jeep and in uniform. Lieutenant Slipka set up five L.P.s a block out in all directions, but nobody has called in any activity yet. No movement anywhere."

"Just ain't the same without Broox, is it Ants?" Smitty forced a thin grin.

"No," Thomas admitted. He thought about the cable he had received from Mike only the day before:

Fi Fi Ky had left him a little over twenty-four hours after their Las Vegas wedding. The boys had been right. She only wanted that precious ticket stateside. Now she was somewhere in Hollywood, trying to break into the big time—American movies. Broox was brokenhearted. And disgraced. He had always considered himself streetwise. And he thought he could spot a con a mile away.

If it had happened to anyone else, Thomas would have read the cable at the next choir practice, but Mikey was his buddy. He would suffer in silence with his blood brother. The only man he told was Stryker, for Mark was like a father to them both.

"Yah, ol' Mikey is probably on the hundredth hour of his honeymoon right about now." Smitty went on and on, forgetting the mission for a moment. "But I still don't trust that Fi Fi broad he flew back to The World with. I don't care what anyone says. *I* never saw her in no Vietnamese or Chinese movies. I think that was all just talk. Hers and Mikey's. And come to think of it, now I *know* why I never trusted her: Only character *I* ever saw her play was a back-stabbing bitch on them Saigon TV soaps!"

"But I'm more worried about Stryker," Thomas revealed. "He just hasn't been the same since he flew across town Code-Three last week. Something's been bugging him. Something heavy. Something serious. And he won't talk to anybody about it."

"Oh, Marcus is a big boy." Smitty ran his knuckles back and forth across the front of his teeth — one of his bad habits when action was pending.

Down on the ground, several hundred yards away, Sgt. Mark Stryker sat in his jeep, watching the street and the warehouse compound the movie moguls from Fantasy Land had set up shop in. He stared straight ahead, watching two tomcats pace circles around each other with their tails in the air, but from the corners of his eyes he saw everything that went on around him.

The movie they claimed to be making could conceivably be a smash hit, the newspaper critics were predicting. Tentatively titled, *Quest Of The Jade Lady*, it would feature a blond bombshell in the lead role of chasing treasure across the oceans and routing evil in the mysterious Orient. All the MPs assigned to Kiwi Kolana were hyped up, ecstatic even. But Mark Stryker had other things on his mind.

Five days had passed since Wann disappeared. They had heard nothing from the man who kidnapped her. Stryker took Richards of the Decoy Squad into his confidence about the case, but he swore the man to secrecy and told no other MPs. In all likelihood, the woman was already dead, sitting in one of the ten-thousand odd abandoned warehouses in Saigon, a buzz saw through her brain. Or worse: stuffed down a sewer pipe somewhere, like so many of the city's murder victims ended up.

The four MPs had scoured the underworld with a fine-toothed comb, but nobody had seen or heard anything—those who would talk to them anyway.

Stryker even had Toi and some of his most trusted *Canh-sats* on the case but they, too, had turned up nothing except the usual false tips that always led to dead ends after hours of painstaking investigation.

The ex-Green Beret had considered taking the matter to the provost marshal. With the might of the thousand man Military Police battalion behind him, heads would roll and they might turn up something. But out of respect for Wann—she would have lost face if word got out a patrolman's widow was dating (and sleeping with) another MP so soon after her husband's death—he remained silent, hoping against the odds he could crack the case on his own.

And now he was on a damned stakeout, helping Smitty, when he should be down in the heart of the city, chasing the shadowy leads his private little obscene caller was phoning into his bedroom every night—not that he was sleeping there.

A movement in his peripheral vision caught his attention, and he glanced back into the compound through the sagging perimeter wire. A beat-up old dame (what he felt Kiwi Kolana would look like in fifty years) was making her way across the vacant movie lot.

Up the street, at the other end of the block, a sedan coasted up into a no parking zone, its headlights off long before Stryker had detected its arrival.

"There he is." Smitty pointed down at a stocky figure in a dress. Long, billowing blond hair flowed over broad shoulders. "She" was walking awkwardly down the bunker plank beside a trailer, holding up the edge of her dress, trying not to trip over it.

"Did he actually shave his legs?" Smitty asked. "*God*

is he ugly! It'll never work."

"That Tim is a card." Anthony Thomas's voice raised slightly above the mandatory whisper, and Biggs cast him an irritated scowl. "His fucking dedication above and beyond the call of duty never ceases to amaze me."

"Kinky faggot just wants to be drag queen for a day," muttered Smitty. He sounded serious, but the men on the rooftop knew he was just joking around, too.

Bryant slowly made his way across the empty lot, taking his time, repeatedly dropping a large assortment of hat boxes he was carrying to hide his six o'clock shadow.

"Kiwi Kolana he ain't." Biggs shook his head back and forth in resignation.

"It ain't gonna fucking work." Smitty repeated his earlier prediction.

"Well, poke me in the ass!" Biggs pointed to the far end of the lot.

A dark form was sprinting across the property, after having just crawled under a damaged section of perimeter wire. His height said he was American. His agility told the MPs he was in good shape. "Whatta ya see? Whatta ya see?" Thomas nudged Smitty, who had borrowed his pair of folding binoculars just before the intruder was spotted. "Is he one of our guys?"

"Dorky lookin' oddball," Smitty replied, handing Thomas the glasses. "I'd say the rat is going after the cheese." He started for the fire escape. "Time to spring the trap."

Thomas placed the binoculars against his eyes and quickly focused them. A GI in his mid-twenties with a long nose and thick glasses came into view. The face matched none of the ten mug shots Kiwi Kolana had picked from possible suspects CID had shown her. Thomas felt the interview by the investigators had been a waste of time anyway. Kiwi was going on gut instincts and poor memories of past overzealous fans. She had never actually met the Sandman.

The GI, dressed in green fatigues and an army baseball cap, rushed up and grabbed the arm of the one he thought was the movie starlet.

Sure, it's dark out, but nobody could be *that* blind! So thought Thomas as, he too, headed for the rooftop ladder now.

Bryant resisted, pulling the soldier back off balance. Startled by the unexpected strength of "Miss Kolana," the GI tugged again and was unsuccessful a second time. He then bent over and charged Bryant, buckling him at the midsection. Knocked breathless, the undercover MP collapsed over the soldier's shoulder, and the GI, grabbing a handful of bottom to steady his "catch," started running for the opening in the fence line. His eyes darted about frantically, checking for witnesses to the abduction.

"*Hey*, asshole!" Bryant finally manage to get the words out after the man had carried him halfway across the dark lot. "Military Police!" he slammed a hatbox into the back of the GI's head. "You're under arr—"

A second intruder flew out from behind a Quonset hut, striking the kidnapper in the side, and forcing both himself and his victim off balance. All three crashed roughly to the ground, and Bryant's dress ripped down the middle.

At first the Decoy Squad MP thought Richards or

one of the guys had gotten a little carried away with rescuing him, but then he saw the cherry-red cape flapping in the wind and half of an exposed buttock rolling across the ground.

"Hey!" he yelled, completely recovered now. "Hey you guys! Close in! Close in! Ten-Two!" He worked his way onto his knees, clutching at the torn dress to keep it out of the way. "I got 'em both! I got 'em both here! Captain Condom *and* our target subject!"

"Move in." Biggs, still on the rooftop and in no hurry to join the mess down below, spoke calmly into his pak-set microphone. "All units move in — suspect fighting at this time. Make that two for resisting — all units move in." Then he folded his arms across his chest and stood back unmoving, content to watch all the white boys on the ground desperately trying to draw blood.

But Bryant did *not* have them both.

His elbows and knees badly scraped, Captain Condom was nevertheless back on his feet and racing for the fence line, his good deed for the day done. The GI with the baseball cap was sprinting in the opposite direction, his shirt torn open.

Stryker and Richards had both set their jeep engines rumbling the moment they saw Captain Condom sneaking down through the Quonset huts, but neither MP sergeant had spotted the soldier with the baseball cap crawling through the breech in the concertina.

They were taken off guard when they slid up through the main entrance into the compound and saw Bryant pointing at the fleeing kidnap suspect.

Richards drew his pistol and aimed at the man's

232

back. Someone who had hinted he might attempt assassinating the president of South Vietnam could not be allowed to escape. But Thomas and Smitty suddenly appeared in his line of sight as they pursued the GI, and he pulled up at the last instant, popping a hollow-point up at the clouds.

Stryker swerved around Richard's vehicle and roared after the naked maniac in the gas mask and combat boots, but by the time he reached the maze of round storage huts, Captain Condom had vanished through the midnight mist.

"Damn!" Stryker slammed his fist against the jeep's steering wheel as he skidded up to a set of the portable structures. They were erected too close together for his vehicle to proceed any further, and he wasn't in the mood to chase the idiot on foot. Not when he had such a head start. Pursuit at this point would just be a waste of time and energy. On the other side of the compound, Smitty and Thomas had just tackled the soldier with the baseball cap and were twisting his arms back to snap on the iron bracelets.

Some men from one of the listening posts rolled up beside Stryker in a marked unit, and the ex-Green Beret was surprised to see John Pruett aboard.

"Looks like the prophylactic perpetrator made good his escape," Pruett observed aloud with a straight face, stepping out of the vehicle.

Stryker did not dignify the remark with an immediate reply. Instead he waited a few moments, then said, "Just couldn't stay away from the streets, huh?"

"This city sings with sirens." Pruett's smile became

a knowing grin. "Never fails, three days into my vacation I always want to be right back in the thick of things."

Stryker's brow softened. He understood.

A shot rang out behind the men, and both sergeants glanced back over their shoulders. Pruett was slowly lowering his frame into an instinctive crouch, but Stryker spotted Thomas and relaxed. The MP was giving the all's-okay sign and pointing to a warehouse with lights burning inside.

"What was that all about?" Pruett's look of concern faded.

"Same thing happened a few nights ago," Stryker explained. "Scared the shit out of us. Turns out these movie people work the weirdest hours—almost like cops. Anyway, they've been filming a murder scene in there all week long."

"Oh." Pruett's eyes narrowed out of routine suspicion.

"So what was it you've been trying to tell me all week? We've never really been able to get together. Slipka told me you've been in the hospital since Monday. Meant to come and visit you."

"Aw, like a typical tourist I went sightseeing where I didn't belong. Some foodstall vendor slipped me *pho* soup with green bamboo shoots in it."

"Green?"

"Do I stutter?" His smile was an imitation of Broox's perpetual smirk, and Stryker grew suddenly tired.

"And they expanded once inside your gut, split and punctured the stomach lining. Fucking old mama-san musta been a fan of Ho Chi Minh."

"You guessed it. But I'm still alive—I made it. And I always come back kickin'!"

" 'Takes a lickin' and keeps on tickin'.' "

"Something like that."

"So anyway," Stryker said, still staring out at the dark, at the spot where he had last seen Captain Condom. It was time to get back to business.

"You knew a Kip Mather?" Pruett asked.

Mather's face flashed in front of Stryker and he nodded. "Damn good cop," he said. "Till a Honda Honey lobbed a grenade in his lap a few months ago while he was sitting in his jeep on a short-seven." He started rubbing his knuckles at the memory, and his face whirled back around suddenly. "What do you mean *knew*?"

"He's dead," Pruett said softly. Stryker's eyes locked onto the other sergeant's, trying to gauge his seriousness. It was not the calm reaction Pruett had expected.

"How?" Stryker's tone was angry but subdued. The single word told Pruett the ex-Green Beret sensed Kip had not died a natural death.

"You knew an operative named Hoyden sometime back?"

Stryker shuddered and the hairs along the back of his neck seemed to stand up, though he couldn't be sure. His stomach felt suddenly queasy, and he became lightheaded. He said nothing. His eyes spoke the answer.

"I knew him, too." Pruett's expression said he understood Stryker's mixture of rage and anxiety at digging up the memory attached to the name. "I was once assigned to the Two hundred ninety-eighth

235

MPs in Savannah. Transported Hoyden from Bellvista Psyche Ward to Leavenworth after you guys sent him home from the Nam in handcuffs and a straight jacket — and after the shrinks found him sane. He took an intense dislike to me, merely because I told him every cop knows the shrinks are all full of shit ninety-nine percent of the time, and maybe he could sweet-talk his way past the PhDs at Bellvista, but I could see right through his act. I told him to his face he was as crazy as they came, but that I was also glad the shrinks had screwed up 'cause now they were sticking his ass in the monkey house, and once the gangs found out he raped and shot a woman they'd show him how it felt. I told that goofy Hoyden I thought he was nothing more than a simple punk, and his 'gonna-burn-down-your-house-when-I-get-out' threats didn't scare me.

"Well, he got out, Stryker. Escaped. Two months ago. Killed a ninety-five Charlie with his bare hands, and a K-nine mut after that. And damned if the bastard didn't burn down my fucking house, too. 'Least I think it was him. All the evidence points his direction. My neighbor fingered his mug shot in a photo lineup. Uncle Sammy opted to reassign me back to the ROK for another overseas tour of duty. It was the Green Machine's way of keeping me alive without risking lost face, if you get my drift."

"What about Kip?" Stryker glanced up at the stars and flares floating above Saigon. He thought about how quickly his old friend had adapted to using the plastic and metal limbs the army furnished him after the devastating assault.

"Hoyden contacted every agent he knew — or had

236

known five years ago—till he found one who hadn't heard about his arrest back in sixty-two. Got the fool to run a personnel data printout on his 'old buddies from the Nam' until he found out Mather was medically discharged and teaching back at The School.

"Hoyden paid him a visit three weeks ago, Stryker. Cut his head off with a machete."

Stryker winced. Beads of sweat began trickling down his forehead.

"Strapped his wife."

"Hoa?"

"Yah. Strapped her to the railroad tracks that run alongside Avenue Delta near the range before he killed Mather."

"*Hoa!*—Jesus!"

"Yanked off Mather's artificial limbs and set him free moments before the train arrived. There was nothing Kip could do in time. It was a coal train, Stryker. Couple miles long. Couldn't stop in time."

"My God." He sighed and it felt like his heart had escaped on his breath.

"Then he chopped up Mather. Stuck his decapitated head where the train wheels had severed Hoa's neck."

Stryker's head dropped until his chin was resting against his chest.

A strange thought flew through Pruett's head: They'd be laughing about the double murder now—the ingenuity of the murderer—if they hadn't known the victims personally. Cops always got together and compared war stories and crime scenes, laughing off the gore and insanity of it. It was the only way to keep their marble collection in one tight, little bag,

237

so the other kids on the street wouldn't steal them. But this was different.

"He's in Saigon now," Pruett continued. "Flew all the way back here, pal—looking for you."

"I know." Stryker rested his hand on his pistol, the adrenaline flowing now, challenge dancing in his eyes. But his expression remained somber and subdued. "Lord, how I know."

10. Suicides Don't Count

"This can't be!" Mrs. Derek Ramsey slammed her tiny fist down across the tabletop, rattling the plates and silverware. A waitress passing by glanced down at her briefly but did not stop to see if there was a problem with the food. "This *cannot* be!"

Benny Harcourt nodded his head from side to side in resignation and rested his chin across clasped fists, contemplating his next move.

The Japanese man sitting beside him straightened his tie and closed the folder on the table in front of him. He did not like the Saigon heat, but the polite smile never left his face. "I'm sorry, but there is no mistake, Mrs. Ramsey. Your husband's policies are worthless. He has not paid a single premium in six months."

"I saw him purchase the money orders!" she argued.

"Well, I'm afraid I don't know what he bought with them, Mrs. Ramsey." The insurance agent ran his fingers along the inside of his tight collar. "But it was not life insurance."

"He was paying premiums on more than a quarter-million dollars' worth of insurance!" she maintained.

"Not the last six months he wasn't."

"Well what about this?" She pulled a small packet

239

out of her purse and handed it to the neatly groomed businessman.

He rapidly scanned the first two pages and handed it back. "A fifty thousand dollar policy." His smile brightened.

"I have been paying the premiums on my own." She did not smile back but remained grim. "I suspected Derek might not be keeping up with the other premiums. He thought they were a waste of money—"

"He always said if he valued his life that much he wouldn't stay in Vietnam as an MP," Harcourt admitted.

"It is worthless." The Japanese man's smile faded slightly.

"Worthless?" She struck the table again and several nearby customers glanced over, straining to pick up tidbits of the conversation. Harcourt shot them an angry glare and they turned away, faces reddening.

"This is a war zone, Mrs. Ramsey, despite the rather pleasant circumstances we now find ourselves in." The insurance agent waved a meaty hand to take in the splendor of the French restaurant on Pasteur Street.

"Grenades have been known to "accidentally" fly into pleasant circumstances such as these," Harcourt told him.

"Exactly." The agent grinned the way a veteran defense lawyer would after tripping up a rookie deputy district attorney in front of a jury. "The policy is not good in a war zone, regardless of the cause of death. I'm sorry. I'll write a memo. Your premiums will be refunded in full. The policy never should have been issued."

The Vietnamese woman in the pink miniskirt and

blouse fumed silently as Benny Harcourt pulled a packet from his own pocket. "What about *this*?" He looked confident.

The insurance agent shrugged his shoulders and examined the policy as if he had all day to accommodate them. "You just took it out five months ago, Mr. Harcourt." The face sheet told him all he needed to know.

"So? The payments have all been on time and current."

"Mr. Ramsey died of a self-inflicted gunshot wound." He bowed his head slightly, out of respect to his widow, though he had his private suspicions about her relationship with the other MP seated next to him. "Suicide. The policy does not cover suicide the first two years."

Benny Harcourt slammed *his* fist against the tabletop this time. A small porcelain cup of tea bounced over as he flew to his feet and stormed out of the restaurant.

A produce truck narrowly missed running over him outside. The Japanese businessman closed his eyes tightly, and his head sunk down between his shoulders at the sound of skidding tires and blaring horns, but the woman sitting across from him didn't even seem to notice.

Stryker dropped a six-pack of warm Budweiser on the podium.

"See what you get when you smoke burglars fleeing the scene of a felony?" He picked the beer back up and tossed it over several rows of helmets to Nilmes.

Two MPs on opposite sides of the room clapped

lightly. The men on either side of Nilmes grabbed a can and slipped them into their large thigh pockets. "Take 'em back to your hootch before you hit the street," Stryker said. "We're already short on jeeps.

"Some of you have been asking about Sergeant Brickmann," he continued. "Well, The Brick is doing fine. His arm wasn't as screwed up in that firefight last month as we first thought. He's currently supporting a harem of geisha girls on some hospital ship off the Japanese coast — *with his lips*. He'll probably be back in the Nam before you know it. The PM said he'd let him work a desk sergeant slot till his biceps were back up to bone-breaking par.

"His mailing address is on the bulletin board outside. Every one of you gutless wonders who hasn't asked about Ron yet better send him a Saigon postcard ASAP, or your ass is mine!"

"Say fella —" An NCO in the back of the room gave his tone a feminine accent.

"Fella." Stryker directed an obscene gesture at the sergeant.

"They don't have no postcards in the Nam, sarge." Thomas wasn't happy unless he was complaining.

"Nilmes came across a rack out at Tan Son Nhut airport, so I don't wanna hear that crap, okay? I don't wanna hear no more excuses." Stryker was a master of the English language, as were most of the MPs after going through the academy, but he felt more comfortable using improper grammar — it was the language of the street. "It's run by a nineteen-year-old cherry-girl with watermelons for chest." He knew a physical description of her would be incentive enough to get several units out there to investigate.

Richards, his fingers clasped prayerlike in front of him, rested his lips against them as he silently watched the huge sergeant behind the podium. With all that was happening in Stryker's personal life—Wann was still being held somewhere in the sprawling capital—he still managed to run the watch and humor his men at the same time. Richards admired him for that. He wasn't sure he could cope the way Mark could.

"For those of you who give a shirt, Broox dusted a Tae-kwondo instructor last week. The final decision just came down from MPI: righteous shooting." Scattered applause filled the room.

"Lucky shot," Thomas muttered, painfully aware Mikey was not around anymore to defend himself.

"Some of you have been bugging me for the results," Stryker went on. "Well, the dude was a seven foot tall Korean with an intense dislike for round-eyes."

Richards rubbed his jaw without noticing it.

"Now, stats that mean something: We're currently carrying eight guys AWOL. Four of them: Zane, Phipps, Mallory, and Palance were last seen getting into a Saigon cab with one of our illustrious and notorious meatmarket princesses—a different one each time. Our highly trained and motivated trooper at the adjacent static post has been neglecting to keep his sign-in log current, though. But he managed to remember one thing about the taxi they all got in: The cabbie was a woman.

"I don't know if all these guys are having a circle jerk in Cholon or what, but they haven't been seen on the street anywhere, assuming the units are leveling with me. And much as I hate to assume anything around this joint." He turned to face the blackboard on the

243

wall, wrote the word assume on it in big block letters, then chalked vertical lines on either side of the U. "Since that could conceivably make an ass out of U and me," he said, pointing to each syllable in turn, "there's one thing I'm sure about around here, and that's that you can never be sure about anything."

"Sergeant Stryker!" An MP in neatly pressed khakis and short hair burst through the rear doors.

"A note here from the VNP." He ignored the interruption and kept his eyes on his clipboard. "Little Oral Annie was found facedown in the Saigon River last night—"

Groans of mock devastation rose from nearly every MP in the room at the news.

"*Sergeant Stryker!*" The company clerk was halfway across the room now. A large rat was scurrying along the floor, trying to keep up with him.

"Jake Drake!" Stryker finally looked up. "What inspired *you* to get a haircut?"

"We got her. Sergeant Stryker!" Drake dodged the question. "At the meatmarket! The bitch drivin' the taxi just got pulled over by one of the town units!"

"Assemble for inspection," Stryker muttered as he rushed from the room amid grumbling complaints from the men who wanted to follow him out.

Once outside the doors, he broke into a sprint and was down at the security gate within seconds.

Reilly and The Uke had a blue and yellow Renault pulled over. In the back seat, two soldiers from the APO were complaining about being stopped for no reason. "Take a hike." Uhernik pointed over at a long line of cyclos parked beside the meatmarket, waiting for passengers.

"Fucking MPs." The soldiers took their time getting out of the cab. "Think they own the town."

A mint green *canh-sat* van coasted up behind the MP jeep and two additional CLHH units pulled in behind the VNP vehicle. All had their red roof lights off, but the girls at the meatmarket cage—like a school of fish suddenly changing direction—shifted to the near screen to watch.

"Good evening, miss." Stryker leaned an elbow on the window frame of the sedan, but his right hand remained on his holstered pistol.

"No speaky English," the woman replied, flashing clean white, perfectly straight teeth up at him. She seemed more irritated about losing two fares than worried about being stopped by the police.

"No speaky English," Stryker said sarcastically, "but you just happen to drive taxis for a living."

"No speaky English," she repeated.

"Your national ID card." He switched to Vietnamese, grinning. She complied immediately, handing him her hack license, too.

Stryker smiled when he saw Jon Toi walking up behind the other side of the car. He copied the ID information into his pocket notebook, then handed it to the Vietnamese policeman. "Ask her if she knows anything about Zane or the others, Toi. Like where did she drop 'em off—did she notice anything out of the ordinary—you know what to ask. I'm gonna run her through WACO for Wants and a history." He walked back to his jeep while crazy Jeff covered Jon Toi.

The Uke had moved up in front of the taxi and was checking some recent body damage.

"She's a real space cadet, Mark," Toi said a few min-

245

utes later. "She claims you round-eyes all look alike."

The radio check through Dispatch had also been a dry run. Not even a street contact on record. "F.I. her ass." Stryker handed her ID to Reilly. "I'm sure she's not the only female cabbie in the city, despite the local customs and culture, but she's all we got to work with right now. Then ride the rest of shift with Schultz. Me, Toi, and The Uke are gonna check her pad." He glanced at the address on her ID again.

"Want me to detain her till you get there?" Reilly was sharp.

"Naw, she lives on the other side of town. Wait till we leave, then cut her loose and—"

The tires of the Renault spun across the pavement suddenly, and the taxi accelerated toward an MP walking back to his jeep.

The Uke whirled around, drawing his pistol during the movement as he responded to the sound of screaming rubber. The taxi swerved over at the closest man, and he bounced off a fender, rolling to the side of the road. Uhernik spread his feet, used two hands to aim, and fired one shot at the windshield. The round climbed high, and he jerked the trigger again, more smoothly this time, though the car was almost upon him.

A hole appeared on the passenger side of the windshield, spiderwebbing the glass, and the car swerved back over to the other side of the road. The men around Stryker flattened out on the ground as the taxi flew past, and The Uke's boots slowly pivoted to follow the vehicle's path. He fired four more rounds, and two of the slugs impacted against the trunk of the car with dull thuds. But the ex-Green Beret was airborne—

leaping into Uhernik's jeep.

The vehicle's engine was still on, idling, and he threw the shifter into gear and let the clutch fly. "Hop in!" he yelled, as he shot alongside the private, and Uhernik grabbed a handhold and pulled himself aboard.

The taxi swerved into heavy traffic and turned left onto Tran Hung Dao, heading in the direction of Cholon.

"WACO, this is Car Niner." Stryker grabbed the dash mike and siren toggle simultaneously, just as a long municipal bus pulled up between the taxi and their unit. Signal lights changed at intersections on both sides. The entire block became saturated with cars, and traffic rolled to a complete stop.

"Go ahead, Car Niner," the dispatcher at headquarters replied dryly.

Stryker watched the Renault swerve down a side street and disappear. "Disregard," he muttered.

"We could commandeer a motor scooter." The Uke pointed at a swarm of Honda Honies lined up and flashing leg at the nearest light.

Visions of Kip Mather's torn and tattered body next to the overturned MP jeep after the grenade explosion several months earlier entered his head. "Forget it," he finally said. "It's just not worth the effort. We got her numbers."

"If they're any good." Uhernik sounded skeptical.

They pulled up to her northside apartment thirty minutes later. The neighborhood was silent. No birds. No traffic. Not even any children playing stickball in the gutters.

The street was narrow. One-story, delapidated flats extended for blocks, all attached to each other with no space in between.

Stryker scanned the row of identical, low-rent dwellings. On one door were numbers that matched the ID information the female cabbie had given them earlier. But there was no taxi anywhere nearby.

He glanced in a trash can sitting outside the flat. A pile of old taxi company logbooks was on the bottom, bringing a grin to Stryker's face.

Without a word to The Uke, Stryker returned to the front door, kicked it in with one boot, and entered the apartment — pistol drawn.

Two thoughts shot through Uhernik's mind. *Should I call for backup? Should I rush around and cover the rear?* He drew his pistol and followed the sergeant in.

The interior of the apartment was dark except that narrow shafts of dusk shot in through bamboo drapes. The living room was sparsely furnished: a cooking table and sleeping mat big enough for one. There were no decorations on the walls. No clothes in the open closet.

Then they found the cylinders.

Sealed in thick plastic and piled one atop the other in a cramped storage room were the fully clothed bodies of Zane and all the others. Their skin white, each corpse had a small purple hole in the center of the forehead. And though their other jewelry was intact, every man's MP ring was missing.

"I saw that cunt yesterday," Uhernik whispered to Stryker as they stood frozen to the floorboards in front of the ghastly scene. "I wasn't sure at first, but the

248

more I think about it, the name and numbers match, sarge. She's the one who picked up that Sergeant Pruett yesterday at the meatmarket."

Stryker glanced at the cracked and faded ancestral photos hanging above a small altar in the corner of the buffet. "He wasn't with the Moanin' Lisa I hope."

"He was alone, sarge."

Investigators swooped in on the scene an hour later, taking photographs, collecting evidence, questioning neighbors. The mummified bodies were carried out one by one, sending a swirl of muffled talk and chatter through the spectators now crowding outside the apartment. The female cab driver did not return home that evening.

The following day, Sgt. John Pruett failed to show up for a scheduled appointment with CID agents investigating the Hoyden affair.

11. Firefight In Phuto

Stryker watched the two civilians bump into each other across the street from the Luc Quach Bank on Tran Hung Dao. One of the men nearly dropped the huge camera mounted on his shoulder. *Not very professional*, Stryker noted.

"Where's that goofy Hollyweird director?" Smitty moved closer. A dozen uniformed MPs stood behind them. "I never liked the guy's looks, to tell you the truth."

"Haven't seen him yet today," Stryker grumbled. He hadn't had his mandatory first-thing-in-the-morning cup of coffee yet. "Looks like they got your second choice in charge, though." He was being sarcastic. Kiwi Kolana's short, chubby agent was taking his seat in the director's chair.

They had canceled shooting at the Bank of Saigon because of security objections from the Vietnamese police, but the manager of the Luc Quach Bank had graciously consented to allow filming of the shoot-out scene at his business after the producer agreed to allow the banker's aspiring-actress daughter a small part in a future scene with Kiwi.

"This whole business gives me the creeps," said

Smitty. "Standin' in the middle of Tran Hung Dao with unloaded weapons yet with these targets on our heads." He pointed to his helmet.

"Never should have got involved with this silver screen horseshit in the first place," Stryker said. "I've been getting the worst possible vibes all week long."

"They should have one of those huge cameras on rollers," Smitty continued. "Even if they made *us* roll out the tracks, at least the clarity would come out more professional, with less vibrations. As it stands now, this whole project's gonna end up lookin' like a B-rated foreign flick."

"No sweat." Stryker's mood brightened and he patted the green canvas pouch on his web belt.

"Mags?" Smitty's eyes lit up with admiration and envy.

"Three banana clips." He winked devilishly. "Ninety tracers."

"Green?"

"Red."

"Beautiful!"

"People! People!" The agent who was doubling as a director today stood up and waved his hands about. "Places! Places! Time is tight! Time is money! Time is valuable! Let's all take our positions now. The first one will be a dry run only, but give it your best shot."

A few Vietnamese pedestrians had stopped to watch the proceedings, but for the most part the Americans were ignored. A lane in front of the bank had been cordoned off by private security guards hired by the producer—a man none of the MPs had ever met—but the busy boulevard itself was not blocked off.

The director, wearing a light green safari outfit,

251

stood up and walked over to the lieutenant in front of Stryker. "We'll be shooting scene twenty-five F." He showed the senior MP a xeroxed schedule. "All your people have to do is take cover behind the items they've been assigned and fire their blanks at the bank robbers when they back out of the building."

A long white van pulled up at the end of an alley along one side of the bank, and Stryker felt his gut instincts do a belly flop. After the lieutenant walked off with the director, he ejected the twenty-round magazine of blanks and silently slid a banana clip of hotshots in instead. "You told WACO to have a couple units close by?" He confirmed with Smitty.

"That's a rog, Stryk."

"Okay!" The director called over his bullhorn as he took his seat again. His hand signaled an assistant inside the doors of the bank, and moments later a flurry of shots erupted inside the building.

Stryker and his men exchanged worried glances. The discharges going off inside the bank in no way resembled harmless blanks! But Stryker held up his hand, signaling for caution. Who knew what Hollywood had developed lately in the way of sound effects?

The doors burst open and four Asians in black uniforms backed out of the bank, some of them dragging large money bags.

The director's hand flew up again, and his fingers dropped to point at Smitty: the signal to fire upon the bad guys.

Stryker glanced around. The cameramen had disappeared. Kiwi Kolana herself was not scheduled to be in this particular scene, so Stryker was not surprised when she failed to walk out of the bank with the bandits.

One of the Asians turned and fired at the American military policemen kneeling behind light poles and parked cars.

Quite a show, Stryker thought. Except that the smoke belching from the bank robber's submachine gun had hot lead in it!

Windshields all around the MPs shattered and caved in. A beam supporting a roof overhang split down the middle as a bullet impacted inches from Stryker's cheek, and wood flew everywhere.

This time the lieutenant held up a hand as Stryker's rifle came up to his shoulder. "Maybe it's just special effects that they didn't brief us on!" he yelled above the clamor of the barking MP-40.

"Bull." Stryker took a bead on the gunman just as a round bounced off the pavement and whistled past, inches from the ear that already had a bullet hole scar in it. He triggered off a slug on semiautomatic, and the man flew forward through the plate glass windows in the front of the bank.

"Maybe someone accidently slipped some live rounds into their weapons," the officer with butter bars on his collar had the gall to suggest as both veteran sergeants crouched behind a car.

Stryker didn't care about mistakes that could be substantiated after the fact. All he knew was that he was being shot at.

"Life's tough all over." Smitty let loose a ten-round burst after Stryker threw him one of his banana clips. Tracers splintered against the brick wall of the bank, showering the gunmen with red sparks. Two more gunmen were catapulted off their feet, only to be replaced by another duo fleeing the giant double doors. Traffic between the bank and Stryker's men skidded to a halt. Women were everywhere—Vietnamese and Eurasian—but none of them screamed. They all dropped behind cars as if out of bored routine. Those not wearing silk or *ao dais* slid under chassis. Most of the Americans quit shooting for fear of hitting innocent civilians, but the "movie actors" in black uniforms unloaded on the MPs with everything they had.

Firing from the hip, those gunmen still standing dragged their money bags over to the van and piled in. Tires began squealing even before their feet were off the ground.

"Let's go!" Stryker headed for the units parked down at the end of the block. He caught a glimpse of Kiwi Kolana's agent in the van. The actress herself was nowhere around.

They chased the van in and out of traffic, through back alleys and the wrong way down one-way boulevards for thirty minutes until the speeding convoy skidded into the Phuto racetrack precisely at dusk.

Several horses scattered as the van crashed through track railings and careened into the bottom bleachers of the stands. A galloping thoroughbred attempted to jump over the zigzagging van, but its hooves crashed through the windshield. Both the animal and vehicle rolled over onto their sides. Metal warped, folded and screeched.

Their instincts and training directing them how to respond, even the youngest of the MPs fell into the best offensive position available, avoiding a crossfire.

The stands had been nearly deserted, and those few gamblers left were now stumbling and leapfrogging for the poorly lit exits.

Glass in the left door of the van blew out from inside, and a fist appeared holding a small automatic rifle: an AK with no stock and a converted snub barrel. The handler began firing in a blind semicircle in the direction of Stryker and his MPs. Rounds danced about, and sparks flew off red railings that enclosed the bleachers.

Stryker responded with a long, drawn-out burst of thirty tracers. Glowing red bolts of light punched at the top of the van, and, amid smacking sounds, bullet holes were punctured through the thin metal, but the vehicle's occupants continued to resist. Stryker sensed they were in the mood to fight to the death, and he was ready to oblige them.

The thoroughbred lying under the van neighed wildly as hot lead flew back and forth, lighting up the racetrack. Stryker glanced over at Smitty just as the sergeant put one clean shot through the wounded horse's head. The animal shuddered then stiffened and lay back suddenly, silenced and relieved of its pain and misery, and those legs which weren't crushed under the van straightened out and went still. Stryker smiled inwardly: He didn't think the notorious Mr. Smithers gave a damn about any animal's plight or feelings. But that was how mean men sometimes were. They loved and would defend to the death creatures that could not stand up for themselves, but they rarely had compassion for dumb humans.

"WACO, this is Kilo-Two!" an MP was calling over his radio nearby. Kilo was the military phonetic designation for Kolana security detail. "At the Phuto racetrack — Signal-Three hundred — send help ASAP! We got hostile fire and VC comin' out the ying-yang!"

Stryker's grin faded at the improper radio language as he slapped the last clip into his rifle. The call for assistance had been unnecessary. He radioed for backup when the chase first started. (Rooks! They missed *everything*.) Already Saigon was alive with dozens of sirens crisscrossing the city as reinforcements converged on the Phuto racetrack.

Blood splashed from the bullet holes in the van as Stryker sent another three-round burst into the vehicle's roof, but no sooner did he take his finger off the trigger than a second AK-47 appeared out the shattered window. One continuous flash of flame erupted at the end of the barrel, and slugs crashed in all around the military policemen. Someone yelled out when a sliver of lead slammed into his shoulder and knocked him off his feet.

"That's it!" Stryker shouted to Smitty. "I'm not risking any more casualties over this fiasco!" His rifle was not really an M-16 but an XM-203: a recently developed experimental prototype that featured a converted grenade launcher with M-79 tube hanging beneath the barrel grips. They were in high demand and short supply in the Nam.

He pulled an HE round the size of a duck egg from a pouch on his web belt, clamped it into the tube and aimed at the middle of the van.

Seconds later, the round, visible to the naked eye as it shot across the racetrack, punched a fist-sized hole through the roof. A heartbeat later the side of the vehicle exploded skyward, and a bright fireball lit up the grandstands before slowly rising off the ground.

"That's for Wann!" Stryker raised a fist in the air,

though he didn't know why he used her name. *I soc mau* you, *Victor Charlie*! I *soc mau* you back to Buddha!"

But no sooner did the smoke begin to clear before a blackened, bloody face appeared behind the sharp edges of ruptured metal.

The survivor aimed a pistol at the MPs and began firing at the white letters on their black helmets.

Overkill.

The word came to Stryker like a migraine as he watched ten gun jeeps, bristling with military policemen in flak jackets and steel pots, roar into the stadium, lights flashing, sirens screaming, and M-60 gunners peppering the van with sustained bursts of powerful 7.62 armor-piercing ammo.

The drivers kept their steering wheels turned hard to the left and their gas pedals floored as they circled the gunman like Indians attacking a wagon train laager. Dirt flew from beneath windows, creating a dustbowl in front of the towering bleachers.

Within one minute, the van looked like an old tub that had been out on a country firing range for years: Filled with so many holes it was collapsing under its own weight.

"So you think they were Charlie?" Smitty yelled over the straining engine noise as they sped across town to the warehouse district minutes later.

"I'll leave that up to CID." Stryker hit the siren toggle a couple times to clear traffic along bustling Tran Quoc Toan Boulevard. "But my gut feeling is that they were. Kiwi Kolana may be a legitimate actress, but this agent she got tangled up with — for whatever reason — is as phony as a three dollar bill. My guess is he's out to make a fast buck any way he can, and running

257

guns, gold, and rice to the fucking commies is popular with the *in crowd* right about now."

"*Was* out to make a fast buck," Smitty corrected him.

"Right. Now we beat feet back to that warehouse where they have been filming a murder scene all week and toss that director asshole for the facts. Yah!" He laughed. "*Just the facts*, man."

They cut their siren several blocks before arriving at the movie lot and coasted in blacked out.

Smitty checked his watch, surprised. "They're still filming—or whatever they're doing."

"Like I said: Movie people work hours worse than cops sometimes."

"And so do crooks," Smitty muttered as they dismounted and slowly crept up to the rear doors of the huge warehouse. Stryker tested the doorknobs.

Locked.

"In the mood for a little Batman and Robin?" he asked.

"The roof?" Smitty looked hopeful.

"You're genius material, Smithers."

It only took them five minutes to shimmy up a drainpipe to the top. The whole time, three women screamed inside the building, but their voices came across fake. Bad actresses.

Then a shot rang out and the screaming stopped abruptly.

"Jesus!" Smitty whispered as they crouched beside a skylight in the center of the roof. "It damn sure looks authentic!"

Below, a large bed was the only item of furniture evident inside the warehouse. Three women—one American and two Asian—were strapped down to it with ropes. They were totally nude. The one in the middle was Kiwi Kolana. The one on the left no longer seemed to have a face. Her chest and what had once been her head was drenched with blood.

Movie cameras on tall tripods stood at either end of the bed, pointed down at the women in different angles. They were turned on and rolling.

A Frenchman, glistening with sweat and wearing only boxer shorts, stood over the women. He was pointing a large caliber handgun at Kiwi's terrified face.

A second Caucasian suddenly appeared and jumped on the bed. Naked from the waist down, he dropped onto the Vietnamese woman and began savagely raping her. "A porno flick?" Stryker muttered under his breath as he flipped the safety off his pistol.

"Well it damn sure looks authentic!" Smitty repeated. He was still looking at the gnarled face of the woman who had been shot.

"That's because it *is* real!" Stryker stepped forward and jumped through the skylight. "They're filming a snuff film, Smitty!" he yelled on the way down.

The ex-Green Beret landed catlike on the rapist's back, snapping it in two. The woman beneath them both screamed and blacked out from the intense pain.

Stryker's arm whirled around, and he fired three shots at the man with a gun, tearing his hand off at the wrist and shattering his lower jaw. The Frenchman flew back out of sight.

"Hands on your heads!" Stryker rolled off the dead man and onto the floor, cautiously fanning his .45 at the cameramen behind the tripods. They quickly complied, not one of them trying to flee out a side door, which took the MP sergeant by surprise.

And then he felt the gun barrel behind his left ear.

"Drop the equalizer, asshole," a high-pitched voice ordered. "And don't look back!"

Stryker almost laughed out loud. *Equalizer?* Nobody had used that term since the fifties. He slowly raised both hands in the air but refused to surrender his automatic.

"Listen buster," the voice squeaked again.

"Geronimo!" Smitty dropped from above, right on cue. His boots landed on the shoulders of the gunman behind Stryker, breaking his clavicles, rendering his gun arm useless, and smashing him to the floor.

Stryker turned around and gave Smitty the thumbs-up. Grinning, he said, "I owe you one," then went down on one knee beside the naked man in the red cape. The guy was out cold.

He slowly pulled the gas mask of Captain Condom and sighed in disappointment.

"The fuckin' movie director!" Smitty recognized the man immediately.

Stryker walked over to the Frenchman on the bed, gently peeled his frame from the unconscious woman's, then roughly flipped him down on the floor. "And I was kinda hopin' it would be Slipka or Raunchy Raul," he admitted. Stryker took a sheet and draped it over the woman, then pulled a commando knife from his boot and cut Kiwi Kolana free.

"Oh thank you, sergeant!" She got up and started toward him, not bothering to cover herself. "Thank you so mu—"

"Shut up, bitch," he snapped, bending over to check the woman with no face. "When I want somethin' out of you I'll beat it out of you."

"Better radio for a Ten-Five for this one." Smitty was beside the rape victim. It appeared she was going into shock. Both MPs recognized her: the banker's daughter from the Luc Quach, where the robbery went down.

"He was supposed to rescue me in this scene." Kiwi turned to Smitty for compassion. "Nobody ever told me they were going to start killing people. Nobody ever told me that was what this movie was all about!"

"You should have leveled with us from the start," he said, dropping to one knee beside the director. "About this schmuck, Captain Condom." He tied a red rubber around the man's ear, then got back up. "About that bank heist over on Tran Hung Dao, about—"

"About *everything*!" Stryker cut in. "As it stands now, you're under arrest for investigation of homicide, Miss Kolana.

"Homicide?" She was almost speechless. "You saw him pointing that gun at my face!" Her finger flashed at the dead Frenchman. "I almost ended up looking like *that*!" She glanced down at the dead woman sinking in a pool of blood on the mattress.

"A shooting just went down here," Smitty muttered. "And everyone involved is subject to charges the same as the dirtbag who pulled the trigger."

"But I was a *victim*, for Christsake!" she cried, her body shaking with each word, huge breasts jiggling up and down with the movement.

"It'll be up to the Investigators." He threw her a robe that was lying on the floor. Then he turned to the cameramen standing speechless behind the tripods. "All four of you douchebags on the floor! Facedown, arms behind your back." He pulled an extra set of handcuffs from his back pocket.

"Whatta ya think?" Smitty was examining the tripods.

Stryker flashed back to the buzz saw murder scenes and the marks that were always found on the dusty floor. He shook his head in the negative and said, "Wrong size, my friend. And you should know better: It's never that easy."

12. The Dangerous Edge

"I'm proud of you, Stryk!" Cob Carmosino leaned out from his hospital bed and slapped the ex-Green Beret on the back.

"Aw, he just got lucky," Smitty argued, but his eyes were smiling.

"Greetings!" The door to the ward burst open and Sergeant Schultz appeared, liquor bottles in both hands. A cheer went up from the other patients on the floor, but their toothy grins would vanish when they discovered the clannish MPs were not about to share with strangers.

Within minutes the space around Carmosino's bed filled with loud soldiers with armbands, over to visit one of their favorite NCOs. Cob was still recovering from wounds sustained in a payroll convoy ambush the month before. The men were filling him with shoptalk. Bringing him up to date on current events. Briefing him on what had gone down in the battalion since he had left the street.

"So here we are securing the crime scene," Smitty said, needing no urging from the men to continue the war story, "when ol' Mark pulls a cherry-red condom from the director's boot, rips it from its package, and

263

wraps the damn thing around the pervert's fucking ear! It was great!"

"*Pruett!*" Stryker shot up from his chair upon seeing the sergeant-from-Korea enter the ward. "Where the hell you been?"

"We thought you were dead!" Smitty appeared beside Mark like a shadow. "We thought you were victim numba nine of that cabbie bitch who—"

"Yah, I heard all about that mess." He grinned sheepishly and bent over to autograph the cast on Carmosino's leg. "The chick didn't say word-one to me, fellas. Dropped me off at the Saigon Zoo, and I been throwin' popcorn and shit at the apes ever since. Didn't much feel like showing up for that stupid meeting with the C.O. It was the fifth one we had scheduled—and *he* hasn't showed up for one yet!"

"Jesus!" Stryker shook his head.

"But I got a theory about the dame." Pruett's expression took on a scholarly look as he glanced up at the ceiling, trying to recall specifics. "Since I got into her cab all alone, maybe she didn't freak off into her other personality or whatever. Maybe she stayed cool—treated me like any other passenger. Maybe she goes into her psychopath routine only when a GI drags a hooker into her car. Hell, I don't know—might not even be the same cunt. *You* guys figure it out. That's what you get paid for, right? Me, I'm on my vacation, whether the Brass know it or not." He sat down on the edge of the bed and lit up a cigarette.

Stryker didn't want to know anymore. He decided it was time to change the subject before some of the enlisted men latched onto a new hero—a role model. "Got some good news from Mikey back in The World," he revealed, after first hesitating a second. He wasn't sure how he wanted to break the news. "He just reenlisted for—guess what?"

"Honolulu," Smitty said with a smile, a faraway look in his eyes.

"Paris," added Carmosino.

"Tahiti," Murphy said dreamily.

Several of the men moved away from The Murph. They were tense when around the MP: He hadn't had an accident in days.

"Rome." Another man spoke up.

"Nope." Stryker smiled proudly, and he tapped the combat patch on his right shoulder.

"The Nam?" Carmosino sat up in his bed. "Broox is coming back to the Nam?"

"What?" Thomas looked like he had just been told his long lost dog had been found.

"Can't guarantee he'll get duty with the Seven-sixteenth again," Stryker warned, "but he's got a twelve-month RVN contract, and they let him fill out a dream sheet on desired units."

Later, as they stood away from the others, by the window overlooking the edges of Pershing Field several blocks away, Thomas asked, "What about his—divorce?" He stared down at the women strolling by and regretted asking the question as it escaped his lips.

Stryker was watching the passing *ao dais*, too, hoping to see Wann's face somewhere in the crowds. "I've been meaning to bring that up, Ants. It seems Mike's old lady had a change of heart after she ventured out on her own for a few days in gloomy Denver." He held up a folded telegram.

"Really?" Thomas was both happy and concerned.

"But the very next day a drunk driver crossed the centerline at Deadman's curve out on Riverdale Road and hit her head-on."

"Was Mikey with her, sarge?"

"No." Stryker looked down at several small girls playing with a monkey in the open market below. "But Fi Fi Ky is dead."

"She wasn't such a bad chick, sarge." Thomas detected the hostility in Stryker's last five words. He decided it was time to spill all—at least all he knew. "She was really a very loving woman, and I think maybe she really cared for Mike. But she was running scared. That Captain Condom bastard was chasing her around town long before Kolana and her troupe flew into Saigon—trying to get into her pants and persuade her to star in his new film—his *snuff* film. She refused, and he put a lousy fifty dollar hit on her head—a lousy fifty bucks, sarge."

"You can arrange anything in Saigon," Stryker admitted.

"What better person to run to than a macho man who always packs heat, right?" He pulled open his uniform top to reveal a Feel Safe Tonight—Sleep With A Cop T-shirt.

Raucous greetings were exchanged as Sergeant Richards appeared in the room, and Stryker and Thomas rejoined the group. "A bit of ironic news," he announced. "Harcourt has been relieved of duty pending an MPI investigation into the circumstances surrounding his partner, Ramsey's death—"

"You mean it was murder?" Murphy cut in.

"No," Richards was quick to reply. "Derek had powder residue on his hands—the whole bit. But it seems

266

there's some question about Harcourt's activities with *Mrs.* Ramsey possibly contributing to Derek's diminished mental capacity — if you know what I mean."

"And what about Mrs. Derek Ramsey herself?" Stryker had heard a few rumors. He was so disgusted with the beautiful woman he refused to speak her first name.

"The Vietnamese authorities are investigating her for possible insurance fraud, but she's still on the street."

The edges of Stryker's frown jumped slightly — his anonymous tip to the *canh-sats* had paid off.

"You know what to do if you see her while on patrol," Smitty said to the enlisted men in the room, and they, in turn, nodded grimly, understanding completely.

"What about Derek's GI insurance policy?" Stryker asked. "What is it these days — twenty thousand dollars?"

"Yah. That's the ironic part." Richards laughed. "Just before his sui — just before his death, Ramsey changed the beneficiary to read Benny Harcourt's girlfriend."

"You're kidding!" Smitty slapped his knee.

"What's her name?" Stryker asked, but he was rapidly losing interest in the conversation.

Richards consulted his pocket notebook. "One Vo Dehb."

Stryker felt like someone had just hit him in the face with a baseball bat!

Vo Debh. Paul Kruger's live-in girlfriend. *Now he could place the voice that had been taunting him for months!*

Paul Kruger had once been an MP in Stryker's

Company. He flipped out during a robbery bust, beating the suspect to death. Then he deserted the MP Corps, fleeing into the Saigon underworld, a hunted AWOL.

Vo Dehb, a waitress at the Queen Bee, took him in just days before the tragedy.

The couple had virtually disappeared after that. Nobody saw them for months. Until a dazed and doped-up Kruger encountered Stryker and The Uke in a dark back alley behind the Miramar Hotel on Tu Do. Kruger, still in possession of his service weapon, pulled the .45 and Stryker shot him on the spot, killing him.

He hadn't lost sleep worrying about Vo Dehb. She had been around. She knew the ropes. She would cope.

Unfortunately, her method of coping entailed phoning him at odd hours of the morning to entertain him with one-sided, obscene conversation. And lately she was taunting him with dead-end clues about Wann, and her new boyfriend: an ex-MI agent.

"Thomas!" Stryker grabbed Pruett's arm and started for the door. "Loan John here your backup revolver so we can—"

"Hell, sarge." Thomas backed up and held his hands out in mock innocence. "I don't carry no—"

"Cut the crap and just hand it over, clown. And come along for the ride. I might need cover. You too, Gary!"

Thomas reluctantly pulled the .38 snubby from inside his boot and tossed it to Pruett. "If you use it, you gotta clean it."

"Do you remember that Vo Dehb's address?" Stryker asked Richards. "I remember the general location but

268

not the numbers."

"Same-same, Mark—sorry. But it was down on Nguyen Cong Tru somewhere." And they were gone.

With the half moon watching over their shoulders, Stryker and Pruett descended on Vo Dehb's apartment alone, but the block was silently ringed with Military Police units, Egor's dust-off was standing by on the roof of the embassy less than a mile away, and Lieutenant Slipka authorized a gunship from Tan Son Nhut for backup. They weren't taking any more chances with Hoyden.

"That's the joint." Stryker pointed to a long, tin-walled building. It was one-story high, with windows that were smog-smeared and grilled over. "Inside are several small cubicles—kind of a communal setup, but Kruger and his cunt had their own door. Only way we found out about this place was after I dusted the dude and Vo Dehb came in out of the cold to claim the body. He's got nobody who gives a rat's ass back in The World anymore. The morgue guys told her it was me who pulled the trigger—*dipshits*. Her phone calls started a couple nights after the shooting, but I didn't make the connection. They were just vulgar conversations—you know: the kind Raunchy Raul prays for but never gets. I don't know when Harcourt latched up with her, or if he knew she was fuckin' with me. I doubt it. Harcourt has turned into a real louse, but he wouldn't go after anybody personally—"

"Unless pussy was at the root of it," suggested Pruett.

"Yah. Anyway, lately the phone calls were getting

threatening. Last week somebody loosened the bolts on my jeep's front tires, but that could have been any cowboy on the street, I guess. I still get this nagging feeling the bitch was trying to cancel my ticket."

"To think she was balling Harcourt blows my mind."

"You think he knew about this place?" Pruett checked his revolver as they left the shadows and started toward the house. He didn't know if Broox carried it loaded or not.

Stryker grinned approvingly when he saw the silver primers sparkle back at him, snugly in place. "Well, Benny had a pad way over on Tru Minh Kỳ, and the guys tell me she stayed there with him, but who knows.

"Christ, to think I locked eyes with her just last week at Ramsey's party! I just couldn't place the face. Or the voice." He sounded very annoyed with himself.

They entered the building through the west end and allowed themselves five minutes to prowl the dark corridor before arriving at Dehb's door. They passed several open cubicles with whole families sleeping on the floor. Incense burned at one end of the building, and somewhere an old mama-san was humming along with phantom tunes in her head. Cockroaches fell from the walls now and then, and rats scurried across the hot tin roof.

When they came to the room, Stryker quietly tested the doorknob.

Locked.

A hand latched onto Stryker's wrist from behind, and he nearly fired a shot through the ceiling.

A short, fragile woman wearing a loose-fitting sarong had appeared from behind them without a sound. Long hair was piled atop her head, and her belly extended out nearly a foot. She cradled a second sleeping child in her arms. *"Kiêu tu ây im láng!"* she whispered harshly, then turned and walked back down the narrow hallway.

"What did she say?" Pruett wiped sweat from his brow.

"She says the people inside have been making a lot of noise and would we tell them to knock it off or she'll call the *canh-sats*."

As they spoke, the door slowly creaked open.

Both Americans backed up and apart from each other, pistols extended at arm's length.

A slender Vietnamese man in his early twenties was standing in the doorway. One eye was swollen shut. His shirt was torn down the middle and soaked in blood. Bruises and scratches covered his face.

"I killed him," he said simply, motioning the two taller Americans inside.

Stryker glanced over the youth's shoulder. In the back of the room, a large man was lying facedown in a growing pool of blood, a long dagger sticking out of his back—the kind street vendors were always trying to peddle on GIs outside the airport, Stryker noted.

Pruett followed Stryker into the small flat and stepped over the body blocking the entrance to the bathroom. He glanced up at an oil painting of the Hong Kong singer Frances Yip, next to a tapestry of golden Bangkok temples. Against the opposite wall hung a bamboo bird cage. Inside was what once had been a small green parakeet. Its head had been viciously twisted off recently.

"He beat me." The youth sounded like he was in a

271

trance. Almost hypnotized. *On the edge*, Stryker observed sadly. On that dangerous edge that separated madmen from the rest of us. People like Hoyden often cut themselves badly when they tripped over that edge. And, in cases like this, they often took several innocents with them. It became a war of the Innocents, in Saigon. "He beat me for days and days. And then I got loose."

"Don't worry about it, kid." Stryker waved his story silent. Then, to Pruett, he said, "Check for a pulse — just to be sure."

The Vietnamese kept close to the military policemen. "No sweat, sir." It sounded like his mind was returning to them. "He's dead."

Stryker noticed a birthmark on his forehead: a tiny discoloration that looked exactly like a unicorn head. "Check him anyway," Stryker told Pruett.

And then they found her.

Vo Dehb.

In the dark back room. She was strapped to an ironing board. A buzz saw blade was buried in her face, the tips of its shiny silver teeth protruding from her nostrils and mouth. Her brain was missing. From the looks of it, the thing had been gone for days. There was no sign of Wann anywhere, but then he came across her scarf on the floor.

As Pruett dropped to one knee to search for a pulse, the body lying on the floor sprung up without warning, and the room filled with a deafening howl.

Hoyden was back on his feet, waving his arms, charging blindly. Blood squirted from the gaping hole where the dagger had exited through his chest.

Pruett seemed to bend over to pick up something

and his boot shot up, connecting loudly with Hoyden's jaw.

The madman stumbled to the side but remained on his feet. His eyes popped open and his arms bent back behind him, groping for the dagger's hilt.

Stryker flew from the back of the room and leaped at the escapee feet first. Both boots slammed into the man's back, and he finally went down. Pruett jumped on top of him just as Stryker drew his pistol.

The two men began wrestling, and furniture tumbled across the room, bouncing off the walls, splintering with loud cracks. Stryker holstered his .45 and dropped on Hoyden's back just as the former MI agent got his massive hands around Pruett's throat and began applying pressure.

Stryker wrapped his right arm around Hoyden's throat, slammed his left forearm against the back of the man's neck, and began squeezing the muscle-laced limbs together. Hoyden kicked out at Pruett, but the sergeant from Korea fended off the blows against his stomach and concentrated on breaking the madman's grip.

He slid his fists up between Hoyden's arms and struck outward, over and over, until he knocked the hands from his throat. And he quickly rolled away, gasping for breath.

Stryker increased pressure on the choke hold, tightening his grip around Hoyden's throat until the man quit kicking, and the MP sergeant felt his own pounding heart trying to burst from his chest.

"He's out, Mark!" Pruett got slowly to his feet.

But Stryker kept squeezing, the exertion taking his own breath away, sapping his own energy as the dead man's life swirled out through the window and his descending soul rattled the floorboards. Stryker squeezed harder, and his vision seemed to go white along the edges. Fuzzy grey dots appeared in front of his eyes, and he no longer saw Hoyden in front of him but Kip Mather. And Hoa.

And the rape victim five years ago. And the man plummeting from the helicopter.

And all of Hoyden's buzz saw victims.

And Wann down on the riverbanks, laying out a blanket in the midst of a rainbow of swaying flowers, hummingbirds forming a halo behind and above her. And she smiling up at him.

And he squeezed harder. Until the vertebrae inside his biceps cracked, and the monster fell completely still and ceased struggling.

"Okay, Mark." Pruett did not try to pull Stryker away but merely rested his hand on the ex-Green Beret's shoulder to prop himself up. "The bastard's dead."

Stryker glanced up at the other MP, stared through him for several seconds, then slowly released Hoyden. He leaned back on his elbows, breathing for the first time in minutes. He started to get up, but Pruett kept him in a sitting position by pushing down on his shoulder.

"Rest," he said simply.

A muffled cry filtered out through the brick wall across from them, in the rear of the room, and Stryker noticed for the first time that it jutted out unnaturally from the drywall in the corners. It appeared to have been recently erected. A pile of loose bricks was leaning beside the doorway to the bathroom, and a bucket of dried cement sat beside it.

The cry sounded again, became a steady wailing, like a child trapped underground, and then someone was pounding on the other side of the wall.

"What the hell?" Both he and Pruett rushed over and placed their ears against the bricks.

"He buried her alive," the Vietnamese youth spoke up suddenly, startling the two Americans. "Some woman—I don't know who. He was keeping her there for later, but I think he forgot about her. He was having too much fun with this one." He pointed at Vo Dehb, her head split wide, and her breasts and vagina covered with black, swollen circles where a red-hot poker had been plunged into them. "How is my sister?"

"She's fine, kid." Stryker began kicking at the wall, but it refused to budge. It had dried quite solidly. "She's in the hospital."

"Together," Pruett said, and they locked arms and threw their shoulders against the wall.

"Wann!" Stryker yelled, praying to any gods listening that it was she inside, as they hit it again and again. "Stand back!"

"Maybe it'd be easier to get to her through the outside wall," Pruett said. "It looked pretty flimsy when we rolled up on scene." A section of the wall suddenly collapsed, and several bricks caved in.

"Mark!" Two filthy, blood-caked arms reached out through the small hole and grabbed him.

Wann's face, high cheekbones and thin lips marred by cuts, scrapes, and bruises, stared out at him, tears streaming from her wide eyes.

"It's okay, Wann!" He reached through the opening,

275

tearing more bricks away until he could embrace her, pull her free from the dark hole. "It's okay — you're safe now, baby."

She stepped out of the makeshift crypt, her legs weak, and collapsed in his arms, sobbing.

"It's okay, baby." He held her tight, smoothing her hair down with his rough fingers, over and over. "I'm here to protect you now."

John Pruett folded his arms across his chest and leaned back in a corner shadow, allowing the two their privacy. In the hallway outside, his ears picked up the clamor of a dozen MP boots running toward them.

The danger had passed, but it was still a very pleasant sound.

13. Tough Men Don't Tango

Stryker tilted his head back as far as it would go, draining the last of the beer from the green bottle with the number Thirty-three across the label. He would start in on his tenth shortly. And he didn't give a damn what they thought about him, either!

Wann tightened her grip around his arm, sliding her fingers up and down through the hair on it. She was still nursing her first drink. And he didn't care what the men thought about the two of them being together in public anymore, either!

Her period of mourning was officially over, he proclaimed silently to himself. It was time she enjoyed life again.

And to Stryker, manning a small candle-lit table in a dark corner of a Saigon nightclub, with beautiful Asian women dancing atop a stage to the live music of CBC or Hammer or The Dreamers, was his idea of how to enjoy life in a war zone.

But that would come tomorrow night. This evening they were at the Pershing Field NCO club, announcing without words their close friendship. So that there would be no gutter talk, no gossip. So that the rumors would die before they got started.

"Let's dance," Wann said, surprising him after a teenaged MP slipped a dime into the jukebox and a Moody Blues song filled the crowded room. Enlisted men were allowed to join the NCOs at Pershing's cop bar.

She had never asked to dance before, but perhaps she was just being shy. Or polite. She had never appeared interested in the people dancing at the nightclubs they frequented before. Only in him. In staring deep into his eyes. In holding his hands in hers while she stroked his wrists slowly, tenderly.

"I don't dance, Wann," he said softly. In the past, he would admit it freely. It was like playing cards, which he didn't do either. And he didn't give a damn what anybody thought. He was a fighter *and* a lover, and he could shoot the eyes out of a Victor Charlie at a hundred meters. Wasn't that all that really mattered in life?

But he felt himself going red along the temples.

"I thought you did a little bit of everything, Mr. MP sergeant." She batted her eyes at him playfully.

Stryker's tongue slithered in and out a couple times, and he ran it across his lower lip. "Oh, I know a few tricks, honey."

Some of the men walked by with their Vietnamese girlfriends in tow, and greetings were exchanged cheerfully, but they sensed he wanted to be alone, and they drifted off to other tables. Wann diluted her drink by pouring some Coca-Cola in the glass. "Why did he do it?" she asked suddenly, with little warning, though he had seen something in her eyes earlier—something troubling her.

And he knew whom she was talking about. "At first

he just came back here looking for me, I think," Stryker said, opening another beer bottle with his thick fingers (and they were not twist-off tops). "But all the beautiful Vietnamese women set him off, Wann. He began seeing the face of that woman he killed in Mytho five years ago on every woman he encountered," he said, offering his own personal theory. "And sometimes the impulse was just too overpowering, and he dragged them off into the night and killed them. I've pondered it for hours and hours, but I guess we'll never really know why he chose buzz saws. Maybe he had a Dudly Dooright complex or fancied himself a lumberjack.

"He kept a journal for the first few weeks he was here, but most of it was just endless babbling that didn't mean anything — to us anyway. CID might make something out of it someday, if they even give a shit or care enough to stick with it.

"Hoyden kept photographs of the women he murdered. Before, during, and after he ran the blade through their skulls." Wann did not flinch or look down but stared into his eyes like they were discussing what to order at a restaurant. "He glued them to certain pages of his diary. I *accidentally* let a few fall into my pocket, and when I found them later," he said, smiling evilly, "I decided to drop them off at Toi's place. He's already got them up on his wall. You should see his little chamber of horrors. I don't know how his wife can take it. Someday we'll pay him a visit and I'll show you the famous back room. We'll all sit down at his gun-cleaning table and suck through a six-pack or something."

She could sense when the booze was beginning to

loosen him up. "I think it's about time I took you home." She pulled his head down like a little puppy and held the side of his face against her breast.

"Well, ain't we gettin' good an' cozy over here!" Smitty and three of his goon platoon had walked in for an unofficial bar check. He slammed a fist on the table in front of Wann and winked his eye playfully at her. "Don't let this big bastard pull his drunkard routine on you, miss. He's always up to no good. I'll take it upon myself to warn you upfront: He'll take advantage of you if he can."

Stryker blew Smitty a kiss, then totally ignored the NCO as he buried his face against Wann's long, silky hair. She frowned knowingly at Smitty, then looked away without saying anything to the man. Everyone in the room knew she had been his woman for quite some time now.

Stryker felt good all over. Biggs, the Zulu warrior, was one of the men standing behind Smitty. The squad seemed to be getting along fine. Smitty had even put the African wildman in for an ArCom, and Thomas swore at guardmount earlier that day he saw the NCO with an arm around the man while they joked in the mess hall line. Of The Troops And For The Troops. Maybe the violence and racial hatred flaming in the streets back home wouldn't affect his Saigon Commandos after all.

"We go now." Wann pulled him to his feet, expertly maneuvering him through Smitty's troopers.

The warm Saigon breeze struck him in the face like a slap, and the smell sent his adrenaline running. "I fucking love you, Vietnam!" he yelled at the top of his lungs, waving a beer bottle in the air. Men in a passing

MP patrol smiled and saluted their favorite sergeant. They didn't know quite what to think. It was the first time they had ever seen him drunk in public. "Look at the pretty flares." He giggled like a child as they staggered toward the main gate, leaning against each other for support.

"Can I get you a unit?" The sentry at the camp entrance recognized Stryker immediately. "I'm sure a patrol's headed your way."

"We'll take a cyclo, thank you," Wann answered for him. "I think he needs the fresh air."

The MP private laughed in agreement. "But do you think he can make it that far?" The long line of three-wheeled vehicles was on the far side of the access road that separated the Military Police compound from the civilian populace, about a hundred yards away.

"We'll be fine." She smiled, but the kid was no longer listening. Pershing Field had its meatmarket, too, and several girls in the background, their faces caked with makeup, were competing for the bachelor's attention, reaching through the torn chicken wire and stroking his shoulders and back.

"Good luck, ma'am," she heard him say as she started down the access road.

"Yes, you should have seen us wrestling around on the floor with that goofy Hoyden!" Stryker had been giving her a round-by-round account of the fight in Vo Dehb's apartment, when a cloudburst suddenly dropped sheets of rainfall across the camp.

Holding her purse over her head, Wann urged Stryker to walk faster. "It's only water, honey!" He laughed, lifting his face and hands toward the sky. "Hell, it used to be our shower, up in Pleiku!" Thunder laughed back at him, and lightning crackled overhead, illuminating the fear in Wann's eyes. Storms brought back the memories. Rain reminded her of her Johnny and the day he died.

A blue and gold Saigon taxi, its headlights sending dull beams through the rising steam, was slowly rolling toward them.

Wann quickly flagged it down, and the driver swerved over to the side of the road. "Get in!" Wann ordered, taking control of the situation.

After they were in the back seat, she checked her purse to see how much money she had. Taxis were always so much more expensive than cyclos. Satisfied she had enough dong, she glanced up at the driver and said, "Mac Dinh Chi and Thong Nhut. I'll guide you to the exact apartment." Her words were Vietnamese.

The driver was a woman, she was surprised to see, with hair as dark and long as her own. She never turned to face her passengers but looked at them through the rear-view mirror. The large, black eyes were unblinking. They sent a shiver through Wann, or was it just the cool air that chased after the storms?

"Yes, you should have seen that crazy Pruett from Korea jump in there and try to box the guy's lights out. I had my pistol out and everything, all ready to paste the sonofabitch right between the eyeballs!" He drew the off-duty .45 from the shoulder holster under his jean jacket. He pointed it at the empty passenger seat in front of them. "Why that crazy fuck coulda got himself killed trying to, and I quote: 'use only the minimum amount of force necessary to subdue the suspect,'" he said sarcastically, mocking the judicial system he was sworn to serve and protect.

Wann shook her head from side to side in resignation. She had heard it all hundreds of times before. From both her men. "Give me the gun," she said forcefully.

"Hell, I would have saved us all a lot of sore muscles and soiled uniforms," Stryker said with a laugh, "if Pruett would have just waited another second or two." He pulled the hammer back on the pistol.

"Mark!" She reached out and grabbed his wrists, and they began struggling — he playfully, Wann seriously.

The female taxi driver had been watching them nervously for the last several minutes through the rearview mirror. She did not notice the large truck approaching, its left side partially across the centerline, into her lane. The blaring horn sounded as the lorrie was almost upon them, startled her, and she jerked the steering wheel hard to the right to avoid the head-on collision.

The .45 automatic in Stryker's gunhand discharged with a deafening blast.

"My God!" Wann screamed as the hollow-point punched through the driver's seat and struck the woman cabbie in the back of the head. The impact splashed her face forward against the windshield, and the taxi skidded out of control into several parked cars, coming to rest in the middle of a traffic circle where several Vietnamese policemen were setting up a curfew checkpoint.

"Aw, shit," Stryker muttered as he surveyed all the damage he had caused from the back seat. He flipped on the pistol's safety and holstered it as *canh-sats* rushed up the smoking car.

Wann, her arms over her head and her face in her

lap, was breathing hard but not injured or crying. She refused to look up at him.

Suddenly sober—or so it seemed—Stryker stumbled from the car and staggered over to the front door. He brushed back several policemen and jerked it open, then reached in and grabbed the driver's left shoulder. He pulled her back away from the windshield and she flopped down on her back in the seat.

A large, gaping hole had replaced her nose and eyes. Splinters of protruding bone further marked the bullet's exit wound. The woman was about as dead as any corpse he had ever seen.

"There it goes." He turned to the nearest *canh-sat*. "There it all goes, brother. My job, my pension . . ." But he was laughing as he talked, and he didn't know why. "It's all being sucked down the sewer," he lamented. "And you know why?" He stepped away from the cab, raised his arms high over his head, and began turning around in slow circles. "Because she's pissed, my friends. Lady Saigon is pissed! Somehow she got a hair up her ass tonight, and it's not enough she had to piss on me!" He dropped his head back and let the rain splash against it. "But she had to let my luck run out! Things were going so damn well, but she fucking had to have the last word, the final say! And you know what, brothers? It's okay!" Wann finally stepped from the car, but she did not approach him. She just leaned against the vehicle and stared at him sadly, too drained to help anymore. "It's all right!" he continued. "Because what goes around comes around, and maybe— just maybe my time has—"

"Hey!" a *canh-sat* had been rummaging through the cabbie's personal belongings. "Hey GI!" he said in English. "Come check! Come check this!"

Stryker, irritated by the interruption, nevertheless abandoned his debating expression and dropped his hands. He staggered back over to the totaled-out car. "What is it?" Wann was by his side again.

"You tell *me."* The *canh-sat* smiled, somehow realizing his discovery would drastically alter the behavior of the MP sergeant every policeman at the roadblock had recognized on sight.

On a gold chain around the dead woman's blood-streaked neck hung over a dozen pieces of gold jewelry. Stryker's eyes seemed to sparkle as he focused on the Vietnam dragons and Georgian cross pistols, and his grin grew ear to ear. He hugged both Wann and the policeman at the same time and shouted a VC battle cry up at the flares sizzling angrily against the falling rain.

On the necklace were the Military Police Academy graduation rings of Zane and all the others.

THE BEST IN ADVENTURE FROM ZEBRA